CAGED

A CASEY CORT LEGAL THRILLER

AIME AUSTIN

AIME AUSTIN
www.AimeAustin.com

LOS ANGELES, CALIFORNIA

ALSO BY AIME AUSTIN

CAGED

A CASEY CORT LEGAL THRILLER

AIME AUSTIN

Caged

This edition published by
Moore Digital Media Inc.
1125 N Fairfax Avenue
Unit 46071
West Hollywood, CA 90046
www.aimeaustin.com

Cover Designer: Wicked Good Book Covers
Cover Images © Depositphotos, Shutterstock

Caged/Aime Austin. — 2d ed.

Genuine tragedies in the world are not conflicts between right and wrong. They are conflicts between two rights.

—Georg Wilhelm Friedrich Hegel

1

THIS WAS GOING TO BE THE DAY I told my momma the truth. I'd waited until she'd stopped wailing. I waited until the cemetery people threw dirt on that motherfucker. I waited until the limo we had no money for slipped and slid through the snowstorm to that man's house on East Eighty-Eighth Street. I waited until the fake ass church mourners left. I waited until our ancient next door neighbor finished wrapping all the leftovers in plastic, taking to her house what we couldn't fit into our refrigerator.

"Steffi, what we gonna do without Clark?" Momma asked. She was on the edge of hysteria. The wailing would start again if I wasn't careful in what I said.

"We'll be okay, Momma," I assured her. We couldn't be any worse off, I figured.

"This here his house," she said, her sweeping arm taking in the kitchen with its fake brick wall and the living room with its fake stone wall.

Clark had liked making our house look perfect like the pretty ones on HGTV. Too bad it had been rotten to the core.

"We can move somewhere else, right?" I wanted to be anywhere else but here. Momma was a nurse. We'd done fine before Clark. We'd be fine after. I didn't say that, though. That would have pushed her over the edge. I had something of my own to say, anyway.

"Where we gonna go? My own momma ain't gonna take me in. She got too many up in there already. Clark's family say we never married, and I ain't got no business layin' up with them anyway."

I'd waited long enough. I didn't want her to wind herself up. I didn't want her to go searching for a blunt to wind herself down. I wanted my momma, the one from when I was a little kid.

"I need to tell you something." My voice was whisper-soft, but she heard me. I knew she heard me because she looked at me out of the corner of her eye and stopped moving for a long beat.

The wood chair legs scraped across the tile floor, ringing in my ears. But for the first time in a week, my momma sat. She stopped talking. She rested her elbows on the table. Cupped her head in her hands.

Her eyes pushed me back. I felt for the fake bricks covering the far side of the kitchen and buried my fingers between the thin masonry grooves, brushing against the unnaturally smooth mortar.

"Clark—"

"How many times do I have to tell you call him Daddy? He was more a daddy than the guy who made you," she said, her voice as rough and grating as the stone pushing against my arm.

"Daddy..." That left a bitter taste in my mouth. I was still waiting for the day my *real* daddy would come and take me from this place. Maybe he'd have a new, pretty wife who talked all soft and made big, hot breakfasts. I'd have a room with a pink canopy—

The *snap, snap* of Momma's fingers brought me back. "What you need to say?"

Now that I'd had her attention, finally had all of her attention focused on me like a laser beam, I wanted to back out, run away. I coughed. The afternoon's lunch pressed at the back of my throat. I swallowed hard, the acid burning a trail down my insides.

"Clark...Daddy...he..." I wanted to throw up. Sit down. Run out the door. This was a very bad idea. I don't know why it had seemed so all-fire important when I'd woken up this morning. But God told me that silence wasn't the way. I listened to God. I wasn't stupid enough to ignore Him. "He made me...he raped me, Momma."

"What you talking about?" Momma's voice rose. "Speaking ill of the dead like this." She got louder. "That man cared for us. Bought us this house." I wondered if all the neighbors up and down the block could hear her now. "Paid for the clothes on your back."

I tried to catch her eyes, but those red-rimmed brown eyes looked everywhere but at me. That laser beam stare was long gone.

"Are you saying I couldn't satisfy my man in bed...and he turned to you—a barely developed girl? I don't believe it."

My throat had nearly closed like the time I ate a strawberry and whipped cream cake at Antoine's sixth birthday party. But I pushed past that feeling. Pushed the words from my throat. "I'm only saying what happened to me."

"What about your sister? She always been prettier than you. She ain't never said nothing 'bout anything like that."

Sydney had never said much that wasn't about complaining or asking for something. She was right about that. "I don't know about Sydney," I said. Clark had said *I* was his special one.

"That girl has a mouth on her. She'da said something. So I'm left with you saying this now. He dead. Put him in the hard cold ground this morning. What you want me to do? Iff'n it were true, don't matter anymore, do it?"

"No, I guess not," I mumbled into my too tight black blouse. No hug. No tears. No...I don't know, offer to get me a counselor. That's what happened on TV talk shows. Ricki and Oprah would've hugged me.

"You ain't pregnant, is you? Did you get knocked up? You blamin' some baby on him?"

"No, Momma, no. I get my period." Not that a little blood had ever stopped Clark.

"Maybe if you'd gotten pregnant, we coulda figured out a way to stay in this house, here."

I was ready to pack my bags. I didn't ever want to go down to the basement of this house again. Clark loved to shop at Tops, buying boxes of food like a hurricane was coming. Getting me down to the basement had been his excuse. One day, my momma had gone out to work and he'd asked me to reorganize the shelves down there. He'd pulled me down to the blow-up mattress we sometimes used for his family and told me that he needed to show me what men and boys wanted, so I'd be prepared.

"Finger, tongue, or prick," I blurted. That was the choice he'd given me. I told him whatever would hurt the least.

My momma flew across the room like a scared pigeon in the park. Her hands hit my face like sharply beating bird's wings and I raised my own to protect myself.

"Don't you ever say that again. Ever!" she screamed and cried. Suddenly, she wasn't hitting me anymore. I dared to lift my lids. Fear and truth and dread filled my mother's eyes. She closed them and ran up to the one bathroom we'd all shared. The slamming door rattled the entire house.

He'd said those same words to her.

I knew then that she believed me.

2

I needed to go for a walk. Now that Clark was gone, Sydney was back—with her kids. If I didn't stay late after school or find something to do with myself, I ended up watching her rugrats while she went out and had fun. My sister still treated me like I was one of her kids, but I wasn't a little girl anymore. Clark had said he'd made me a woman.

Momma surely treated me that way. She didn't ask when I was coming or going. Didn't ask to see my progress reports or report cards anymore. Didn't ever come into my room. Weekly, she left a wad of money on my dresser. I assumed I was supposed to take care of myself. At fourteen, I figured I was grown enough to do it.

Forget the walk. I needed a little afternoon break from moving and thinking. *Jurassic Park* was on in a few.

"Where you going?" Sydney asked. She had my niece Sheron on her lap. That girl wasn't a baby and was too big to be lying all over her momma, but nobody asked me. In the second I was standin' there, her little boy Jaylen pushed his sister off their momma and was pulling at my sister's top. Sixteen months old and that boy ain't gave up the titty. I kept to steppin.'

"You didn't answer me," my sister yelled through to the kitchen.

I pulled the extra butter Orville Redenbacher from the cabinet and slammed it into the microwave.

"Are you cooking something?"

No, I wasn't cooking nothin'. Sydney could get up off her ass and make some kind of food for her kids. God did not put me on earth to serve them. I wasn't in the mood. I was getting tired of cooking and cleaning behind those kids. I didn't say anything, though. Talking had only gotten me into trouble. Momma was working double shifts at the hospital. She said she needed the money to pay for this house. That Clark's family was practically stealing from us. But I think she didn't want to have anything to do with me. In two and a half months since the funeral, she'd never once looked me in the eye.

"Going to have some popcorn. That dinosaur movie's coming on." I loved that the star of the movie had a little black girl for a kid and no one ever questioned it. Maybe some rich white man would adopt me. Build me an amusement park. Save me.

"You ever think of moving down into the basement?"

I wrenched open the microwave door, snatched out the popcorn, not caring that it burned my thumb. I'd learned to take pain. "No."

"Sheron is sayin' she can't sleep with Jaylen waking up all times a night."

"No."

"Hear me out. I'm sure we can fix it up real nice. There's already a blow-up bed down there."

"I said no!" I must have screamed because it got real quiet. Even the kids stopped making all kinds of noise.

"What's wrong with you lately? You've been off since Clark died. Comin' and goin' as you please."

"I'm glad Clark's dead."

"Not even playing with your niece and nephew like you used to."

I got a big yellow plastic bowl down from the cabinet. Poured in my popcorn. Sprinkled on season salt and garlic powder. Squeezed on the extra butter.

"You're not going to answer me?"

"I don't have nothing to say except it's time for my movie."

I tossed the toys off the leather couch and got comfortable. I quickly got lost in a world where fake dinosaurs were the worst thing that could ever happen to a teenage girl. Right when that fat guy from *Seinfeld* was about to be eaten, the screen froze. I didn't need to look too far to see my sister standing near the TV, remote in one hand, hip in the other.

"What?" I was seriously going to kill this girl. She all but ignored me all the years before she had them kids. Spending half her time with her daddy and her daddy's family. Coming home with grins and gifts, while I pretended Momma's man of the moment could be my own.

"Can we talk about you moving?"

"No way in hell am I sleeping down there."

"Why?" That whine used to get Momma to give her things. Probably worked on her daddy and them Higgins folk. But my last name was Wells and I wasn't falling for it.

"Because I said so." I was not in the mood to fight. I did not want to have to come up off this couch and hit this girl. But if she tried to shove me down in the basement where Clark had tied me to the pipe next to that air mattress, I couldn't be responsible for what happened next. "Turn it back on."

"No."

"Syd. Don't mess with me. You turn that set back on or I'm gonna toss your kids into the yard behind the house. They can be dinner for those pit bulls."

"They're Rottweilers."

"Either way."

"You're not serious."

Why were people always playing with me? I picked up little Jaylen from the floor and started to tote him out the back door. I was halfway across the backyard when Syd ran out and rescued her little pup.

"What in the hell is wrong with you? I leave here for a couple of years and you turn into a serial killer."

As close as they were, Momma didn't tell her. I wanted to punch her and cry at the same time. My fucking relaxation was ruined. I needed to get the hell out of here. This house was smothering me.

It was fake warm like it could be either summer tomorrow or snow could fall. I didn't care. Took myself out down East Eighty-Eighth. Turned left on Wade Park. Weren't ten seconds before some man was honking his horn at me. Dogs in heat, they all were. I gave at least three guys the finger before I got to MLK Park.

Sat on the swings like I did as a kid. I kicked off and swung back and forth. Reminded me of the time Sydney's daddy brought me along to one of his family picnics. He'd treated me like I was his kid that day. Made me a plate of barbecued chicken. Pushed me on the swings. Got me one of those three-color popsicles where your mouth look like the Fourth of July exploded in there after you're done. But after that day, he only picked up Syd. Left me alone with Momma and whoever.

"You want a push?"

I whipped around. I hadn't heard anyone coming. A tall, narrow boy stood off near the diagonal poles holding up the swings. I was usually on my guard in parks. Never knew who was messing around in these places. People think they can do all kinds of things when there aren't any cars goin' by. But this boy with his neat cornrows and pressed tan pants looked all right.

"Nah, I'm fine," I said, digging my canvas sneaker in the sand, pushing off a little with my foot, giving myself a little swing.

"You mind?" he asked, gesturing to the empty swing next to me.

I shook my head. Pushing off again, I got up a little height this time. I'd forgotten how much fun it was to fly.

The boy started swinging too. I glanced his way. He glanced mine. We reached a silent, tacit agreement. Soon, we were in a little race to see who could go higher. I was flying so high I only saw the blur of trees, clouds, and sky. I was sure if I kept pumping, I'd flip over the bar. That stopped me cold. Without momentum, my swing snapped back with a jerk. Slower and slower I went. My arc got smaller and smaller. Dragging my feet brought me to a stop.

The boy stopped too, jumping from the swing, bouncing on his feet. He wore one of those shirts with an animal on the chest and a flip-up collar. Wondered how he didn't get beat up in those clothes. My best friend Antoine had gotten beat down for a lot less.

"Dion," he said, looking at me, but not in a way that made me feel like he was thinking about me naked.

"That your name?"

"Yeah. Yours?"

"Steffie," I said. Immediately, I wished I hadn't said that. The nickname sounded stupid out loud in front of this boy. "Stephanie," I corrected.

"You live around here?"

"On East Eighty-Eighth," I said, not giving him my address. I wasn't that stupid.

"You hungry?"

I was. I never did get more than a little bit of that popcorn. By the time I got home, Sydney and her kids would only have left me some salt and those hard, burned little nuggets that didn't pop. "Kinda. But there ain't much to eat around here."

"I got a car."

A car. Nobody had a car who wasn't slinging. But Dion didn't have the shifty eyed look or baggy pants of a drug dealer. "How you get a car?"

"I was sixteen," he said, as if that were enough explanation. Like everyone in the 'hood got a car when they turned the right age.

"Your parents buy it for you?"

"You could say that." He blinked slow. "I did my chores and they got me the car as promised."

My stomach growled. "Sorry," I mumbled, embarrassed. "My sister and I got into a fight. I left without finishing my popcorn."

"Let's go then."

I hesitated a long moment. 'Don't talk to strangers' was an early lesson Momma taught me. "I don't know—"

Sensing my hesitation, Dion held out his hand. "Dion Fortune," he said. Then recited his address and phone number. "Not a stranger anymore."

He started walking and I jumped off the swing and followed along, curious about his car. I liked riding through town. Beat walking, or taking the bus. I liked watching the brick and wood buildings speed by, the pattern of the tree branches sweeping over the car. Made it feel like there was going to be something good at the end of the ride. Felt like that when Syd's father was with us. He liked to drive all over Ohio, to get some buckeye candy, to see his family, to see the countryside.

A beep sounded and a green car's lights flashed. Nice. Dion pulled open the door and I slid into the passenger seat. Leather. This was real nice. I'd only been in a ride this nice once. One of Momma's great-uncles or something had a Cadillac that he took us for a ride in. That had been like riding on a cloud. Dion got in and started the car.

We drove past Mickey Ds and Burger King. "Where we going?" I asked. I couldn't figure why I wasn't afraid. Something about him put me at ease. If Clark had been driving, I'd have opened the door and jumped out even at forty miles per hour.

"Relax. Enjoy the ride. We going someplace good," he promised in his smooth voice. Kinda sounded like a white guy or a black guy from the Heights.

So I did. I watched the big pretty houses and parks roll on by. I pressed a button and my window eased down without a sound. I didn't have long flyaway hair by no stretch of the imagination, but I pretended I was a California girl as the warm breeze blew through my scalp. I turned to look through Dion's window at the green line train. I wondered where all those people go. They gotta live in all these big brick houses in Shaker. I wonder what it was like in there. Roaring fires. Meals without yelling. No pretend daddies who wanted you to do nasty things.

Even the schools out here were pretty. On a Sunday, kids were laughing and running around the splotchy spring grass. Nothing like the school I was at where people stayed away—always on the edge of truancy. We drove even further and for a fleeting moment, I wondered if Dion was looking for a place to dump my body. Oprah would have frowned on this. There'd have been no hug for getting into a car with a man, only a stiffly wagging finger.

I glanced over at him. He wasn't much of a talker. Dion was humming along to "Wild Wild West" with Dru Hill and Kook Mo Dee. Good music. I bopped my head along as we passed over the highway. As smooth as can be, we pulled into Red Lobster. *Fuck yeah!* I'd only been here once when Clark was in a celebrating mood.

The place was old, didn't look nothing like the commercials on TV. But that had Cleveland written all over it. Run down on the outside. This city needed a makeover, bad.

Dion opened my door and held my hand as I got out. Now that was class. After we got seated in a restaurant booth, I looked at the menu. And started to sweat. It wasn't because it was seventy degrees in March. It was because I didn't have but a couple of dollars in my pocket. I hadn't been planning on doing more than walking off my anger at Syd.

It was like Dion could read my mind. He said, "Order whatever you like. I got you covered."

When the waitress came over, I ordered the alfredo and scampi combo. Dion got lobster. I saw him pass a coupla bills to the woman and within seconds, a big fruity drink appeared in front of me.

"What's this?" I asked.

"Taste it."

I picked up the straw she'd left and pushed it through the whipped cream down to the Italian ice-looking part below. It was so tall, I had to pick up the glass and bring it to me. I took a suck. Nothing. Dion laughed. I could feel the heat climbing up my neck. I took a bigger suck the second time. It was good. Like dessert in a glass.

"What's this?" I asked. "It's tasty."

"Strawberry daiquiri," he answered.

I took another few pulls until the glass was nearly empty. Was a minute or five before it hit me. I leaned and whispered across the table, "This got alcohol in it?"

Quick nod from Dion.

"How you manage that? I'm not twenty-one." I glanced both ways, making sure no one was listening. I didn't need to have the police bring me home. Momma had laid off me all right, but the police would bring on some unnecessary complications I did not need.

"Have one of them biscuits," he said, pointing to the basket on the table. "That'll help."

The biscuit was full of cheese. Damn, I'd forgotten all about this. It was real tasty too. Way better than I got at home. But it didn't stop my head from swimming.

"So where you go to school?" I asked Dion, trying to have a straight conversation even though my tongue felt anything but.

"I graduated."

"Oh. How old are you?" Maybe he was like Doogie Howser or something. Graduated early.

"Eighteen," he said. "Not much older than you, right?"

"I'm fifteen," I said. Well, almost. But I didn't want him thinking I was no kid. Being a freshman in high school was bad enough.

Another drink came to the table, then our food. I must have been thirsty because most of that drink went away before I knew it.

Dion wasn't shy about tearing into his food. He dipped the pink and white meat in butter. Looked like he was enjoying himself. "What you and your sister arguing about?" he asked between taking in food and licking the drips from his fingers.

I put my fork down. That brought down my mood. "Nothing," I mumbled.

"Look, I'm sorry. They say it's easy to talk to someone you don't know. They can be fair. Don't judge you."

I sighed. "After my momma's boyfriend died, Sydney, that's my sister, moved back into the house. She brought her two kids with her. They been sharing a room. Syd got her old room back, and Momma got the big bedroom. She want me to give up my room for the kids and move down to the basement."

"It fixed up?"

My stomach clenched, and I pushed the plate aside. It didn't matter if that room looked like the living room from the *Brady Bunch*, I wasn't going down there. "It's wet and dark," I said. "I don't want to be down there with the spiders." I shuddered. But it wasn't about the bugs.

"Then I don't think you should move," he said with finality. He sat back and crossed his arms. "You got as much right to be there as her. Maybe more." He pulled meat from a shell. "How old her kids?"

I told him.

"Damn. I've seen kids share a room 'til they was six, seven, eight. They don't need they own rooms."

"But what if Jaylen cries at night? Syd says it wakes up Sheron."

"She got a king size?"

I nodded. My sister got a king size from her daddy on her birthday one year.

"Then she can share with—Sheron, was it?"

He was right. Just like that, I knew what I'd go back with. Syd liked having her own room so she could stay up watching TV half the night. But Sheron could sleep with her. Jaylen could have that crib to himself. "You're right. Or she could sleep with the baby. Since she's up and down nursing him."

"That boy still on the titty?" he asked, twisting his mouth.

"I know. I keep telling her. But I bet she like it as much as him. She ain't got no grown man in her life."

"You want dessert?"

I got the rest of my dinner packed away in a doggy bag and took a look at the dessert menu. My appetite was back.

Dion was true to his word and paid the bill after I finished the chocolate chip lava cookie. I rolled up the window on the ride home. That little spit of summer weather had blown away in the wind. It was chilly outside and I didn't have nothing more than this thin T shirt I'd put on when I hadn't planned on going anywhere past the couch.

"This your house?" Dion asked.

"Yep." He'd found my address though there wasn't anything to mark it.

"I really liked spending time with you, Stephanie," he said as he cut the motor. I glanced across the street. My momma's car was in the driveway. "What's your last name anyway?"

"Wells," I answered. "What about you?"

"Fortune."

"That for real? I thought you was kiddin' back there in the park."

"Maybe my name helped get me money from the universe," he said. "I'd like to see you again."

I hastily spit out my house phone number. He didn't even try to find a pen. I half hoped he remembered it. Half hoped he forgot it.

I opened the car door and was going to push it wide when a hand landed on my wrist. Here we go. Man can't buy you nothing without expecting something. I turned around, ready to spit that at him when he handed me my doggy bag. "Don't forget your food."

"Thanks," I said, suddenly ashamed of myself.

"Goodnight, Stephanie Wells. So glad I took a detour through the park today."

I slammed his door and crossed the street toward home. Maybe all men weren't like Clark or the guys trying to get me into their cars. Maybe I shouldn't have judged the male half of the race so badly.

3

"Where you going?" Momma asked. "It's Wednesday night."
She was hunched over some kind of take-out that she hadn't
offered to share with any of us.

"Going to Dion's place. He's got air conditioning."

It was going on ninety degrees in Cleveland. Momma
still had the storm windows in. Without a man to pull them
out, we'd probably smother in here this summer.

"You never bring this boy around. You say he's in elev-
enth grade?"

I put enough whine in my voice to sound truthful. "Ma,
he's at my school." I wasn't exactly going to tell her my boyfriend was twenty-two. It had been a couple of weeks before
he'd told me his real age. He'd said he was afraid I'd quit
seeing him if I knew. I hadn't yet told him how old I was.

Dion was right about one thing though—age was just a number.

"Do I have to talk to you about boys?" she asked, giving me a knowing look.

"Clark already did that," I said.

Momma put down her food, wiped her hands, and walked upstairs. I took the liberty of removing fifty dollars from her wallet on my way out the door.

"Momma still thinks you're at my school," I said, settling into the couch at Dion's place an hour later. I was still sweating from the long bus ride over. "Where's the air at?"

"I only have air in the bedroom," Dion said.

Something fluttered in my belly. I wasn't sure what I wanted from Dion. But I knew what he wanted from me. I wasn't stupid. He wasn't going to wait forever.

"You turn it on."

He nodded. "I got Mulan. You said you wanted to see that."

My stomach stopped tumbling and my heart went all soft. He didn't make fun of the stuff I wanted to watch like Syd would. I suffered through all those shoot-'em-up, blow-'em-up movies with my head turned most of the time. And he got me the cartoon movies I liked without laughing at me.

After pulling off my sneakers, I took myself to his bedroom. I'd been in his room a couple of times to change clothes and stuff. It wasn't any big deal going in there. While he put the tape in the VCR, I pulled up the covers and got comfortable. I pushed play and watched the previews. He stepped out and I heard the blender in the kitchen going.

"I got your favorite," Dion said. He handed me a Mudslide, a drink that tasted like melted ice cream. It was so good. I took the straw and sucked it all down even before the movie started. My guy knew me though, and had another in my hand in an instant.

"Momma and Syd want to meet you," I said, licking the foam from my upper lip. So what, Dion Fortune wasn't sixteen, or eighteen. He was twenty-two. I'd seen his driver's license. But he'd said I wouldn'ta talked to him if I'd known his age. And he was right. My track record with men weren't so great. But Dion was different. He liked silly movies and video games like kids my age.

"That's the thing I like about you," Dion started. "You're your own person. You act more grown than your age. I ain't against family. They important. But I don't want to weigh our relationship down with weekend barbecues and chicken dinners."

Half of me wanted him to meet my momma and Syd. I wanted to show them that somebody nice wanted me. That I could make my own decisions. That I could pick a man who didn't leave me with a couple of kids and no support. Who didn't mess around with all the females in the family. The other half wanted to keep him all to myself. Not taint him with the crazy.

"No sweat. Momma's working back to back shifts at the hospital. Don't see her much anyway."

Dion put an arm across the back of my pillow and I leaned into him. Floated on that Mudslide high. During a break, he brought me another drink.

"I can't do another," I whispered.

He pressed pause. "Sure you can. Why don't you go..." He pointed toward the one bathroom in the apartment.

I was still embarrassed to use the toilet around Dion. I didn't want him to know that I was human like that. It was probably stupid. I closed the door tight on the white-tiled room. Wished it was like at home where all sound was drowned out with a noisy fan. But he lived in one of these old buildings where the bathroom vent was a window.

I did my business and pulled up my pants. The grout swam before my eyes. Maybe I needed to cut back on the drinking. Usually, I could hold my liquor, but today I was feeling it. I flushed as quick as I could, wishing the sound away. I wasn't one of those girls to linger in the mirror, but I caught a quick flash of my reflection—dark skin, white teeth. I hated looking. It was always different than I felt on the inside. On the inside, I was like Syd, light, pretty in a floaty kind of way. My voice was soft, my lips shaped like a bow not like a bubble. I slinked past the reality staring back at me.

I closed the door and went back to his room. That third drink slid down like a dream. I wasn't even hot anymore. I imagined I was Mulan, bold as a warrior, not meek as a victim.

The movie ended too quickly. I wanted to see it again, but that would have to wait. I wouldn't ask him to see a girl movie twice. Not until we got through two movies littered with dead bodies. After that...maybe.

"Gotta get home. School tomorrow," I said. Felt stupid for mentioning school. Good thing I didn't throw in homework or tests. I didn't want him to remember he was dating someone in high school, a freshman nonetheless.

Before I could throw my wobbly legs over the bed and get my shoes on, the bell rang. The shrill sound nearly scared me sober. I hadn't ever heard it before. Dion didn't get a lot of visitors.

A guy, taller, beefier, scarier than Dion was in the living room by the time I tied my sneakers and came in.

"Steffi, this my man Sledge," he said.

I didn't want to go all nerd by holding out my hand like we were at a business meeting, so I just nodded. "Why they call you Sledge?"

The guys laughed. I didn't like the sound of their voices. "He studies Kung Foo or Karate or something like that. It's his move."

"Well. Nice meeting you." I was about to walk toward the back door off the kitchen when a firm hand gripped my arm, stopping me. I couldn't have moved even if I'd wanted to.

"Don't go. Dion said you're a friendly girl. I want to get to know you better."

Friendly? I didn't have any friends. My one friend's parents had moved him to the suburbs. I wasn't cute. Didn't have no money. No one other than Antoine had ever wanted to be friends with me.

Pulled my arm. His grip was like a vise. My stomach tightened like it had when Clark had come into a room. Sledge looked down at the hand circling me and laughed. Like he was a puppy who'd grown into a dog not knowing his own strength. "Sorry."

"Come help me in the kitchen a minute," Dion said.

I followed him there. He pulled the glass top of the blender from the fridge and put it on the stand. "Press 'Ice,'" he ordered. I found the sticky plastic top and pushed it on. He popped out the middle. I did what he said, pressing the button and watching as he added more vodka and rum to the ice and coffee brown mix in the pitcher. The mixture whirred together until it looked like a shake from any fast food restaurant. He poured three big glasses. He shoved two in my hand. "Give one to Sledge." When I hesitated, Dion said, "He's kind of like my boss. So go be nice to him."

I ain't never asked much about what Dion did for a job. He worked nights, wore nice clothes, and had a nice place. There weren't no hollowed-eyed crack hoes living here, so it didn't much matter to me. But I wondered now what Sledge did in their business. Like the wife in Bewitched who always had a smile for Darren's boss, I took the glass to the living room.

I glanced at the time on the cable box while I handed a drink to Dion's boss. For the first time in the longest, I wished my mother gave a shit about where I was at night. I wanted one of those parents who'd send out the troops if their kid was even a minute late for curfew. But I didn't have either a momma who'd worry or a curfew to break.

"Here," I said, handing off the drink.

"Come sit next to me."

Dion ain't say nothing so I sat on the leather couch. The cushions pulled me in like a hug. It was always hard to get off a here. Even harder with someone big next to me. Sledge pushed in next to me. His whole side was next to mine. There weren't no air out here. I could feel the sweat making our bodies stick together.

"Dion say you fifteen going on sixteen, huh?"

I nodded, then sipped my own drink. I didn't want to talk to him, exactly.

Dion put on some music. It wasn't the usual rap or hip hop. More like that stuff my momma listen to when she and Clark was locked up in they room. Marvin Gaye or Barry White or somebody from the olden days.

"You and Dion doin' it?" Sledge asked.

I whipped around, looking for something from my boy-friend. Why was he letting this guy get all fresh with me? "No."

"You a virgin or something?"

I tipped back the glass. If I didn't swallow something, I'd throw up all over this place. I knew Dion loved me, but having his girl barf all over his precious leather sofa wouldn't go down well. He was cool. But he wasn't that cool.

Sledge's laugh was low and scratchy. "I guess not." He slipped a hand on my thigh and squeezed too hard. "I want to get to know you. Dion and I are tight. A friend of his is a friend of mine. You get me."

Breath sweet from rum and chocolate warmed the side of my face. I swallowed again. I tried to push up from the couch, but I was too dizzy. Sledge turned and pushed down on me. His lips slid all over my face and neck. His hand tried to pull my legs apart. Strength I never knew I had came from somewhere and I pushed myself up and away from the grop-ing hand and mouth of Dion's friend.

"I gotta do my homework," I said, running out the door.

"I gotta do my homework," Sledge mimicked in a fake high voice. I didn't care if he made fun of me as long as I didn't have to see him again.

An hour later, after a bus ride full of people and their funk, I was never so glad to see that damned house of Clark's. I didn't even make it to the front steps before all that Mudslide came up outta me on the weeds Momma called grass. I wiped my mouth with my bare arm and un-locked the kitchen door.

Home.

Safe.

4

With each passing day, I hated school more. I couldn't wait for the day I could graduate. I was kind of thinking that when I turned sixteen I would quit. I didn't want to be no nurse's assistant like Momma cleaning up people's piss, shit, and blood. But maybe if I could get a job now, I could start saving up for the time I could move out, find my own place, start my own life.

"Where Antoine?" someone yelled in my direction. There was enough evil in the voice that suggested the person who was calling my way wasn't the least bit interested in where my best friend was.

Suddenly, two of the biggest bullies from ninth grade surrounded me. "Where's your sissy boyfriend?" the other asked.

I raised my head. Looked them both in the eye. I wasn't afraid of them. "He gone. Transferred."

"Gone to some faggot school?" the first asked.

"Maybe somewhere he can wear a dress," the other said, giving me a good shove before walking off.

I took the hit in stride. I'd put up with worse over the years. I loved Antoine, but being his friend hadn't ever been all that easy. He liked boys and hadn't done much to hide it. After he got beat up pretty badly, his aunt from New York got him into some fancy sleep away school. He'd called me once when he first got there. He sounded happy. I tried not to sound jealous or mad that my best friend had left me in this place with girls who only cared about getting boys. And boys who only cared about getting in their pants. I hated all of them. Without Antoine though, there wasn't much left to like about school.

I stood at the bus stop flipping my pass around in my jacket pocket. Couldn't wait to get away from this place. It was another hot one today. But fake hot again. Like I'd be sweating for a while, then it would be freezing cold as soon as the sun went down. I liked dropping by Dion's place after school but after what happened Wednesday, I wasn't in a big hurry to go back.

The number ten bus came, making my choice for me. I'd go on home. Maybe I could start on that civics project on elections. As if voting made a difference. But I'd work on my election project like it did. No teacher wanted to hear from me how my neighbors voted down at the church every November, but still had pot holes that looked like lakes in the rain and no police when you needed them.

There was a Lincoln in the driveway when I rolled up to Clark's house. Ignoring the little twist in my stomach making me nauseous, I kept on to the kitchen door. It was propped open with a single shoe. The smells coming out of there made my stomach twinge but with hunger this time. Momma had made her gumbo. Her momma had been from Louisiana. That stew was one of the best things—ever. Sometimes, I thought a lot more things would be right in my life if Momma made that gumbo more often.

I couldn't wait to get in there and dig in. Maybe Momma had forgiven me. Or maybe this was her way of saying sorry.

"Gumbo–" I never finished. I was caught up short by a big man sitting at the small kitchen table. How quickly that Navigator had slipped my mind. Of course the food wasn't for me. Momma never cooked for us. The truck owner took up nearly the whole room. As tall as Clark had been but about twice as wide.

"Steffie. C'mon here and meet Tyson."

He looked up at me and nodded. "Tyson Overbey," he said between swallows.

"Hi," I said, shrugging my backpack on to the floor.

"Go put that in your room," Momma said. She ain't care nothing about keeping a house neat, clean, or orderly until there was a man up in here. Then she was a female Felix Unger.

"Can I get a little gumbo first?" I asked.

The man put down his spoon and turned to look at me over his shoulder. "You obey your momma," he directed.

Oh Lordy, he was gonna be one of those. I picked up the nylon bag. My hunger pangs were going away, fast. My momma managed to go to work, pay the bills, and keep us all in food and clothes until a man came along. Then she acted like she didn't have a brain in her head and we all had to follow the rules of whomever she'd taken up with. Clark had been the worst. Syd's dad the best. Tyson looked like he'd fall somewhere in between.

I lugged the bag upstairs and took my sweet time changing from my school clothes into a t-shirt and sweats. I pulled off the bra that was digging into my back and tossed it toward the hamper in the corner. I needed to get something new, but was too embarrassed to go for help at the mall or ask my mom.

Unsure of what I was supposed to do next, I stood on the bottom step near the kitchen. Mom was scurrying around the kitchen. Getting...I'd forgotten his name on the way upstairs...a big mug of Coke to wash down his dinner.

"Why are you standing there watching us?" he asked.

"I..." didn't have an explanation. I walked into the room and stood next to the counter. The lid was firmly on the pot. "Any gumbo left?" My appetite wasn't back, but I wasn't going to turn down something that didn't come in a box, wasn't orange, or hadn't come out of the microwave.

The new guy looked me up and down. His eyes zeroed in on my titties. They'd been growing bigger. I could see that in the mirror. I could feel that in the bra strap that had been digging into my back. I wished they'd go away. Didn't seem like they'd been causing me anything but trouble. Clark didn't waste no time getting his hands all over them, telling me he couldn't wait until they got bigger than plums.

"What you looking at?" Momma asked. Her voice had the slightest edge to it. Just the littlest bit.

Warmed me inside. Made me almost hopeful that I would come first this time. "Wondering what her boyfriend see in a girl with no more than wasp bites."

His laugh was a deep guffaw. Momma joined him. Sydney came down, her two kids clean from a bath.

"What so funny?"

"Nothing," I snapped. I'd told Momma about Dion because I wanted her to know that somebody loved me. That someone had my back.

Momma pulled out a purple bowl with a white-girl princess stuck on the side for Sheron and a red and blue superhero one for Jaylen. She spooned stew in each, careful to pull out any shells. The kids dug in eagerly. Sydney helped herself.

"You want any more, Tyson?" Momma's voice had gone from scratchy to sugary. My teeth nearly ached with it.

He took his sweet time before waving away the offer.

I waited for Momma's go ahead before I got down a bowl for myself. I scooped out a small portion and sat on the only remaining chair. The one with the tear in the vinyl. It poked against my leg, not quite hurting, but irritating me nonetheless.

"Girls," Momma started. "I've been working hard these last coupla months. Tyson's agreed to move in. To help with the bills and all that. I can maybe drop some shifts and finish up my R.N."

Tyson eyed me from the head of the little table. "Looks like you need a man around here. Someone to father these kids," he said.

I looked at the big man, his knuckles scarred by I don't know what and wondered why he wanted to move in with some woman. Didn't he have any family of his own at his age? Men always want something, but I didn't know his game yet. He didn't have a beer in hand. Maybe it wasn't drinking. Looked at his big biceps in his t-shirt. Maybe not shooting up either. But that didn't mean he wouldn't spend all Momma's money or try to get a two-fer like Clark. Wasn't itching to find out.

I shoved my unfinished gumbo aside. The last thing I needed was another daddy coming in here. I'd had a few too many. As soon as Tyson and Momma went outside to get something from his truck, I ran back upstairs.

"Where you goin' now?" Sydney asked, watching me tie on my sneakers.

"Somewhere no one's trying to be my daddy."

5

While Tyson was carrying a suitcase in one door, I was running out the other. None of them would miss me. Syd would be busy getting her kids to sleep. Momma would be busy locked in her room getting the new man situated. And that situating was probably going to involve a lot of screaming and headboard banging against the wall we shared. I could do without that tonight. When I was younger, I could pretend Momma was playing handball indoors or hopscotch with my pretend daddies. But after Clark, I knew exactly what was going on. Standing by while it happened made me want to throw up the little bit of gumbo I'd swallowed.

By the time the number seven bus delivered me to Dion's neighborhood and I made the walk to his building on Overlook, it was getting dark—cold like I'd thought it would. I hit the buzzer inside the front door, but no one answered. I didn't know what time he started work. I looked around, not seeing him or anyone who looked like him coming up the front pathway. Maybe I was too late.

I pushed open the door into the cool night air. Walked down Euclid Heights past a bunch of brick buildings and folks dressed up nice for dinner and the movies. Came up on a place called the Centrum. Looked like a lot of other abandoned movie theaters in Cleveland. I didn't know what was inside, but I knew it wasn't any movies.

Good thing was that there was a payphone outside. I fished for a quarter in my pocket. Dialed Dion's pager, putting in the number on the keypad careful like making sure I got it right. Then I had to stand by the phone looking like I was going to use it. I practiced what I'd say if someone tried to pry my hand from the receiver. Fortunately, it wasn't long before it rang.

"Fortune." He sounded very adult, not like the boy I'd known for months. Called myself a hundred times a fool for bothering him at work. My momma woulda killed me if I'd called her at work and the house weren't on fire.

"Dion, it's me, Steffi. I needed a place to stay tonight."

I wondered if I'd gone too far. He was my boyfriend, but I hadn't never stayed the night. I hadn't ever been to his apartment when he wasn't there. There was a long time before I heard anything on the phone. I was afraid he'd hung up on my schoolgirl problems. The last thing I wanted to do was slink back home, have Syd laugh at me. Listen to my mom sweettalk a new man.

"I'm working," he said. No offer to give me a key. Didn't tell me to wait. I didn't want to have to beg.

I did all I could not to sound like a whining, pouting child. "Can you pick me up? I won't get in the way. I could stay in the car." Another long pause.

A long sigh whispered through the phone before he finally spoke. "Where are you?"

I told him.

Not ten minutes later, his car pulled up. Sledge and a woman were in the backseat. It was too dark to see more and I was too grateful for the ride to ask where we were going when Dion edged away from the curb.

Sledge was whispering fiercely to the woman in the back. I had no idea what they were talking about but I was grateful I wasn't her. Her swollen lip told me that she'd gotten on the wrong side of the man. I was happy that I was with Dion. We didn't have any of that kind of drama. After listening to Momma's screaming matches with one man, then another, I didn't want any of that in my life.

Latching my seat belt, I sat mute. I knew better than to ask where we were going. I'd ride around in this car all night if'n it meant I didn't have to go home right now. I could face them all again tomorrow.

The dark scenery of Cleveland's east suburbs flashed by. A tractor-trailer truck roared by, pushing us all sideways a little. Dion cursed. The woman squealed. Sledge murmured something that kept her quiet. Tyson could be a trucker. Momma had messed with one of those. He was gone five days out of seven. Wasn't as good as Syd's dad, but he wasn't there to bother me too much.

The darker it got, the more difficult it was to see what was around me. Didn't seem like we were going anywhere in particular. Finally, we slowed down, pulled up to a house. The woman in the back got out and went in. Then we drove to another. The click-clack came first before I saw anyone. Like in one of those stupid cable horror movies, a woman ran down the walkway in the highest heels I'd ever seen. I looked up from the shoes to the clothes. She was dressed like one of those movies too. Too tight skirt. Shirt half opened. I tried not to shiver. Half expected Jason to jump from the shadows and slash her. But there was nothing deadlier than mist out there. Sledge opened the door and the woman hopped in the car.

I didn't want nothing to do with Sledge, but my curiosity got the better of me. I turned back to see the woman pulling a small wad of bills from her bra. He counted it. Lifted his butt off the seat, kicking Dion in the process, and jammed it into his front pocket. The streetlight coming through the sunroof glinted off something metal in Sledge's pants. A gun.

At the kick in the seat, Dion looked up at the rearview mirror, but didn't say a word. Put the car in park and drove again. I tried to wrap my brain around what I was seeing. Momma gave her money to whoever was in the house. So I knew about that. But Momma didn't wear really high heels or half her clothes while doing it. She was usually in her blue work scrubs, pulling money from her pay envelope after she'd cashed her check at the place around the corner. And no guy ever brought a gun in the house, not that I knew about anyway.

I looked at Dion, wanting to ask him a question. But the look he gave me back told me to shut up, stop being such a kid, be quiet. So I did what his eyes told me. I didn't say anything as we stopped by another woman who knocked on my window.

Reflexively, I pushed the button letting it down. She started to hand money through to me, but stopped short. Guessin' I wasn't who she was expecting.

"How much *you* get?" she asked me.

Get? "I'm Dion's girlfriend."

"I'm in the back," Sledge yelled. I hadn't realized I was taking up his seat.

"I can sit in the back," I added quickly. Sledge didn't seem the kind of guy who I wanted to be on the wrong side of.

"Get in the damned car," Sledge ordered. The woman yanked open the back door and got in. I didn't turn my head this time.

I shifted in my seat instead. I wanted to go home. Momma and Cyrus or whatever his name doing the nasty next to my head didn't seem so bad. I probably could have gotten a good-sized bowl of gumbo in me when they went upstairs. In the morning, she would have blamed the smaller-than-she-remembered leftovers on him. Or she would have been in that goofy haze where I could have gotten away with anything.

I looked out the window, but didn't recognize a single building. I fingered the RTA pass in my front pocket. It was the single biggest expense from Momma's allowance. But it let me go everywhere without needing a ride. I was sure if I jumped out at a corner, I could find a bus to take me downtown and get me another home.

Might take a couple of hours, but that was probably better than getting involved in whatever mess Sledge was up to. I wasn't sure if he was slinging, but I did *not* want to call my momma from jail. She might not pick me up. And from what I heard about juvey, I wasn't wantin' to be stuck there for months or years. Who knew how much rock Sledge may have had in the trunk of Dion's car.

"I can get out here," I said to Dion when he stopped at an unfamiliar corner.

"We only got a few more stops before we can go home," he said, not looking at me. He put his foot down, driving fast when the light turned green.

"I need to go. I didn't tell my momma I was going. Don't want her to send the po-lice out for me," I said. Dion looked at me kinda funny out of the corner of his eye. He probably knew as well as I did that Momma wasn't sending no cops out for me. She probably wouldn't notice I'm gone for a good day or so. Even then, I'm not sure what she'd do. Try to call Antoine's family? Ask Syd to try to find me? None of the above? With Clyde or whoever moving in, that could be more than two days.

We all rode for several blocks in silence.

"Let her out," Sledge finally said from the back seat. "We got business to do. Don't have time for babysitting."

That remark about me being a baby stung hard, like a slap. But I fingered my bus pass again. My ticket home. Dion didn't say nothing about seeing me later, or calling me. Just swerved over and popped the locks. I swung open the door and stepped out. The little green car swung away from the curb before I could get the door closed right. Damn. Literally kicked to the curb.

Before I could look up and down the street right proper for an RTA sign, a guy approached me. He got my arm in a tight grip before I could think to back up away from him.

"You with Sledge?" he demanded to know.

My mind zoomed from one place to another. Was he a rival of Dion's boss, ready to stick a knife in me for crossing territory? Did Sledge owe him something and this guy expect *me* to pay?

I said, "I was with Dion. He my boyfriend. Sledge was only in the back seat."

He considered me a long time. Didn't let go none though. "Dion working on his own then?"

I shook my head as dramatically as I could muster. "I don't know nothing about they business. I was only getting a ride."

"Why they drop you off here, then? You planning to work this area?"

"I'm only looking for the bus. I ain't working nowhere," I replied.

Another long considering look from him. I might be dark-skinned, but the bite of his fingers in my arm would leave a bruise in the morning. An empty city bus roared up to the stop a few feet away. "You better catch your bus, then."

Wrenching my arm away, I ran for the open door of the vehicle.

I flipped my pass to the driver. The old black man was probably somebody's grandpa. He shook his gray-haired head. "Damn girls get younger by the week. Oughta clean up this strip," he muttered.

Insulted, though I couldn't quite place why, I asked. "What's the last stop?"

"Tower City."

He looked at me a little closer. I pulled the thin jacket over my top. Why was everyone looking so hard at me today? I regretted taking off my bra earlier. A tight brassiere was probably better than none at all. Looking like he made up his mind about something, he asked me, "Where you going?"

"Home," I said. Then changed track. "East Eighty-Eighth and Wade Park."

"Change at Ninety-Third for the ten. That'll take you home faster."

"Can you–"

"I'll let you know," he said, leaning toward the windshield and turning the huge steering wheel to the left.

I stomped to an empty seat. It was a long time before the driver said anything. I thought he'd forgotten about me, but I heard, "Girl with the green jacket. This is your stop."

Thank God there wasn't anyone hanging around at the second bus stop. I was tired of men today. If I never saw another one, it wouldn't be too soon. It had gotten legit cold by the time the ten bus dropped me off.

Momma was making some noise that made her sound like a pig as I tiptoed down the hall to my room. I ignored the grunting and changed into my pajamas. Laid my head down for a second, but couldn't sleep with the slap of the headboard. Slipping out of bed, I pulled my Civics book from my backpack. Got some paper I borrowed from the library computer lab, some colored pencils from the top drawer in my dresser, and went down to the TV room.

Maybe I could make heads or tails of the constitution. I cheered up considerably when I found gumbo left in the pot. I moved my stuff to the kitchen table. My mouth had been all ready for something to relax me. Dion always had something good prepared for me. I looked in the fridge. Alcohol appeared like clockwork the minute another daddy moved in. I took a beer. Dared anyone to accuse me.

Full and relaxed a half hour later, I decided to draw a map of states that needed the Voting Rights Act. Most times being able to draw could get me close to an 'A' all by itself. I didn't think I'd be sleepy for a long time, so maybe I could write a good essay besides.

6

"You ain't called." Dion's voice came from the receiver. I was shocked as shit when the phone rang and it was for me. First of all, ain't no boy ever really called here for me. Excepting Antoine and that didn't count. Second of all, Dion didn't call. I paged him. If the phone rang twice and stopped, I could come over. That was how things worked. Third of all...well, third, I figured he'd dumped me after that Friday night when I'd caused so much trouble at the bus stop. It had been nine days since he'd had anything to do with me. Life with Momma had taught me that if a man didn't call, they was probably done with you.

"I been busy with school," I said. It wasn't exactly a lie. I'd gotten that 'A' on my Civics project. I didn't even tense up and squeak out my oral report like I usually did. I'd also been busy avoiding Tyson. He didn't seem to have any kind of job to speak of. He said he worked nights in a restaurant, but he seemed to be up with Momma in her room more nights than not. Which wasn't so great, because my last bra had broke and I was working up the nerve to ask her to go shopping with me. But I had to see her first to ask her. I wasn't quite desperate enough to beg a favor off Syd. I'd probably owe her a lifetime of babysitting if I did that. She didn't do anything for anyone without expecting something in return.

"I need to see you. I miss you," Dion said, bringing me back. He missed me? He'd never said anything like that before.

Even though no one was here to watch me, I felt shy, vulnerable. My stomach fluttered. I said, "I can come over now." I looked at the clock on the stove. It still had the old time. Tyson wasn't handy like that. Clocks an hour behind would have driven Clark nuts. The reality of a new guy living in his house would have driven Clark nuts. In that moment, I liked Tyson a lot more. "The buses run slow on Sunday. Maybe I'll be there in an hour or so?"

"I can't wait that long to see you, girl," he said. "I'll pick you up where I parked that first time."

I calculated how long it would take to get to that spot next to the park. "Okay, I'll see you in twenty," I said. Tearing up the stairs, I looked through my pathetic closet. Suddenly, I wished I'd listened to my sister, Antoine, anybody, about the importance of having the right clothes. I'd never much cared. And around here, it had always been a little better to look shabby. Didn't work on Clark, but it kept Momma's other boyfriends from looking too close.

Girls wore all that makeup and tight clothes and wondered why boys was always up in their business. I shook my head. I think maybe I kind of wanted this boy up in my business. Well, I wasn't entirely sure about that. But Momma kept a man around by keeping him in the bed.

If I wanted Dion to stick around my young ass for more than a minute, I'd have to maybe make a little trade. The flutters in my stomach rolled into a ball of queasiness. But I pushed away the thoughts of Clark. Maybe if you liked the person, the touching would feel good. It had to. Momma and Syd sure were all up in the bed with men. My twenty minutes was ticking by fast. I didn't want to be late and I needed something better than my jacked-up middle school clothes.

I peeked out in the hall. Momma's door was shut tight. I tiptoed to the bathroom and looked in the hamper. I flipped the lid and there it was: the nice white polo I'd seen Momma wearing at breakfast. She'd gotten some egg yolk on it while making grits, eggs, hot links, and toast for Tyson. I pulled the shirt out. Smelled like perfume. I sniffed at it and the tightness in my tummy eased.

I rubbed the green bar soap from the sink hard on the small corner of the shirt and in a minute the egg was gone. I pulled off my too tight t-shirt and pulled on Momma's shirt. I modeled in the mirror, arms on hips, cheeks sucked in. Not half bad. Most days, I hated being dark, but with the white shirt, I looked good.

Gross I know, but I continued to dig around. Pulled out a pair of flared jeans. They fit better than I thought. Distractedly, I wondered when Mom and I became the same size. I always thought of Momma as bigger than me. Like when I was a little kid. But Clark had said he was making me a woman. Guess he was right.

Since I was long past trouble, I lifted the heavy blue bottle of Momma's favorite perfume from the toilet shelf and sprayed a couple of pumps at my neck and on my wrists. Once I was done, I didn't tiptoe on the way out of the bathroom. Momma was in her room for good. No way she was going to come out and harass me about where I was going. Syd was out with her kids and they daddy. No telling when she'd be home.

On my way out the kitchen door, I glanced at the stove clock. Damn. I was going to be late. I didn't even mind the hoots I got from the cars. To the last guy in the beat up Chevy, I even threw a 'back at you,' to him. He looked almost too interested to drive with his eyes bugged out of his head. I was glad when the woman behind him honked.

Something cold trickled on my scalp. I raised my head to see if a bird was pooping from a tree. That was the kind of luck I had. It was rain, though. A lot of it. Looked as if the heavens had opened up. I glanced behind me. Nothing but gray houses, gray skies, gray rain. Clark's house was a distant memory. I ran. My sneakers squished with every step. I stopped for a moment under a huge tree. Nothing but a mist underneath there. I pulled at my hair, but the naps let me know it was ruined. I'd done my best flat-ironing it into something like Halle Berry's hair. But I didn't have one white parent helping keep it straight.

My polo was wet. I hadn't yet gotten around to getting a new bra and I wasn't hiding nothing. I wished there were undershirts for people my age. Momma's jeans had picked up mud around the big cuffs that dragged when I ran. Damn, she was going to kill me if she found out I'd borrowed, then ruined her clothes. Her and Sydney were the same like that. Leaving my temporary shelter, I darted along through the park to the street where Dion's car had been parked the first time. I tried to remember if his building had a dryer.

I was so happy to see Dion's green car on the street, I almost cried. Maybe I could get warm and dry in there. I hoped the water wouldn't ruin the leather. When I bent down to look in, he was bebopping and tapping to music only he could hear. I rapped on the window. He rolled it down, rap spilling out like mist from a full freezer.

"You look good, girl," he said. But Dion wasn't looking at my eyes or hair.

Reflexively, I pulled my arms across my chest—an elbow in each hand.

"Can I get in?" The shiver that stole through me wasn't for effect.

"Sure, yeah," he said, popping the locks. I ran around to the other side of the car. "Sorry about that."

Something was off in the way Dion was looking at me. My skin pulled tight on my arms as goose bumps rose. "Can you turn up the heat?"

He pushed a few buttons and soon, I couldn't hear the music over the roar of the air. I let the heat blast at my arms. Leaned my head, trying to dry my hair some.

I would wrap myself in a bathroom towel as soon as we got to Dion's place. Maybe I could even borrow that green robe he hooked on the back of the bathroom door.

"Let me make you something hot," he said once we were in his place.

Nearly dry, I curled on the couch and watched the rain taper off. Of course it only rained in the five minutes I was outside. My luck had always been like that.

Dion handed me hot chocolate. I took a big sip. Burned my tongue in two ways. First on the hot. Second on the booze. "What's in here?"

"Bailey's," he said.

"It's really good." I blew on it and took another sip. So very good. "You got any marshmallows?" I asked. The look he gave me made me regret asking the question. Marshmallows were for kids, I guessed. I should have known that. Dion put on some music and went to make some phone calls. Probably work. I finished the cocoa.

"You want another?" Dion asked when he came back.

"I'm good," I said.

"Then let's go for a ride," he said with a long sigh.

"I'm okay hanging out here," I said.

He shook his head swiftly. "I can't always hang out. Sledge needs me to do some work today."

The chocolate and milk and alcohol solidified in my belly like a fried chicken joint buttermilk biscuit was in there. "Can I ask you a question?" I whispered.

"What you need to know?" His tone was curt. "Spit it out."

Took me a minute to get my guts up. I didn't like to anger men who had friends with guns. "You slinging?"

"Damn girl. Nah, I ain't slinging. I don't want to fuck around with them dealers."

I nearly slipped off the couch in relief. Cops wouldn't pick me up asking me to explain fifty pounds of MJ in Dion's trunk. "Let's go for a ride then," I said. As we walked toward the car, I floated down the street, relaxed and happy. Maybe we'd pop over to Red Lobster again. Or maybe get something even fancier like steak. My mouth watered with anticipation while we drove through the growing darkness.

With every year I lived here, Cleveland grew darker at night. More houses stood empty. More businesses closed. More vacant lots popped up. Street lights broke and never got fixed.

In school, there was so much talk about the big cities having built this country, steel this, coal that. When did they become small towns again? New York and Chicago couldn't be like this. Detroit maybe.

I stopped looking out and closed my eyes. In a few years, I'd move out and be able to find out. Sometimes, I wondered where I'd go first. Maybe I wouldn't need to go anywhere. I glanced at the side of Dion's face. Would he want to get married one day? We could buy a house in Shaker, maybe. Have a couple of kids. I could stay at home with them all day. Love them like kids deserved to be. Take 'em to the park. Read them books.

"We're here," Dion said, shaking me from my thoughts. How much booze had been in that hot chocolate? I was feeling like I'd had three drinks instead of just the one.

"Where's here?" I asked. I was disappointed that we weren't near the front door of a restaurant. I peered a little more closely at the building set way back from the street. 'The Sleepy Time Motel' the sign read, even though the 'l' and 'p' were missing. Heat rushed up my back, under my arms, prickled my scalp. I'd have been more comfortable doing it in his place. It was familiar, at least. But maybe I wasn't good enough for his place. Probably had a nice-looking girlfriend his age who he was with in that bed.

"What's here?" was my second question. It always came down to this, didn't it? Men only wanted one thing from Momma. Maybe two things—some money for booze and to be all up in her room all night. Clark had only wanted one thing from me. He promised that it would be the same no matter who the man was. Guess he was right about more than a few things. Wanted to kick him in his grave.

Dion laid a hand on my arm. "You'll have a great time, don't worry." I sighed deep. If I wanted to get out of Momma's house, I needed to grow up and learn to do this. At least I knew what was going to happen. He'd want to rub my titties, rub me down there, then stick it in. I hoped he didn't want me to put his thing in my mouth. That part had always made me gag. I pushed hard at my belly, willing myself not to throw up.

"Oh, okay," I said. If I didn't love him, at least I liked him. He was nice to me. Nicer than most people had been. He knew what I liked to watch, drink. All this time, he'd never asked for a thing in return. I guess I owed him this even if it had to be in some skank ass motel.

Dion opened the car door for me like he had that first time. The rain hadn't started up again, but water hung heavily in the air, making a fog I could barely see through. We walked across a planter strip. I nearly tripped over the wood chips and asphalt berm. Dion's grip on my arm was hard as he helped me straighten up.

"Sorry," I said. Didn't know why *I* was apologizing. If we'd parked in the lot, I wouldn't have had to make the trip across plants and chips and stuff.

I shivered again as Momma's jeans brushed against an old car, water soaking to my skin again. We'd weaved between parked cars until we got to a blue door. '142' stood out in raised letters. Dion slipped a card into a slot above the handle. The light switched from red to green with a soft beep. I walked into the room ahead of Dion. I'd never been in a motel before. The biggest thing in the room was the bed. My eyes pinwheeled around, looking for something else. A cube of television sat atop a rickety dresser. That was all. I sat on the bed and looked down at my canvas sneakers. Couldn't think of anything else to do. The carpet was stained. I tried not to think of what could have made those puke green and reddish brown circles.

Dion sat next to me. "Just remember I'm here. Everything is going to be okay."

I kept my eyes trained on the plastic that was flaking from the ends of my shoelaces. After a time, I nodded. Met his eyes. "Okay."

He patted my thigh. "I'll be right back." Dion opened the door. Left. I wondered what he was going to get. Dinner? Condoms? I took off my shoes and laid back against the pillows. It took everything to ignore the smell of the bedspread. Reminded me a bit of Syd's room. Like someone had peed, thrown up, and hadn't done a real good job cleaning it up.

The other door in the room must have been the bathroom. I wondered if I should shower. The bed creaked as I stood. It *was* a bathroom, but the mostly white towels hanging from the bar were small. I touched one—scratchy. Without a bathrobe or something, I'd be as cold after a shower as before. Plus there weren't no place to dry the clothes. I jumped at a loud noise. A fan had started blowing cool air in the room. I ran over. The knob turning the cold to heat was broken. I slipped on my shoes and walked to the front door. Maybe I'd tell Dion I wanted to go home. I didn't want to be there especially, but I didn't want to be here either.

The handle turned under my hand. I stepped back to avoid getting smacked in the face. Sledge walked in. Dion was behind him. Then five different guys came in behind them.

"Dion, I want to go home." I didn't care that my voice sounded like a whine. This wasn't fun anymore.

He didn't look at me. Sledge closed the door behind everyone and stood guard. Weren't no way I could get behind him. "I need to go pee," I said.

The guys passed a forty back and forth, drinking and laughing. I ran to the bathroom and closed the door. I sat on the toilet before I wet my pants further. I didn't flush. If I stayed in here, then maybe I wouldn't have to deal with what was out there. The sweet smell of weed trickled under the door. I heard a new bottle being opened. The top twisting, letting out the fizz.

"C'mon out here, girl," Sledge called.

I'd have thrown up if I'd had something to eat. But Dion hadn't taken me to dinner. I pushed open the door. Two of the guys were laying on the bed, passing a joint back and forth. The others were passing that second forty back and forth. Sledge got the joint and handed it to me. "I don't..." I tried, pushing it back into his hand.

Sledge dropped his hand. "Take a hit."

I put it up to my lips and sucked in. My lungs burned. My eyes were going to explode. Only coughing made it better. The guys all laughed. Great. I was the kid trying to hang with grownups. When one guy passed me the forty, I took it and drank greedily.

"Yeah, girl. Drink up," a guy said. Another tipped it against my mouth. It spilled all over my shirt.

"Shit, yeah," another guy said. They stopped talking to each other and all zeroed in on my chest. "Nothing better than a black girl wet t-shirt."

I didn't need to look down to know that my titties was on display. I looked toward the door, searching for Dion. But he wasn't nowhere in the room. Sledge pulled my hands behind my back. The other guys started to circle me. One grabbed one of my titties and squeezed hard. The squeal escaped my throat before I could think about what I was gonna do. Another put his hand in the top of Momma's pants and pulled. The button popped off. Momma was going to kill me.

"Pull 'em down," one guy said.

"I don't—"

Sledge pulled tighter. "No one want to hear anything from you."

"But—"

One guy popped me in my mouth. My tooth cut my lip. I stuck out my tongue, tasting blood.

"Put that pretty pink tongue on me instead," the guy with the fast fist said.

Sledge let me go. Finally. I jumped up and tried to run to the door.

"You ain't goin' nowhere, girl. You're the life of the party."

Two guys grabbed my arms and pulled me back down on the bed. I tried to tell them no, but my heart was stuck deep in my throat. Next thing I knew, someone had pulled off my shirt. I was so cold. Another took off my pants. I got even colder. But I couldn't pull my hands back to cover myself. There was a knee on one of my arms. A meaty hand held the other.

Then the faces got too close for me to see any details. Everything blurred behind the tears. Hands and mouth and teeth were everywhere, squeezing, prying open, laughing.

Liquid spilled on me, then the bottle went somewhere a bottle should never go. I closed my eyes and wished myself anyplace but The Sleepy Time Motel. No one was planning to let me sleep tonight.

7

We stepped over to the little room where the motel keep old coffee and new condoms. The coffee was free. I pulled a white paper cup from the stack and filled it half full with the thick, half-day-old sludge, the other half with sugar and creamer.

My momma was missing a leg behind the sugar. If I didn't want to go out like that, living half my life in a wheelchair, I needed to lay off this shit. I took a sip. Tomorrow, I'd go cold turkey for sure.

Dion paced back and forth in the small square lobby. I held the lukewarm coffee under my nose, trying to chase away the heavy smell of ammonia and disinfectant. I hated that damned smell. Reminded me of hospitals and jails, two places I'd spent too much time.

"You didn't give me enough time to prep her," Dion complained. He was shifting from foot to foot. The linoleum floor creaked with every movement. I hated this seedy little place, but that Indian guy behind the counter took my money and didn't give a shit what I did up in here. Wasn't going to get that kind of welcome downtown. I shifted my mind from building a better business to the kid in front of me.

"You getting soft or something?" I asked, poking him in his little concave chest. I barely touched bone through that polo shirt he wore. Thing had to be three sizes too big. Someone needed to tell these peewee guys big clothes didn't make them big guys. "What kind of preparation you think she needed?"

He bowed his head so long, I almost thought he was praying. Finally, he looked up at me. The little diamond chip he wore in his ear winked in the pink fluorescent light. "You kind of threw her to the wolves."

"I needed to compensate for the fact that she wasn't a virgin," I said. "They needed something exciting to get the money flowing."

Dion nodded like the 'yes man' he was. "It's just…"

"I don't see you giving back none of that cash stuck in your pocket." The roll I'd given him bulged out in spite of the size of the baggy jeans.

"They really pay three hundred apiece?"

I got close, crowding him. "You saying I shorted you?"

"Na, man. I ain't sayin' that." Dion held my eye. Had to admire that.

"Na, you ain't saying shit," I said. I was harder on Dion than some of the other boys I had working for me because he was one of my favorites. If anything ever happened to me, I'd put him in charge of the business. He might be small, but he wasn't afraid of nothing, not the cops, or the other guys running girls, or a gun being pointed in his face. That fearlessness more than anything else would keep him safe and on top in this business. Cowards got killed.

Dion pulled his pager from his pocket. Pushed the buttons, hooked it onto his coin pocket with a shove. "How long you going to leave them in there?"

"Ninety minutes. After Dashanique, I can't take any chances."

Dion didn't look in my direction at the mention of that girl. Worst fuckup of my career. I had a pretty strong stomach and that night still turned it. It's what had bound us together like brothers, though.

"Them niggers acted like animals," he said derisively.

"I told these cats here that there'd be cameras. They're hoping for a video to stroke out on. I just want them to know I have their balls nailed to the wall." Weren't no one going to fool me twice.

"Is there really video?" Dion asked.

"Yes, there's video. Look at it this way. If something happens to the girl and my name get caught up in this, then I can send that to the po-lice. If one of them gets the stupid idea of trying to frame me, I got them with a minor. And even if none of them knuckleheads tries anything stupid, I might just need a favor of my own down the road."

"Shit, you always thinking ahead." Dion's voice was full of admiration even if he kept his face impassive.

"How many times I got to tell you that business ain't about today only. That's why these street level dealers so dumb. They have a lot of cash today. Lose their patch, or their freedom, or their lives tomorrow. You got to run whatever you're doing like you're in it to win it."

"You sound like that white guy with all the teeth selling the videos in the middle of the night."

"Look, I ain't buying into no franchise scheme or something like that, but there's some truth to what he say."

"What? How to get a big house, boat, car?"

"I ain't got no boat. What he say is that people gotta keep control of they shit. They can't go blaming everyone else for what happens. If I get arrested, it my fault. When that girl Dashanique got hurt bad, it was my fault. Could have turned out a lot worse than it did. But I fucked that shit up. Ain't never going to let that kind of shit happen again. And if it do, because we can't always control the customers in our business, I'm taking out insurance."

Dion fumbled with the pager again. When he finally got that hook off his pants, he announced, "Been eighty minutes."

"Go knock on the door."

"Am I going in?" Dion was doing that shift and shuffle again. I was going to have to work on that. A man stood tall and strong, not shucking and jiving like he was on a southern plantation.

"No, that's they ten minute warning," I said, pointing to the glass door.

The minute he walked out, my pager lit up. Momma. I signaled the desk guy who pulled my phone from the desk. He started to hand me the charger plug, but I didn't want that just now.

"What's going on?" I barked at my niece.

"Auntie Velma refuse to take her insulin today."

"It's just a quick stick. Does she want to lose her second leg?" Getting Momma around in her three story house without a wheelchair was already a hassle. Double amputee didn't sound like no fun to live with. "Did you get that injector pen like I told you?"

"Auntie said not to," she whined.

"Who's paying you?"

A big huff of frustration followed a long silence. "You are, Sledge. But Velma said that was good money we could use to get the roof patched or fix the leak in the basement."

"Do I need to pick up the medicine on the way home or can I trust that you'll get it done?"

"I'll do it now," she said after a long pause.

"Good," I said, satisfied with the acquiescence in her voice. "What roof problem?"

"There's a stain in the attic ceiling." My niece rushed on. "I didn't tell you about it because you was busy. But it's just a little spot. Probably be gone come spring."

I gripped the little plastic phone tight. I'd already gone through a couple of the plastic gadgets—throwing them across the room. I didn't want to spend any more money on deductibles buying new ones. The insurance company wasn't going to believe a third claim. I certainly wouldn't. Paying out more than you take in wasn't good for anyone's business.

It was time to lay out orders. With proper motivation and a list of tasks to complete, life ran smoothly. "Get the injector that doesn't hurt. Walk across the street and ask the guy in the white house—"

"Clive?"

"Yeah. Him. Ask him who did his roof last year. If it's holding up. If it is, get that guy's name. Call me and give me the roofer's number. You got all that?"

"Going to the drugstore now," she said.

Pleased, I pressed the button. I slipped the agreed upon cash to the desk clerk, and he handed me my charger. I tried not to bounce on the balls of my feet. I was ready to go. I had girls to pick up and money to collect. Dion and I didn't usually stick around too long, but with first timers, you never knew how it would go. Protective of the investment I'd made in them, though, required keeping an eye out.

I looked at my pager. On cue, Dion walked back in the lobby.

"Sledge, you're gonna wanna see this," he said.

I didn't tell him I didn't want to see shit. Wasn't manly to say that you liked money, but not the details. Needed to get into the clothing or electronics business. They sold their shit here but kept the dirty business in China and India.

"She alive, right?" I asked.

"Yeah . . . but something ain't right."

Swallowed back any bad feeling and got ready to face whatever was coming.

8

Miles Siegel

July 10, 2004

Casey's gasp brought me around. I didn't know how long I'd stood there looking into that void.

"Lou?" I looked at FBI Agent Valdespino for some kind of explanation. My mind was having a hell of a time making sense of what I was seeing.

I dropped Casey's hand as Valdespino motioned me a few feet away from the container. "Our best guess is that someone is smuggling illegals into the country."

"Cleveland? I thought this kind of thing only happened in the border states. You know, California, Texas, Arizona. The places where they've got patrols, snipers, fences, walls."

"Maybe that's precisely what brought them here."

"But why are they…here?" I asked, pointing down at the ground beneath us. The odor had started to hit me. There was probably a makeshift toilet in there. From the smell of things, it hadn't been emptied out lately.

"The M.O. on these things is that there's a guy in charge. Probably hires them out for work, keeps the money. When…if they ever pay him off…they can have their freedom."

"As what? Another undocumented person in the U.S.?" From all news reports, that wasn't a great position. Fear of immigration. Subject to exploitation at work. I couldn't see how that was better than Mexico or Central America which seemed more peaceful now than when I was a kid and Contras were nightly news fodder.

"Maybe it's better than what they came from," Casey said. I'd nearly forgotten she was there. All that pacing in anticipation of our date. All that worry over what to wear seemed irrelevant in the face of whatever this was. This was more than Timberlands versus Vans. More than worrying that my curly hair was too unruly. This was the other side of humanity.

"What are you going to do with them?" Casey asked Valdespino. Or maybe that was meant a little bit for me too. Why couldn't Rachel have answered her phone? That woman never missed an opportunity to climb the career ladder. This looked like a ten rung leap.

Interrupting my thoughts of avoidance, Valdespino said, "Take 'em down to headquarters. Scour this thing for evidence. Figure out if we need to arrest them or deport them."

I looked at Casey. But she wasn't looking at me. She was frowning heavily, her entire face pinched. "Why aren't any of them coming out?"

That was the one hundred thousand dollar question, wasn't it? If we were freedom, why weren't they running to us with open arms like Elián González?

Valdespino looked at me. Like I could give some direction. "Let's take them downtown. I'll meet you there," he said, for lack of a better option. He nodded and dispatched his guys.

"I'll take you home," I said to Casey. This was a hell of a day for her car to break down. What had been a gift dropped in my lap—an open invitation to take this woman home—was turning procedure on its ear.

The drive to her apartment was quiet and the kiss I placed on her cheek perfunctory. How I'd imagined the night going and how it had turned out were so far apart, they didn't even exist in the same universe.

"So...I'll see you," Casey's voice was hesitant. I hated that tonight's situation put that unsureness there. I wanted her to know that my interest wasn't going to wane. Even if I was knee deep in some big immigration case.

"My head's somewhere else right now," I said.

She dipped her head as if to reassure herself of something and looked up at me again. Her blue eyes were clear, focused. "Gotcha. I'd say have a good night, but...I don't think it's going to be one."

I nodded in mute agreement. She shoved the passenger door closed and made short work of the ten feet of concrete between the street and her building's door.

Twenty minutes later, I was standing in Valdespino's office in the FBI's brand spanking new digs, cooling my heels. He'd set up a series of interrogation rooms. Each woman was in one. I was waiting to get the go ahead that we could start questioning. No doubt some office secretary was pulling stacks of 302s—the FBI's interview form—out of storage. They refused to record interrogations. Made cases harder to prosecute in my opinion and upped the mistrust factor, but I worked for the US Attorney's office and didn't have a direct line to Robert Mueller. Not that the FBI director was dying to hear my rookie opinion anyway.

Valdespino came back in, interrogation forms under his arm and keys jingling in hand. "We're good to go."

"Where's the kid?" The dark eyes of that child haunted me. Whatever my parents' faults, I'd never been without creature comforts. That boy or girl had no comfort at all. What parent would subject their child to life in a tin can just to escape another country? I couldn't imagine it got much worse than that abroad.

"Child protective services," Valdespino said, opening the door and walking down the hall. I tried to shake off my bias against foster care. The one or two stories Casey had shared had put a healthy fear for that child into my heart. Anything had to be better than living in a metal box unfit for human habitation, though.

Valdespino inserted the key into the first doorknob. Twisted. We walked into the room. A lone woman sat. Her arm was chained to the desk; she wasn't going anywhere. I knew that hollow-eyed look from my cop days. Total and utter defeat. Whatever hope she'd had about finding a better life had disappeared long ago.

"I'm Miles Siegel, Assistant United States Attorney." I stuck out my hand. It hung limp for a long moment, before I pulled it back toward my side. "What's your name?"

The woman finally raised her eyes. They were sunken, haunted. She looked at me. Shifted her eyes to Valdespino, then either closed them or took in a lot of fake wood grain melamine.

I took in her appearance. She was white, with dirty-blonde hair, blue eyes. After Valdespino's talk, I was expecting someone dark-haired, about my color, a typical Mexican woman. I searched my mind for other countries people fled from. The Ukraine? Chechnya always seemed perilously close to collapse. But I was an American, what did I know?

"We're here to help you," I started, slowly enunciating each word. "In our country, no one is required to be enslaved. We can help you find a place to live, maybe get you transport back to your home country."

"Can I get a first class back to Texas?" The drawl caught me off guard. I traded glances with Valdespino. My look said: So much for your stupid theory. His look was: Win some. Lose some.

"What's your name?" My question was rapid-fire this time. I clicked the pen point down, slid the pad Valdespino had given to me closer.

"Look. I like living. It may not be too much of a life right now, but I'm not interested in having my light put out just yet."

"Who's going to turn out your lights?" Valdespino asked.

"I ain't sayin' no more until I get those tickets."

"You were serious?" I asked. Valdespino shot me a look. This one said: rookie. My Philly cop had been a lot better than my Cleveland AUSA. These federal suspects were a little bit more cunning, smart, outspoken than their Philly street level counterparts. Those people never spoke a word unless under threat of…well, under threat.

"Never flown first class. Think I might like it," the woman rasped. Sounded like she hadn't talked in a while or was sick. I resisted the urge to back up my chair a little.

From my experience with free government tickets, we should all be grateful we weren't traveling by military jet with a five-point harness keeping us in our seats. I looked at Valdespino again. He nodded. Well, that was some pull. Maybe I needed to have the Feebs arrange my travel.

"Fine." I was done with all the soft-pedaling. I didn't want to be here all night trying to fit pieces into a puzzle. I wanted the key to solving the mystery. "Why are you living in a container?"

"Cause Sledge put a lock on the door."

"How long have you been there?"

"Don't know. A year, maybe."

"Why is he keeping you in there?" I wasn't blaming the victim, but someday, a juror would want the answer to that question.

"'Cause he don't want us to leave," she said like I hadn't graduated kindergarten.

I worked my face to neutral. No one had asked this woman her opinion in years. That was obvious. She liked hearing herself talk. Having a little of the power that had probably been taken from her. I leaned back and crossed my arms. It was her show.

"I told you my name." I jerked my thumb sideways. "This here is Lou Valdespino. He's with the FBI. You?"

"I used to be," she paused. Her voice got whisper quiet. "Krystal Marsh."

"What does this Sledge call you?"

"Candy. Candy Sweet."

"What do you do for Sledge?" I had a sneaking suspicion it wasn't piece work at a local factory. Not that there were many of those left up here in Cleveland.

"Whatever guy he wants," she said.

Prostitution and container didn't jibe. "Excuse me for my confusion. You're a...prostitute?"

"Whore, working girl, hooker, escort. Words don't matter none. I know what I do." What she did was a misdemeanor. The Feds didn't touch it, much less the counties. This was low level local all the way.

"How often do you work?" Valdespino asked. I wanted to pull him out of the room and ask him what either one of us was doing here. What we'd come across was sad, tragic even, but not a federal crime.

"Day. Night. Whenever," Krystal said.

"How?" Valdespino shot back.

"He unlocks the door. His muscle, a young-looking guy, puts us in a vehicle. We go to a hotel. That kid walks us to a room. There's one man or sometimes more waiting. We do whatever they want. If we're lucky, we can get a shower and a little something to eat before getting put back."

"This Sledge is your pimp?" Valdespino asked point blank.

"Jailer, more like."

"Why can't you leave?" I asked. "Don't most pimps let the girls go home at the end of the night?" I regretted asking the question, but my curiosity overcame my temperance.

"Because his money walks away. Sometimes, it don't come back. He learned to keep his money close. Sledge makes more than anyone out there on the street."

"Why?" I probed. Valdespino wasn't an idiot. He must be seeing something I wasn't.

"His girls will do anything."

I tried to wrap my mind around all this. I'd always thought guys visited prostitutes to get stuff they couldn't get at home from their wives or girlfriends. Now there was a greater circle of hell? Working girls who do what regular prostitutes won't?

"What's anything?" Valdespino asked. He looked unfazed. I was fifteen seconds from losing my wine and dinner.

"Mostly kinky stuff and gangbangs," she said.

A niche is what this guy Sledge had. At least that's what it would be called in the white collar world. It was both ingenious and infuriating.

"Does that include children?" Lou asked.

Finally, something cracked Krystal's hard-as-nails demeanor. "Yeah, young girls too." Bam, we'd just graduated from minor misdemeanor. We were now right in the thick of federal crime territory.

The rest of the conversation was logistics. The bare bones of Sledge's operation, and getting Krystal's front-of-the-plane ticket while extracting her promise to testify.

When we left the room, I looked at Lou. "We've got a federal crime."

"No shit. You looked a little doubtful in the beginning."

My tilt of the head was my only acknowledgement that I'd needed some convincing.

"I'm thinking trafficking, kidnapping to start," Valdespino said. "Probably RICO." RICO may have once been the sole providence of the mob, but everyone organized into some kind of crime was under the statute now. And what so-called Sledge had here sounded nothing short of organized.

I was more than ready to leave Valdespino to his job. "Brief me on the rest tomorrow, if necessary. But Monday for sure. I'll loop Chas in as well."

Valdespino gave a little mock salute, jingled the keys, and opened door number two. I didn't envy him. He'd get the raw stories. My second-hand report would be dry, dispassionate, and fact-heavy. I liked it that way. It was half the reason I'd left the PD and joined the AUSA. I walked the brightly lit, sterile halls and out the door to my car, only one of a few in the nearly empty lot.

I know it was wrong to drive to Casey's house at this hour of the night. But I didn't want to be alone with my imagination. Without hesitation, she buzzed me in when I called up. When I finished the four story trek, she was already waiting at the door, glass of wine in hand. Didn't look like she was ready to turn in for the night either.

"You want—" she'd started to say before her cat snaked out through her bare feet and out the door. My mom had been a cat lover and owner for years. For that reason, my reflexes threw me into action. I was quicker than the feline and had her...no, him scooped up, claws facing away from me quicker than a quick draw cowboy in an old Western movie.

"Thanks. I was gonna ask if you wanted wine."

I stepped in and dropped the cat, which promptly ran down the hall toward a back bedroom. "That would be wonderful, thanks." Damn, I sounded like a polite houseguest. I glanced at the watch my mom had given me for law school graduation. Polite houseguests did not show up at midnight.

"Make yourself at home," she said, doing her own polite host bit.

I sunk into a dining room chair. "Do you mind?" I asked, gesturing to my Timberlands. What had seemed sharp in the morning was just heavy now.

"No, I don't mind. You shouldn't be driving, anyway." She gestured to my wine. Casey disappeared in the kitchen, coming back with the half full bottle. She plopped it between us with a loud smack on the table.

"Does that mean I can stay?"

"The futon is comfortable." Casey tilted her head in that way she had. "Let's talk about what happened tonight."

I hesitated a long time. Criminal prosecutions were tricky. Like any other lawyer, I owed a duty of confidentiality to my client. But my client was the United States of America. Joe Citizen wasn't privy to all that was done to protect him.

But Casey had already been there. She'd probably made a reasonable guess what was going on. As if reading my mind, she said, "I told you I'm not in federal court. Departures downward and upward make me nervous. What you say stays here."

"Those people you saw tonight...they weren't illegal immigrants. They're victims of sex trafficking."

"Oh, shit," she said, falling silent.

We both sat with that through two more glasses of wine.

"The kid too?"

I only nodded. Who wanted to think about that in any detail? I surely didn't.

I started talking to get the horrific thoughts that had started swirling in my head. "Lou thinks we may have a big thing here. Kidnapping. Human trafficking."

"How many months does all this carry?"

"If the kid is under fourteen, life in prison."

I could see Casey close her eyes in a silent prayer of thanks. It was good to know that even a defense attorney had a line in the sand. Many of them didn't.

"Do you think they'll let you handle the case?"

Not that I hadn't asked myself that same question, but it still stung—a lot. I'd lost my first big case earlier in the year. I'm sure my boss Chas Fitzgerald would ask the same question as well. After all, Rachel was the one on call. "This is just the kind of thing Rachel would love to sink her teeth into. But I've done some of that preliminary leg work. It would be best for the case to leave me on it." That was my ego talking and I knew it. But I wasn't about to admit that in front of the woman I wanted to be impressed with me.

Wine nearly depleted, we sat for long moments.

"I'm sorry tonight got cut short," I said. I was really, very sorry. It was a few months past her breakup and I was hoping tonight we could start fresh.

Her hand snaked out to cover mine. It was pale compared to my tan one. "I'm sorry too."

I curled my toes in my socks and closed my eyes. I pushed those women out of my mind. I don't know what in the hell had happened to them, would happen to *them*. At least *we* had a chance.

9

I wish someone had told me law school wasn't lawyer school. Three years at Cleveland Marshall taught me little to nothing about the real world of courthouse work. I had to take a class to pass the bar. I had to stock up on Continuing Legal Education courses to learn everything: juvenile, divorce, criminal. Despite all that practice, I was in over my head, again. I didn't handle criminal cases in federal court for precisely the reason I'd shared with Miles.

The sentencing guidelines scared the shit out of me. One fuckup and my client could be in for ten years instead of five. But when this guy had called, he'd said he had a civil matter. And he did…in the way that the federal government confiscating your…alleged…drug money was a civil forfeiture.

I scrutinized the guy sitting in front of me a bit more closely. "So tell me again Mr. Singleton, what happened?"

We were on our second or third go-round with this one. If maybe I heard it one more time, I'd get that little kernel of truth that would pull this whole story together. Make it more Perry Mason and less aliens tried to have my baby.

"I'm just Morris," he started. "Like I said, I was getting on the bus to Detroit. We were about to pull away when the feds knocked on the door."

"The driver opened it?" I scratched down notes. Maybe I could make hay with the bus company. They must have some search and seizure policy to protect their passengers from unwarranted harassment.

"He grumbled about leaving on time. But yeah, he opened it."

"Then?" I prompted. This was the unbelievable part of the story. Letty had written this part in the pre-interview sheet, but it seemed unbelievable no matter how many times I heard it.

"They got a dog sniffing around everywhere. Next thing I knew, they were pulling down my bag."

"What was in there?" I asked, though I had a very good idea.

"Clothes and my money," he said like everyone traveled the highway with only those two items in their luggage.

"How much money?"

"About twenty gees," he said, looking as aggrieved as a person would upon losing nearly twenty grand.

I tried to keep my face neutral. What I could do with the walking around money drug dealers kept in their pockets. But then, maybe I'd be on the other side of this desk.

Refocusing, I continued, "And why were you traveling on a Greyhound bus with that much cash?" I tried to keep my voice dispassionate. But the whole story had been unbelievable the first time around. It hadn't gotten better in the retelling. I leaned that much more forward. Maybe I'd missed something in all my fantasizing about what I'd do with that kind of cash.

"I *told* you. I was thinking about moving. I needed some money to put down on a place if I found one." I considered that. Then dismissed it. Even if I believed that bullshit, no judge would. Time to poke holes.

"Do you have a car?" I probed.

He shook his head like I'd asked him if he had a space ship. "Nope."

"A bank account?"

"Nope. Can't trust banks." This wasn't the first time I'd heard this one. A lot of my clients and their families didn't trust banks. I'm not even sure *I* trusted banks, not after the way they'd treated me when I couldn't pay my loans for a stretch. But I wouldn't carry cash on my person either.

"What happened after they took the money?"

"Feds handed me a receipt. Told me to wait for that letter there."

The letter was sitting on my desk. He'd kept it smooth and flat in a little binder he held in his lap. According to the short text, his money had been seized pursuant a federal statute that allowed it to be taken if there was suspicion of drug activity. A claim form was attached to seek return of the funds. But there was the sticky part. Getting it back.

"The letter only says eighteen thousand." I tapped at the one and eight printed on the page.

He held out his hands as if to say: What could I expect? The seizing officers had kept a little for themselves. I'd grown up learning to expect honesty in my public officials. The last year I'd been enmeshed with the corrupt Brody family had cured me of that. Now, I wouldn't put it past a few officers padding their paychecks. Seemed minor compared to Eamon Brody's abuse of power.

"Where did you get this money?" I asked. I wondered if I was starting to get jaded. Because, like the feds, I'd assumed he was dealing drugs and lying to me. If the cops were criminals and the criminals were criminals, that didn't leave much space for justice.

"Working. Been saving for a while now."

"Do you have pay stubs?" I asked.

He shook his head. "I'm off the books."

So many of my clients worked without documentation. They were the very definition of the shadow economy. Their employers skipped taxes and reporting. My clients did, as well. Everyone was happy until someone needed a pay stub for proof of gainful employment, to get an apartment, to get their kids back. Then the whole backdoor economy was a huge pain in my ass.

"You understand it says here to get it back, you have to show where you got it, right?"

He nodded.

"So...if you show up and you can't tell a judge where this money is from, they're gonna assume it's drugs."

"But you can tell them the truth, right? You can be my lawyer and explain why I should get it back. They'd believe you."

If only everything were that easy, Mr. Morris Singleton.

There was an expert in shingle hanging attorneys, Alan Cordova. This guru had always said us solo practitioners should be the filter. Sure, we couldn't handle every case, but we should interview everyone coming in the door. In theory, I could control the referral fees, keep the good cases, and boot the bad. Cordova's book never told me what to say to a potential client when I didn't know what in the hell I was doing in the topsy turvy world of forfeiture where I was required to prove my client wasn't a drug dealer.

What I was doing is that I was about to boot this guy out the door—refer him to one of those super ego driven, super expensive defense bar stars. Probably wouldn't get his money back any better than I could, but they'd be confident while losing. Singleton interrupted my thoughts on the best way to finesse getting him out the door.

"How much do I need to give you to get you to take the case?" Morris pulled out a fat roll and began peeling off hundreds. I stopped him at three thousand and told him that was enough. I called Letty in and she made out a receipt while stuffing the cash in a bank envelope. Because I wasn't messing with the IRS or the feds. I always documented my money trail.

In the end, I determined I could lose as confidently as the big guys. Morris signed the retainer agreement, and just like that, I had my first federal case.

10

Red velvet cake caught my eye. I'd recognize my favorite dessert anywhere. I leaned into the break room to investigate. A couple of slices were missing. It was ingenious, the cake. Cream cheese frosting were the white stripes in the American flag. A blue field was at the top left corner of the cake. Ready to pick up the cake knife, I glanced at the calendar on the wall. The first twelve days of July were crossed out.

Meant this cake was nine days old—at least. Appetite gone, I fiddled with the latest office gadget. Everyone talked about this single service coffee machine like it was the second coming or the BlackBerry.

"Gonna have the cake?" Rachel Schaefer appeared in the breakroom's open doorway.

"It's a July fourth cake," I said.

"And . . ." she stared at me, her wide eyes unblinking behind her glasses.

"Independence Day was nine days ago by my count," I said, lifting the coffee to my mouth. Wasn't bad for a frou frou brew. Maybe there was something to not sharing hours-old coffee from a pot.

Schaefer lingered at the door.

"I'll get out of your way, if you want cake or something," I said. I needed to get back to my desk anyway. Go on about the government's business of putting non-violent drug offenders behind bars. I blinked, grateful Schaefer couldn't read my thoughts. It's not that I didn't think those who did the crime shouldn't do the time.

It's that prison had turned into a business. I was one of the cogs in the wheel grinding away. I'd hoped that federal cases would be a little more sophisticated. That crime fighting on a national level wouldn't be a repeat of the 'buy bust' cycle I'd witnessed in my former cop shop.

"I think I'll skip it," she said. "So Chas said you're from Philadelphia?"

I nodded, though I thought the question was about a year too late. "Born and raised. Parents are still there."

The way Schaefer shifted on her feet, I had a very good idea what her next question would be. I wanted to reach into my pocket and pull out a quarter. Heads she'd ask about my race. Tails about my religion.

"You found a church or synagogue in Cleveland?" she asked, pussy footing around what she wanted to know.

Tails, I won. "I don't worship," I said, deliberately opaque. My dad would have balked at the question. He rested on the contention that answering those kinds of questions could get you on a cold cattle train traveling through Germany and Poland. But he'd grown up having lost all of the extended family who hadn't taken the cross-Atlantic trip when they'd had the chance.

That wasn't exactly my reason for answering. I didn't think Ms. Schaefer had any kind of final solution in mind. Honestly, I didn't want to talk about who I was or where I was from. I wanted to figure out how I'd be able to keep the 'container case' as people around the office had started calling it. My hunch was that her interest in me was much more myopic. No more dodging and feinting, I turned and stared her straight in the face. "Has Chas talked to you about the case I picked up this weekend?"

"You?" There was the slightest edge in her tone.

"Lou couldn't reach you. I was in the neighborhood," I explained.

"I was at a Sabbath dinner at my cousin's house. They're seriously Orthodox and I couldn't smuggle my BlackBerry in there," she said.

Maybe I needed to check myself. Could be that she asked about the religion thing because she wanted sympathy, not because she was trying to dissect my genome. "FBI wanted someone on the scene. They thought it was possibly some immigration scheme. But it wasn't."

"Let me get some coffee and I'll see you in the conference room in ten," Schaefer said.

I went to my desk, got some preliminary stuff Lou had left for me on Monday, and took a seat at the table.

The rest of the AUSAs filled in. Most had cake with their coffee. I hoped someone had the Cleveland Clinic on speed dial.

Without preliminaries, Chas started speaking the moment he closed the door. "Miles and Lou walked up to a doozy this weekend. The FBI stumbled upon a sex trafficking ring," he started.

"Stumbled?" Schaefer asked.

"They were behind the motel working on a drug sting. Something about the container drew their eye. Heard banging on the door. Exigent circumstances and all that."

Only a bit of luck that those women and child were found. My heart skipped a few beats as I wondered what would have happened if they'd never been found by the police or some well-meaning Good Samaritan.

"Who's leading the investigation?" Schaefer asked.

"Lou and a few of his guys are on the case," Chas answered.

"I was on call last weekend," Schaefer said.

"You know the policy," Chas started. His voice had gone soft like he was talking to a preschooler. I looked left and right at my fellow AUSAs. Even though I was the rookie on the team, I knew better than to condescend to Schaefer. She took everything as a slight against women.

"What? That if one person doesn't answer the phone, you go to the next on the list."

"Yes, that policy, Rachel. Lou's guys tried you twice. They didn't want evidence to walk away while they waited for you to return their call. We had child welfare coming, ambulances. There wasn't time to waste."

"So are you going to keep…Miles on the case?"

She might as well have said out loud that I'd tanked the Brody case. The fact that the guy had ultimately shown his true colors and gone away, and the fact that she and Chas had been co-chairs during the *actual* trial while I sat behind the bar carrying water, seemed to have been collectively forgotten. Every time a new revelation from some victim or former Judge Eamon Brody's legal maneuverings made the headlines, *I* got the sympathetic nods and head shakes.

Of course, none of them had tried to bring down the black sheep law breaker of one of the most powerful families in Ohio. But I didn't say that to them. I didn't say any of that now. I took the hits like a man. I'd faced worse than these petty slights on the job.

"The U.S. Attorney and I will discuss case assignments. Right now, I'd like to know from those of you on the Organized Crime and Corruption Strike Force, have you heard of this ring? This guy..." he rattled his papers. "Sledge Hammer?"

"Not his real name," one of the deputy AUSAs quipped.

Bunch of comedians these guys were.

"Nah," one said.

"He must not be high level. Maybe he's working for someone else. We'll check the database," Isaac Wray said. I'd never talked to Isaac much. He was one of those guys involved in the modern day mob stuff: Chinese heroine runners, Mexican cartels. He didn't say much or take many cases to trial. He and the rest of the strike force spent time listening to wiretaps, sifting through financial records, and trading up from the bottom of the heap.

"You do that," Chas said, pointing to him with a gun-shaped hand. My boss was self-assured in a way that said prep school at Hawken, undergrad at Princeton, and law school at Yale had been a foregone conclusion at birth. My parents had raised me to share that kind of pedigree, but on a half-black half-Jewish kid, I didn't wear the mantle of privilege in quite the same way.

"For the time being, Miles, you'll be the lead on this. You and Lou have worked together before. Why don't you start getting detailed victim statements, and pulling together stuff for the grand jury?"

I hadn't gone to Yale, but even in Philadelphia, I'd learned that you needed a defendant. "So I'm going to John Doe the defendant?"

"It shouldn't be too hard to find out who he is. Between Isaac and the women, it will all lead back to a single source. Cleveland isn't New York or Los Angeles. Hard to hide here."

As if on cue, the BlackBerry I'd sat on the table next to my legal pad lit up and buzzed. "Valdespino," I said. I stood, gathered my stuff, and strode from the room. The longer I stayed in there, the more likely I'd get pulled from the case. I was happy to blow the meeting.

"Valdespino. Miles. What do you have?"

"We need to talk to that little girl before she goes home."

"Where's home?"

"Illinois. We found her parents. They'd reported her missing eight months ago."

"I'll be right over," I said, doubly glad I hadn't had any of that stale cake. I was pretty sure this interview was going to make me sick.

11

"You ran The Place to Be?" I asked, trying not to smile at the man sitting across from me. A felony indictment wasn't a laughing matter. But some of the bar names I'd come across in Cleveland were worthy of a chuckle or two. Owners named bars like it was a giant cosmic joke on a cloudy post-industrial city.

"That and The Dive Bar, but cops shut both down for now."

I tried not to wrinkle my brow as I assessed his level of sophistication. "Cops?"

"Not the police. But the county health inspector, the state liquor control, city building code enforcement all found a bunch of violations."

I looked at the indictment. The state of Ohio was throwing the figurative book at Jarrod Carter. Promoting

Prostitution was only one among the long list of felonies. "Exactly what kind of club was The Place to Be?"

"The usual. We had liquor, food, and a TV in the front. Place was full up on home game nights."

In Cleveland where sports dominated the daily conversation, that was saying a lot. There was no shortage of places where a fan could get a drink and watch the game. I nodded and he continued.

"Kept busy on the nights the Browns, Indians, or Cavaliers were playing. LeBron kept the barstools full."

I had no doubt the high school senior turned star player could draw a crowd almost anywhere in town. "What did you do on the nights there weren't games?" I asked. The *Plain Dealer* and suburban newspapers were full of gotcha stories on restaurants that failed health inspection. Roaches and rodents were reader magnets. But the police didn't care much about vermin. Not in my limited experience, anyway.

"I had a couple of girls dancing in back," Carter said matter-of-factly like women were interchangeable with greasy gray short order hamburgers.

"Clothes on or off?" I asked. Ohio wasn't Vegas. There were strict rules on nudity—none and touching—none, including and especially stuffing one dollar bills in a G-string. Hadn't encountered it personally, but it had been a question on the bar exam. Probably made some examiner chuckle to watch hundreds of eager law graduates scribbling in blue books about the seedier side of the law.

Back then, I still thought I'd had a shot at white shoe glory. Assumed that question was the last I'd see of criminal law. Shaking my head slightly, I turned my attention back to the young black man sitting in front of me.

"As covered as required by law," he said. "They were in bikinis, nothing less."

Nothing more either. I nodded, scribbling absentmindedly. I'd toss out the illegible notes the minute Jarrod Carter walked out the door. I wasn't writing exactly. Instead, I was trying to figure out what about the guy in front of me jarred me a little. He was your garden variety defendant charged with a laundry list of crimes. But unlike the others who'd sat in that chair, he wasn't belly aching about the Man, or the unfairness of the system, or asking me if I had a Gloria Allred type defense up my sleeve.

"You posted bail and pled not guilty at arraignment. What are you looking to do in these cases?" I asked, then sat back and waited for the inevitable barrage of Johnnie Cochran-esque requests. They all wanted DNA testing, a slew of private investigators, and a legal team the size of a baseball lineup.

"Fight the charges. Take it to trial," he said. Nothing more. The usual litany absent, I sat forward, more confused than ever.

How in the hell had he walked through *my* doors on Public Square? He wanted to hire me? I hadn't had a single real trial in the years I'd practiced. I'd been up in front of juvenile judges plenty of times arguing on the behalf of parents sometimes, kids others, but that didn't count in the minds of those in the main county courts.

Those juvenile judges bent the rules of evidence so far, a downtown lawyer would hardly recognize the pretzel of Ohio Revised Code sections that came out of that place. Without a jury, I'd only had to convince a single person of my client's position. And I'd been on the losing side of more cases than I'd like to admit. I vowed not to ask him how he'd heard of little old me in a downtown full of attorneys in tall buildings.

"I can do that. All defendants are innocent until proven guilty," I said. "Let's talk about fees." I tried to infuse my voice with confidence. I was learning to ask for more money. The trick was keeping the quaver out of my voice as I set my fees in the thousands.

Carter didn't flinch at the sum quoted and I wondered for the hundredth time if I'd undervalued my services. From his broken-in brown leather messenger bag, he pulled out a black binder. I was trying to figure out what in the hell it contained when he placed it on the desk and swung the hinged front cover open. A stack of pale blue business checks appeared. From another pocket of the satchel, he pulled out a fountain pen. Like live theater, he completed the check, signing it with a flourish. When he tore it from the book and passed it over the desk, I fully expected the name 'John Hancock' to be inscribed on the signature line.

I looked at the fifteen thousand dollar check for a brief moment, before slipping it into a manila folder. Bang for the Buck LTD was the entity paying for my legal services. He liked the cute names.

"Is this a single member limited liability company?" I asked.

He nodded. "Only me," he said, putting his papers and checks back into the bag.

"I'll need to draft a personalized agreement regarding payment and representation," I said. I wouldn't turn down a check that big, but I did need it to be one hundred percent clear I was representing this man, not his company. Prosecutors could slip through the tiniest cracks and I needed paper to putty this one over. "I'll have it in the mail to you before end of day."

I stood, concluding the meeting. Shaking his warm hand, I pulled away first. It was just this side of too familiar. "How did you hear about me?" I asked, breaking my own rule from moments ago. "I like to thank those who make referrals." For the life of me, I couldn't connect us without more than a dozen degrees of separation. It wasn't only because he was a black eastside defendant and I was a white Shaker Square transplant. It was the level of his case. He was charged with multiple felonies and wasn't interested in taking a plea deal. My criminal clients were mostly from the arraignment room and ready to take any deal that kept them from the penitentiary.

"You came highly recommended from the Brodys," he said. Then he dipped his head in farewell, showing himself through the waiting room to the door.

Of course it was the Brodys. Here I was thinking my reputation had preceded me, that maybe he'd seen me tear it up in the arraignment room. But nope, walking out the door was a reminder of my second worst humiliation. I was a hundred percent sure he'd probably supplied some of that back room 'entertainment' for my ex-fiancé who'd liked them young, black, and willing. Probably hadn't been at the country club with my former fiancé's family though, I thought ruefully. The Brodys weren't that egalitarian.

Guilt at being a crap lawyer gnawed at me for a second. I should have been devoting more thought to Jarrod Carter's innocence right about now. Dancers weren't prostitutes. It was one of those anti-feminist distinctions lost on police and prosecutors. But he didn't need me to believe in his lack of culpability. He was paying me to get him off. I'd have to figure out how.

12

"You're the parents of Kelly Tucker?" Valdespino asked formally. He shook the mother's, then the father's hands before scraping the metal chair legs against the floor and seating himself at the table.

"Yes, I'm Courtney. This is Elliott, my *ex*-husband," the mother said, putting a lot of emphasis on that tiny prefix. She was small, mousy, and very nervous.

"Have you seen Kelly?" I asked from my perch against the sill of the two-way window. Valdespino's glance was full of censure. I knew he wanted me down there at the table next to him looking the parents in the eye.

But I couldn't quite get there. I wanted to know why it had taken them more than a week to make it from Illinois to Ohio. Maybe they'd come by stagecoach.

"We came to your office as soon as we checked into our hotel," Elliott said. Hunching his shoulders, Kelly's father leaned forward. "What state is she in?" he asked. "We didn't want to go in blind."

"How long has she been missing?" I asked.

Elliott and Courtney looked at each other. Blinked.

Neither uttered a word for long seconds that stretched out to nearly a minute.

"*Ell-i-ott* had custody over the Christmas holiday," Courtney said, her voice rising. "He somehow failed to notice that his daughter wasn't there. Didn't notice that she hadn't picked up her presents from under the tree. Too taken with that new wife and baby of his to notice his *first* born child wasn't at his new mini mansion."

"Courtney." Elliott had a firm hand on his ex-wife's.

"For *three* days. This is why I divorced you. You never noticed us either. Didn't stop you from taking on that teenage piece of ass—"

"That piece of *ass* is my wife. You'd do well to respect that. You're talking about the mother of my children."

It was like an episode of that tacky ass show, *Divorce Court*. I cleared my throat with zero effect. Valdespino banged a meaty fist on the table, rattling the chain concealed underneath.

"Can we get back to Kelly?" He looked at both of them. "When is the last time either one of you saw her?" He spoke slowly, spelling out the words as if he were communicating with first graders. Personally, I think he'd started at too high a grade level.

Courtney started to speak. Valdespino shot her a look. She closed, opened, closed her mouth like a dying fish.

"Maybe Christmas Eve?" Elliott said. "She'd asked permission to go to a friend's house. I'd told her she needed to be with Kirstie and me because it was our little girl Juno's first holiday. Kelly stormed up the stairs to the guest room. When my wife checked in on her later, she said Kelly was online with her friends."

"Then what happened?"

If Courtney could have shot actual daggers with her eyes, her ex-husband would have bled out on the new linoleum floor. "We plugged in the lights. Juno went crazy when we turned on the radio. She danced and bebopped in her little diaper. She opened her gifts, but played with the paper instead of the toys and books."

I cleared my throat again. This time, Elliott stopped talking.

"Did you go upstairs to get Kelly to come down that morning?" Valdespino asked this question even more slowly than the last.

Elliott hunched even more. He didn't make eye contact with a single person in the room. His head shake was nearly imperceptible.

"What about later?" I asked. "Did you eat breakfast as a family?"

"Kirstie made Juno's favorite, pancakes. They were shaped like Christmas trees, wreaths, little snowmen."

"Lunch?" I probed.

Elliott shook his head.

"So you never went to check up on Kelly?"

"When I went to her room later, her phone and laptop were gone. I'd figured she was mad at us and went back to her mom's house. I did feel a *little* guilty. But she had to understand it was my first Christmas with my new family and I wanted to make it special."

"You threw us out like garbage, Elliott. That's how I felt. That's how Kelly felt."

"Then why didn't she come back to you, Courtney? Maybe because she didn't want to watch you drink the afternoon away."

"Those two glasses of wine are called 'mother's little helper' for a reason. If you'd ever been with her more than a couple of hours, you'd need a drink too."

I stood and marched over to the table. I leaned my forearms on the cool metal. I was done with *Leave it to Beaver* gone wrong. "How many days do you think she was gone before you reported her?"

Kelly's parents looked at each other. "Eight days," Elliott mumbled after counting on his fingers.

Courtney rushed in, "We waited until after New Year's. We thought she'd run off to her friends in Chicago or something. That maybe she was sulking somewhere. She had her phone and a credit card."

"Did you call the credit card company to see if she'd used the card?" Valdespino asked.

Both parents shook their heads.

"What happened?" Kelly's mom's question was a murmur.

"Was she seeing someone?" I asked.

"There were a couple of boys," Courtney started. "Doug? Maybe? A kid with one of those little cars used to come pick her up sometimes."

Valdespino clicked the top of his pen. "What kind of car?"

"One of those small hatchback cars a lot of kids have. Maybe some kind of Volkswagen? That British thing. Alfa Romeo?"

Elliott looked over at his ex. "Is this the guy with kind of greasy blond hair?"

Courtney nodded.

"It was a newish Saab. Tan? Gray? With tan and black interior." He nodded, more sure of his memory now. "I talked to him about it." To Courtney, he said, "That's a Swedish car, by the way."

"Anyone else?" Valdespino interjected before they could devolve into another kindergarten yard scuffle.

"There was another guy. I never met him, though," Courtney said. "She'd text him, then go meet him somewhere. She promised me it was always in public, so I didn't pressure her. I didn't want to be one of those moms who cross-examines every guy who walks through the door. We had to trust her judgment at some point."

"How old is Courtney?" I asked.

"Fourteen," Elliott answered. I was silent. Because any parent with half a brain had to know they couldn't 'trust the judgment' of a girl barely into her teens. I let that one lay there because all of the errors in their parenting were about to stare them dead in the face. They'd be living with their choices for years to come. Or rather Kelly would.

I paced while Valdespino got the particulars he'd need for a more thorough search. Kelly's phone number and carrier. Her e-mail address, at least the one they knew about, her Friendster and MySpace info. He pried from them everything they knew about her social life—all of it.

This Sledge Hammer—the operation mastermind— hadn't pulled the girl from her bedroom window and locked her up. Kelly had gone willingly into the arms of one man who'd probably turned her over to Hammer. That nugget of information Kelly hadn't spilled yet. We needed to talk to her to start getting a picture of this operation. The middle man was a corner piece of the puzzle and we needed him.

13

"Casey?" I heard my name being called. Took me a good few seconds to figure out who was calling me.

I put my bag down on the marble floor and turned around.

Miles.

A little shiver went through me at the sight of him. We stood there, two feet apart, for a long awkward moment. Finally, he reached and patted me awkwardly on the shoulder.

"What are you doing *here*?" he asked.

By here, I assumed he meant federal court, his domain and province.

"I have a civil case," I said, glossing over the nature of Morris' matter. "My client went to make a phone call. We're due before Judge Lambert in about ten minutes." He turned his wrist and looked at his watch. That Tag Heuer had once gotten him in trouble with his ex-girlfriend when she wasn't quite his ex and she was still my client. He'd left it at my place and Lucille Ball-type antics had ensued, without the red hair, or humor.

"Sorry about last weekend. One of the vic's parents came to town."

I really liked Miles, but we'd only been at the beginning of trying out an actual relationship when that FBI agent had opened that container. Miles, Lou Valdespino, and a bunch of suited feds had been all over the news. I didn't think he'd see the light of day or life outside the new federal building for some time. I tried not to let the disappointment on my face show. I wondered if this was what it was like dating Superman. He was hot and a great catch when he wasn't off fighting crime. Lois Lane probably had a lot of lonely nights.

"Want to try again on Saturday?"

"Sure. Call me later," I said, tempering my hope, and walked over to the courtroom where my client was waiting.

"He on the other side?" Morris asked.

"No, he's not in this case, but he's a Federal Prosecutor," I said, not lying, but certainly implying I was much more of a player than I actually was. That chance meeting with Miles turned out to be the bright spot of my morning. It promptly went downhill from there.

From the moment I stepped into Judge Ruth Lambert's courtroom, I was behind the eight ball.

"You're late, Counselor," she'd said the moment she came to the bench. I glanced at my watch rather than look at the clock behind me. The hearing was for ten a.m., which was the exact time on my watch. My client's eyes bugged out. I could tell he wanted to say something, but I shook my head.

"I apologize, Your Honor," I said, injecting all the contrition I could muster into my voice. For a long moment, I wished I'd bitten the bullet and called my ex-client and Miles' ex-girlfriend, Claire Henshaw. She would have probably shed light on this judge, after all—she'd worked in this courthouse for the months she'd clerked for Judge Grant. But never wanting to appear weak was turning out to be a big flaw. And now here I was caught unawares.

I tried to keep from upchucking the muffin I'd stuffed down on the RTA this morning. This would teach me not to buy food that was sold cheek and jowl with a self-serve lottery dispenser.

"We're here in the *in rem* action against eighteen thousand U.S. Dollars," she said. No hello or how you do, I guess. I didn't even know the name of the prosecutor standing at the next table. Miles probably knew the guy. They'd maybe been trained together. Again, I kicked myself for not getting as much information as I needed before walking through those heavy wood doors and metal detectors.

Pride was going to be the death of me and my law practice. I raised my eyes to the high plaster ceiling and promised God I'd learn to ask for help now that I actually knew people who could provide it.

Judge Lambert flicked through a lot of papers. "Appears your Administrative Claim and Verified Claim are in order."

I sighed inwardly. Wading through the civil forfeiture procedures and laws had been like traipsing through the rainforest—barefoot and blindfolded. Not that I'd exactly know what wading through the jungle was like, world traveler that I wasn't. But I imagined it dense, murky, and impenetrable.

"Your Answer lists several defenses, Ms. Cort. But no jury trial demand was filed. Are you prepared to argue today?"

"Yes," I said, not at all prepared.

"The Government claims that your client was transporting eighteen thousand dollars over interstate lines for the purpose of purchasing drugs."

"He was carrying twenty thousand dollars, Your Honor," I said before I thought better of it.

"Are you saying the United States has falsified its papers, Counselor?"

"No, Your Honor."

"The FBI crime lab found trace amounts of cocaine on the currency," Lambert continued.

"The nineteen eighty five study by the DEA revealed that nearly half of all bills circulating in this country have trace amounts of cocaine on them. Subsequent studies have put the percentage even higher at nearly eighty percent. My client maintains that his bills were thusly contaminated though bank counting machines, ATMs, or the like," I said.

Lambert waived a hand dismissively. I looked over at the prosecutor, wondering what in the hell he was doing here. The court didn't need any adversary to knock me about. The judge was doing a fine job without him.

"Where did your client get all that *bank-tainted* money?" the judge asked with what I assumed was a hint of sarcasm. "You state that he has no bank account."

"Your Honor, it was money saved over time. Under the law, he is not required to use a bank to keep his money," I started. I spent the next five minutes giving examples of cases where money had been seized where the owner had no evidence of provenance. I bet she or any American would be hard pressed to trace the origin of every bill in their wallet.

"Those people sound like they had righteous excuses. I can't say the same of Mr. Singleton," she said.

Part of me felt vindicated for being able to pinpoint the weakness of the case when Morris Singleton had walked into my office. That alone would have earned me an 'A' on any law school exam.

The other part was pissed on his behalf. The way the federal and state government set up forfeiture laws, it was a free-for-all with law enforcement getting between eighty and one hundred percent of Americans' hard earned cash without having to put up so much as a fair fight.

"Without evidence of ownership, I'm dismissing this action. I will delay the judgment entry for sixty days. If Mr. Singleton can come here with a boss, or a pay stub, or evidence of inheritance, I'll take the matter under reconsideration."

With that, the judge stood and walked from the bench.

I hoped my face wasn't beet red from Judge Lambert's dressing down.

"What does all that mean?" Singleton asked me.

"It means that you aren't getting your money back unless you can show how you got it."

Singleton was quiet as we made our way to the exit door. Before we stepped out onto the street, he plucked at my sleeve. "That ain't fair."

"It may not be fair, but it's the law," I said.

"Is that it?" Morris asked. "Like that, the ATF can have my money. I have to prove where I got every last dime, but they don't have to prove that it was involved in drugs?"

I nodded. It was exactly like that. In a game of poker with the government, they held all the cards. A couple of years ago, I would have stood in the hall holding my client's hands as they wailed at the unfairness of it all, but I had another case to handle. If I wasn't in Judge Brody's room by eleven on the Jarrod Carter defense, he might just revoke my client's bail to spite me. Because if I knew one thing about the Brodys, they were all about the spite.

"Call me this afternoon or tomorrow morning and we can talk about ways to prove how you got the money," I said, before nodding in farewell.

Pulling open the single remaining exit door that hadn't been barred since 2001, I walked into the heat. It hadn't gotten too sticky yet, but this walk would probably make me sweat in the thin white blouse under the green and white checked suit. The suit was a little big on me, but my thinner size was accompanied by a thin wallet on account of Key Bank taking most of it every month.

Two blocks and one creaky elevator ride later, I was up on the twentieth floor of the Justice center. I'd traded the squat federal courthouse and its beautiful WPA interior for the utilitarian seventies vintage government building that doled out justice for the county's litigants.

The hallways up here were always quiet. The defendants in custody came up a secure elevator straight from the jail, so the blue carpeted corridors were usually empty save for a few friendly lawyers chatting. Opposing lawyers usually saved all their arguing for the back areas, hallways, and jury rooms behind the courtrooms. I ran through an empty courtroom to Judge Brody's clerk.

"Got held up in federal court," I said importantly. The mention of the other building got the kind of response I was looking for.

"Don't worry. Judge Brody's been waiting for you. Have a look for your client and we'll get on with it," he said.

Back out into the hallway, I scoured up and down until I found him leaning against the windows, taking in the view. This side of the courthouse looked out over a park and the new Browns stadium. On a nearly clear day like this, it wasn't a half bad view.

"Mr. Carter, we're up."

"What are we doing today?" he asked. He lifted that same battered leather messenger bag from the floor and followed me.

"Pre-trial. The judge will want to make sure that we have discovery, that we've provided any of our own, the prosecution—"

"I want to go to trial," Carter said, cutting my explanation short.

We were at the door. "Let's go in," I said.

The prosecutor was already at her table. It was a woman I'd never met before. After I'd settled my client at the far side of the defense table—the chair farthest from the jury box—I walked over to a woman in a severe navy suit. Lucky duck worked in the building, and was as cool as a cucumber. I knew I looked like a badly wilted daisy in comparison.

"Casey Cort," I said. "I represent Jarrod Carter."

"Nicole Long. Your client ready to plea?" No breath between her name and whether Jarrod Carter wanted to walk himself into jail.

"Um, no," I said, taken back by her directness. She didn't exactly do small talk.

"Let me know. We have him dead to rights on this one." She bent to shuffle a few folders around, glimpse at a few papers. "You should know I have a ninety eight percent win ratio."

"Congratulations?" I said, suitably intimidated. Prosecutors did this all the time. I sometimes wondered if it was in their playbook after wear severely cut suit, but before stalling with discovery.

"All rise!" the bailiff called once the court reporter was in place.

I walked back over to my table, gently touching my client on the back, making sure he stood before the judge got too close to the bench and annoyed at Carter's lack of deference.

"Casey, nice to see you again," Judge Brody said. "We've miss you around the house."

That greeting, I knew, could have gone either way. But it was nice to know that I was still in the Brodys' good graces.

Feeling a thousand percent vindication, I threw a small smile in the direction of the prosecutor's table. I'd been of two minds when I'd learned that my ex-fiancé's father was assigned to Carter's case. He'd either be really nice to me for keeping his son's secret or he'd throw me to the wolves for my betrayal of his brother Eamon Brody. This recognition in the courtroom and on the record was the best possible outcome of last year's engagement debacle.

"And your name again?" He nodded toward the prosecuting attorney.

"Nicole Long," she said with a touch too much impatience for a courtroom. "I tried a case in front of you a couple of years ago."

Judge Brody squinted at her. "Where have you been?"

I watched Long squirm for a second. Then I started wondering the same thing. Maybe it's why I hadn't met her. There were, of course, nearly two hundred attorneys in the prosecutors' office. It was unofficially called Cleveland's largest law firm. But the number on felony rotation was a bit smaller and Nicole Long had never come across my radar in my short time doing criminal defense.

"I was in Child Support Enforcement," she said.

I tried not to reel back in shock. Now that was interesting. CSEA was a bottom rung assignment. Some started there, but didn't stay long. If she'd been up here trying cases, then twenty blocks east in CSEA prosecution, I wondered whom she'd angered. I turned away from Long and looked back up at Judge Brody. But he didn't have a sliver of recognition on his face. If she hadn't crossed arguably the most influential family in the county, I wonder whom she had crossed. I looked at the severe suit, and the nearly jet black hair pulled into a bun so tight, it was an instant face lift. I started imagining all kinds of transgressions.

With my mind going in all sorts of directions, it was a good minute or two before I focused back in on the judge. "Is there a deal?"

"Mr. Carter can plea to the charges as they stand," Long said. "If he pleas today, we'd recommend concurrent instead of consecutive sentences on the charges."

"Did you forget in your absence, Ms. Long, that I have sole discretion over sentencing?" The Judge's ostensibly solicitous tone was laced with unkindness.

"No, Your Honor." Long's answer was noticeably quieter than her non offer had been.

"Casey. Have you made an offer?"

I took a deep breath, ready to voice the most unpopular answer around these parts. "My client is unwilling to plea. He would like to take his case to a jury."

Judge Brody's flaring nose was the only indication of his displeasure. Now that I was standing in the courtroom and not imagining my worst face plant, I recalled a lawyer telling me the prosecutor's records were so high because over ninety percent of clients took a plea. And each of those plea bargains was counted as a win in their book. I wondered how the defense bar viewed it. Because the corollary was a two percent win rate. I was batting a thousand or zero depending on how you looked at it.

The judge signaled the bailiff who went in the back and brought out the judge's clerk.

"How long do you need to prepare, Ms. Cort?" Ah, I was Ms. Cort now. First name basis friendliness ended when I started doing my job.

I looked at my client. "I'd do it tomorrow," Carter said. Of course he'd do it tomorrow. He didn't have to do much more than show up and not look too guilty.

"Six weeks," I said.

Judge Brody and the clerk whispered over the calendar. "I'm on vacation in September," Judge Brody said. "You can either have November after my next civil trial or you can have three weeks from today."

Carter tugged at my summer wool tweed. "Three weeks."

I tried to keep my quick inhale of shock surreptitious. I guess it would be best to get my first jury trial under my belt sooner rather than later. Win or lose, that fifteen thousand dollars would be mine. It would go a long way to paying down credit card debt and buying champagne to celebrate. Or more likely bourbon to commiserate.

"We'll take the earliest date, Your Honor," I said.

"Ms. Long. How many witnesses?"

The prosecutor flipped through her files until she'd found the right one. I could feel my eyes narrowing and I tried to smooth out my face. So that little flip and stare had been out of the prosecutor intimidation book, as well. Maybe Long was all show. I'd have to think about that when

I was preparing for trial. "We have fifteen witnesses, Your Honor."

"Four days then. We'll start jury selection on Monday August ninth at ten."

I dutifully wrote the date in my calendar in the red pen I used for court dates, closed the monthly book, and tried not to throw up.

14

Jarrod Carter
July 19, 2004

I sat on the horn. The blaring sound filled the neighborhood. Shook the birds from the trees.

Nothing.

Damned delivery truck was blocking my driveway. But I wasn't getting out until this car was put away. No way I ever left my ride out on the street. Despite Momma's protests over it being a waste of money, I'd fixed up the garage. Made it waterproof and had a working garage door installed. I never understood those people who kept their prized Cadillac on the street and shit they couldn't get rid of in the garage. I'd seen enough evictions and foreclosures with sheriffs throwing stuff out on the sidewalk to know there wasn't nothing worth saving in a garage. It ended up moldy and rotted out in the street nine times out of ten.

I sat on the horn again. Damned white truck. Who in the hell was getting a delivery that took that long? I tapped my fingers on the steering wheel. Maybe he was delivering more than a box.

I turned off my engine and lifted my leather bag from the passenger seat. First, I looked through the stuff about the court case. I probably should have been more worried about going to jail. But I'd been lucky so far. From what I could see, they really didn't have much evidence on me. I tossed those aside to look at later. Instead, I fingered through the heftier stack of bills that wasn't getting paid. That was a much larger concern. I needed a half-legitimate business to funnel money through. No one looked kindly on a black man with a lot of cash. That shit hadn't changed since slave times.

A guy in red and green shorts finally got into the truck and pulled away. I eased up the driveway and put the Lexus in the garage. I didn't like to drive the car while I worked— made people think I had cash on hand. I didn't plan to go out in something as stupid as a robbery.

"How'd it go?" Alisha asked, standing on the back deck while I punched in the combination closing the garage door. I regretted telling her about the charges. But I didn't have too many people to talk to and after drinking a forty, I'd spilled the beans to my niece.

"Where's Momma?"

"She in her room watching *Passions*."

Relieved I wasn't going to have to whisper, I said, "It was fine. We go to trial in three weeks."

"So…what do you want me to do if you don't come home at the end of it?" Alisha said to the toes of her canvas sneakers.

"That's not gonna happen."

"But you're having a trial in front of a jury, right? Like you see on TV—twelve people in a box saying if you guilty or innocent."

"Of course, I'm going to do that. But I got a lawyer who's friends with the judge."

Alisha's eyes widened in surprise. "How you do that?"

"I read the paper like I'm always telling you to do. This lady was dating the son of a judge, then she wasn't. Unless she was some straight up slut, I didn't think they'd hate her."

"And that father's your judge?"

I nodded. "Yup. Picked her like a flower. She had the kind of office that made me know she'd be grateful for the work."

"Three weeks, though?"

"I can't fool around with my business closed and this shit hanging over my head. I'll put it behind me and get back to work."

"But…"

"Look. I ain't planning to go nowhere. But," I started, putting on my Eddie Murphy white guy voice, "In the unfortunate event that I gotta go away for a couple of years, it's all set. My deputy will take over the business. I'll make sure he gets money to you for Momma, the house, and everything."

"I ain't met your second in charge," she said.

That's because I kept everything compartmentalized. It didn't take more than a few episodes of *Law and Order* to figure out that people didn't properly exercise their right to remain silent. If the right hand didn't know what the left hand was doing, then wasn't no hands snitching to the police.

"I'll introduce you," I said. "What you got for dinner?" I was hungry. I wouldn't admit it to anyone but I couldn't eat breakfast like usual before I went to court. I'd rigged things as far as I could in my favor, but like with anything, there was some stuff outside my control. It was those things that stole your appetite and sleep.

"Fried some walleye and hush puppies," she said.

Alisha was as good a cook as her dad had been. I think he'd been in the kitchen in the Navy or some shit like that. Way better than my momma had been when she'd been able to cook for herself. I turned my head and pushed my way into the mud room, vowing not to think about her right now. She was deteriorating fast. No matter what me or Alisha did, my mom wasn't able to control her diabetes.

I sat down at the dining room table. In a minute, Alisha brought me a plate with plenty of fish and tartar sauce. She didn't load up the plate with French fries like they did at those cheap fry joints around town.

"I'm gonna need you to move to the room off the porch," I said between bites. I eyed my niece. If a black person could turn pale, she'd done it.

"What if someone break in and kill me?"

"In Cleveland Heights?" I challenged her. My niece had an irrational fear of being killed. Made me crazy on the one hand. But she kept the house locked up tighter than Fort Knox on the other, and that was good as I kept some files here.

"No. There wasn't no murders. But there were one hundred and one break-ins," she said. I was beginning to be sorry I'd spent so much time training her. She'd finally gotten care of Momma and the house under control. But now, she also read the paper and looked up stuff on the Internet.

I think all that reading about crime made her more scared than safe.

"Maybe you want to go back to your step-momma's house?" I asked, gesturing toward the back door.

She huffed, then went and got us glasses of store brand lemon-lime soda before sitting at the table. "Fine. What you want me to do with her extra clothes and stuff we moved out there?"

Alisha didn't quite cower the way she used to. But after living with me and Momma for five years, I guess she would have to have grown some backbone.

"Get a dumpster. Give it to the Salvation Army or Antioch."

She stood and got one of those grocery list pads my momma loved. The kind with rosy cheek elderly white ladies in blue flowered aprons. "What else?"

"Get a few bunk beds delivered and moved up to the attic. Install a reinforced fire-proof door at the bottom of the attic stairs. Make sure the lock has a key on both sides. I need you do to this by the end of the week." I ate another filet in blissful silence. "Nah, make that ASAP. Don't care what it costs."

Alisha didn't mess around when she realized I wasn't playin.' She was up, out of the chair, and on the phone in an instant.

I pulled my own cell from my pocket and called my deputy.

"You know those white serial killer vans you see on TV?" I asked my second in charge.

Grand took a deep breath before speaking. "Yeah, what about them?"

"I need you to get me about four or five—whatever you can get for about a hunnerd gees. We're going into the delivery business."

15

"Can you please state your name for the record?"

"Kelly Tucker."

"What's your date of birth?"

"June fourteen," she paused for a moment before I nodded. "Nineteen eighty-nine. I guess my mother and father partied like it was nineteen ninety-nine ten years early." Kelly's delivery was deadpan.

I hid my smile. Somewhere in there was probably a funny girl. Was she gone forever? "When did you leave your father's house?"

"Christmas Eve," she answered, any earlier trace of humor gone.

"Where did you go?"

Kelly looked under her bangs at her father, then mother, then Valdespino, then back to me. "A friend picked me up."

"Had your parents ever met this friend?" I asked, though I was pretty sure of the answer. My parents hadn't met every friend I'd had in high school and I'd been a nearly squeaky clean kid.

"No."

"Did he go to your high school in Geneva?" Though I knew he probably didn't. The dangerously cool kids were *never* in high school.

"No."

"So where did you meet? You didn't tell me his name?" I probed for that puzzle piece.

"I met him on the World Wide Web."

"What does that mean?" A website. A chat room. We needed something.

A long teen-aged sigh showed me another flicker of the girl she probably used to be. "One of those stupid teen chat rooms? Okay? All my friends are in there and we talk about shit."

"When did this guy appear?" She wasn't going to give him up easily.

"I don't know. Silver was always there."

"Is Silver a real name?" I probed delicately like a mom taking out a splinter.

"No one uses their real name. You pick out a cool username."

"What was yours?"

"SwissKelly six one four."

"Swiss?"

"As in Geneva? Switzerland?"

And she threw in her birthday for good measure. Ah, the logic of a teenager who hadn't taken the stranger danger talk seriously. I scratched down the information. I could see that Valdespino was writing as well. He'd be serving subpoenas on the website, the company's Internet Service Provider, as well as the parents' before the day was over if we got enough information from this interview.

I didn't want to lose momentum, but I needed to word the next question in the right way so the girl wouldn't shut me down before we'd even got started. "Were your friends also friendly with Silver?"

Nod. "He...was a cool guy. Gave us passwords to Warcraft and other RPGs."

Kelly looked as comfortable as she was going to get. It was time to get to the nitty gritty. "When did you meet Silver in person?"

"The first time?" A flick of the eye toward her dad. I'm sure she'd lied by omission. Or maybe her parents had never asked.

"Let's start there."

Kelly looked under long bangs at her parents. We were about to get into territory they probably knew nothing about. "We went down to Chicago a couple of times. Met him at Club Mist."

"Club Mist?"

"It's a place where you can go and dance and hang out without needing a fake ID."

"How close were you and Silver?" I asked, preparing for a lie here.

"Just friends," she said. Expected that answer. My guess would be that he'd come on hard, buying drinks, pushing sexual contact. She'd maybe been flattered by all that attention she wasn't getting at home.

"Who called who on Christmas Eve?"

"We were all online. Everybody's family was so boring. We were talking about what we were going to do during the Christmas break. Silver suggested we get the party started early. We were supposed to. . . " I waited while she gathered her old expectations and fit them to what had really happened. "I took the train to Chicago. He met me there. We went to a coffee shop first. Got hot chocolate. With extra whipped cream." She threw a look at her mom. I gathered junk food had been one of the many teenage battle grounds.

"He had a car. We'd ridden in it before. From one of the clubs to the train station on some days. But Club Mist was closed on Christmas." Kelly closed her eyes for a long moment. "I should have known that." She plowed a fist against her forehead. "So stupid."

I wanted to keep her from the endless spiral of hindsight. Keep her moving forward in the story. "Where did you drive after Club Mist?"

"Silver asked if I was interested in a road trip. I said I was game. I didn't have to be back at school for a week."

It was an effort not to swivel my head over to her parents. What did they make of a kid who thought she could be gone a week without anyone noticing? "Where did you go?"

"We drove for a long time. I fell asleep. The heat was only half working in the car. And there wasn't much to see when it started snowing." Kelly paused for a long time. I didn't want to interrupt. She needed to tell it her way. "It was like two in the morning when Silver pulled into some motel. I was so happy to have heat and a bed, I didn't think anything of it."

"What happened next?"

"We got up. Went outside. He threw snow balls at me. We went to some all-night pancake place."

"How was the food?" I asked. We were getting to the hard part. I wanted to give her the time and space to come to terms with what she needed to tell us.

"Good. I had these amazing apple pancakes. Syrup, butter, powdered sugar—the works."

"Then?"

"Then we went back to the Sleepy Time. A guy named Sledge was there. Big black guy. Scary as all hell. He tried to be nice, but there wasn't nothing nice about him."

I tried not to twitch, but I must have done something, because Valdespino gave me a sharp look. From one tall black guy to another, I had a moment of sympathy for this Sledge character. No matter how it went down, he was going to be judged on his looks long before we got to the shit he was doing.

"Tell us more about Sledge," I said. Funny how she was ready to throw this guy under the bus, but was defending the asshole who drove her to her destruction.

"He grabbed my arm one second. Offered me some pot in the next. I tried to convince Silver to leave, but he was smoking and drinking. I didn't think he could drive us back to Illinois. It was snowing and he was high. I was relieved when Sledge left, you know. I mean, no disrespect, black guys are cool. But he just wasn't."

I didn't need that bone thrown my way. I closed my eyes for a moment, obliterating the room around me. Refocusing on who the bad guy was in this picture. Remembering the girl was a victim. Ignoring the casual racism. "Did anything happen that night?"

"Nah, we slept through breakfast. Got up and rode that little train you have to the water. Ate down in some old factory. Watched a stupid comedy show. Drove back to the motel. But when I woke up the next morning, Silver was gone."

"Did you have a cell phone?"

"Yeah. Dad here—" she jerked a thumb toward her father, "—got me the new Razr."

"Did you call Silver?"

"I texted him a bunch of times. Looked for his car in the lot. Figured he was getting breakfast. But by eleven, I didn't think that anymore. I got hungry and opened the door. Sledge was on the other side," Kelly said. I waited a beat, two. But she didn't have any more to say.

After a long moment, she spoke. "I can't talk about this with my parents here." Her voice was small, childlike. She looked up at the ceiling. At first, I thought she was going back to obnoxious teen, but the shimmer in her lower lids told me she was trying not to cry.

Valdespino touched the parents on the back. He hustled them out of the room before the mother started crying or the dad punched something or someone. I don't know what he said in the five minutes all three were gone, but Courtney and Elliott didn't come back in with him. It was just us and the girl now.

"Your parents agreed we could talk to you without them," Valdespino said. "We're not here to try to get you to relive what happened. We're here because we want to get this guy Sledge."

"He's not the only one. He has a helper. Little guy named Grand."

I scratched that down on my pad. "You get a first name?"

Kelly shook her head.

"Let's go back for a minute. What can you tell us about Silver?"

"I'm sure he didn't have anything to do with this," she said.

Ah, God damn it. She was still in fucking denial. Valdespino saved me from having to be the bad guy.

"You think Silver had nothing to do with this here?" he asked, jabbing his meaty index finger hard against the table.

"He's my friend. He was my first…boyfriend. He never did a bad thing to me. Never touched me in a way I didn't want to be touched. I knew him for a long time before he drove to Cleveland," Kelly said in apology. We'd have to circle back on that one.

I made like I was checking off notes on my pad. "So we have Grand and Sledge. Anyone else in this operation?"

"Not that I know of."

I took in a lot of air. Tried not to move my chest. I didn't want to be overly dramatic. Make this into a Lifetime movie if that's not how it had played out. I shifted my head back to how I used to do things. Ask questions. Gather facts. Valdespino and I would work the law and facts into conclusions later. Stuff that would take this outfit down.

"What happened when you opened that door?"

"He pushed his way into the room. Took me in with him. It wasn't like I made to leave, but the way he pushed me down to sit on the bed, I got the feeling that I wouldn't be able to walk out that door and get a ride to the airport."

"And then?" I prompted.

"He said that Silver wasn't coming back. That he'd gone on back to where he was from. I got up then, ran to the little window. That car we'd come in wasn't nowhere to be seen. Sledge got up, pushed the brass bar across the lock. At that moment, I really wished that I'd stayed and opened presents with my little sister…"

"What did he say after you turned back around?"

"He said, 'You know the score, right?' and I was like 'What?' and he said that if I was nice to his customers, I wouldn't get hurt. I kind of thought he was maybe dealing pot or meth. Like maybe he needed a girl to run around and make some deliveries. Because police wouldn't suspect a white girl dropping by people's houses in the suburbs. I could see that he'd probably get harassed by the cops."

I looked at her. Was it naïveté or hope that had made her mind go in one direction, nearly one hundred and eighty degrees from the truth?

"Then he got real close. He leaned in and kissed me. It was really gross. No offense." She threw a sheepish look in my direction. I didn't look at Valdespino. I didn't want him to think me a liability on this case and get Schaefer in here. I'm sure half the guys out there thought a woman would be better at this. Talking to victims. Relating to them.

"I was all like, 'What are you doing?' and he was all, 'Testing out the goods.' I kind of freaked out. I told him I was ready to go home. He could do his own damn drug dealing. Because I was looking for a little adventure, you know? But I wasn't no whore."

"Were you in the container for all six months?"

Kelly looked away. Her eyes rolled toward the ceiling, like she was scanning the overhead lights. Her fingers examined the grooves handcuffs or a pen had made defacing the nearly new table top.

"No. I've only been in there since...I'm not sure; I think there were some leaves on the trees. We were living in the hotel rooms. Customers would come and go. Grand or the hotel guy would bring food. But then one of the girls got away somehow. I think she got one of the customers to somehow get her out."

"Do you know the name of the girl who escaped?"

Kelly shook her head.

"Or how she managed it?" Valdespino added.

Another head shake.

"The container," I prompted.

"So Sledge comes banging in. Gathered all the girls together. It was the first time I'd seen any of the others."

"How many?"

"Maybe eight?" Single shoulder shrug.

"Okay."

"So he hit the dresser with a baseball bat. He'd never done anything like that before. He gave a talk like he was the king of the Chicago Board of Trade instead of a gangster. He said something about profit and loss. About capital investments. Then he said our living situation was going to change. I thought maybe it was going to get better. Like it would be some big sorority house with a woman with flowing sleeves arranging our 'dates.'

"Then Grand opens the door. Had another guy with him who had his own hand on a gun on his hip like it was TV or something. I didn't think he'd do anything. But I didn't want to get shot either, so I followed the single file line. Across the parking lot and around back was this big metal crate. Like the kind you'd see on the back of a tractor trailer. He lifted a heavy iron bar and the door swung open. There was a light strung up on the ceiling. And a wood thing with fabric in it…"

"A screen?" Valdespino shot me a look. I wanted to kick myself. I didn't want to lead the witness, but the question had slipped out because I was seeing what she had seen.

"Yeah, that's what my mom called it when she used it to hide the pipes in the basement when they finished it. We went in there. There were some mattresses on the floor. Once we were all in, he closed the door."

"How often did you get out?"

"At night, Grand would walk us to a hotel room, and we'd see one customer right after another. Used to be some time in between. But not anymore. When one went out the door, there was almost always another coming back in behind them. I don't know what Sledge and Grand said to them, but the customers weren't that interested in talking anymore. They were ready to get what they'd paid for and get on home."

"What did they pay for?" Valdespino asked. He was a braver man than I. It was the last thing I wanted to know. In my head, I could tick off the crimes. RICO, kidnapping, criminal conspiracy. No death penalty. And I didn't need that really. Under the sentencing guidelines, this Sledge and Grand were probably going to be in prison, if not for the rest of their lives, then for nearly as long a time. Sometimes, I thought the zillion year sentences that made the news were insane. Not in this case. Sledge and Grand would deserve every year of hell they would get.

Shutting this thing down was good enough for me. I didn't need a list of charges a mile long. But not for Valdespino. He asked Kelly again. She dropped the water bottle. Lou went and got a bunch of paper towels to throw down on the liquid oozing across the linoleum tiles. I pulled another bottle from the impromptu crate of water in the corner and handed it to her. Kelly Tucker took a long gulp, then told us exactly what it was these men paid for.

16

I was deeply regretting that giant coffee I'd picked up from Arabica. My stomach hurt, I had to pee, and I was shaking like the lightning rod on Key Tower. But I hadn't slept a wink the entire weekend and had thought the coffee a wise choice. Instead of laying down in my bed like a good little lawyer should before her first jury trial, I'd polished my opening argument more times than I could count. I'd worked on my cross examination, then spent Sunday's all-nighter going over jury questions, making sure not to cross the line between information gathering and illegal probing.

Before approaching the courtroom, I took a moment in one of the corners of the hallway on the twenty-second floor and burped as quietly as possible. I could have used a good ten minutes in the bathroom. But only the judges had private commodes. We lawyers had to share with the jury. And pushing my nervous bowels was not at all how I wanted to meet the *venire*.

Didn't want to lose the respectability I'd hoped to gain when I'd purchased the navy knee-length dress with its sturdy white piping and matching blazer. I looked down at the faint sound from near my hip. Something was buzzing in my purse.

"Hello?" Damn. I could hear the exasperation in my own voice. This was not my solicitous, client-pleasing voice. I shouldn't have answered it at all, I realized about three moments too late. I'd planned to turn the damned thing off the minute I spotted my client. I wondered who in the hell was calling me. It had taken everything in my power to convince my mother that she didn't need to get dressed up and sit in the gallery to 'support' me today. I didn't want to have that conversation a second time.

"Good luck."

The voice belonged to Miles. We'd tried dinner on Saturday night, but I'd been too distracted to enjoy the food or his company. Though I felt bad, I called it a night at nine and spent the next thirty-six hours pacing my apartment trying to walk out the nerves. All I'd ended up with was a Charlie horse in my calf and sexual frustration knotting up the rest of my lower body.

When I'd knocked on the door of my neighbors across the hall, the doctor half of the couple, Jason Corry, ran to get me some vaunted therapeutic tool that would be a miracle cure for my sore legs. That 'tool' turned out to be a bright green tennis ball. I was ordered to massage my calf. The knot went away, easing half of my frustration. I resumed my walking and worrying—alone.

My boyfriend's voice brought me back to the present. "Should I have said break a leg?"

I looked down at my conservative low-heeled shoes and hoped I didn't trip walking between the defense table and the podium. "No. Good luck is fine."

"Do you want me to sit in?" he asked.

Why did everyone want to watch me fail so badly? 'Cause I couldn't figure a way that I would succeed with a client everyone would assume is guilty. Not to mention the prosecutors' nearly one hundred percent win rate.

"No, thanks. You should get to work finding the container mastermind," I said. Having an Ivy League graduate Assistant United States Attorney sitting behind me watching my every move would make me a thousand times more nervous than I already was. I didn't think Jarrod Carter wanted a messy bundle of raw nerves trying his case today.

Not only was I worried about Miles seeing me in court, I needed him to solve that case. Maybe finding the guy behind that prostitution ring would make my nights easier. Not a few had been filled with nightmares of being closed in a metal can. That image would take years to leave my brain.

"Gimme a call when you can. I'd be glad to bring dinner to your place. Food shouldn't be something you have to worry about during a trial."

Damn. He was being nice and I was thinking bitchy thoughts in my head. Navigating a relationship and a career was way too hard. I tapped the plastic earpiece impatiently with a nail. I needed to get back to the career part. "I think my client's here. Gotta go," I said.

Jarrod Carter practically sauntered off the elevator and down the hall. I let out a breath. This was one client who wouldn't have me running to my office to pull one of my father's discarded emergency ties from the bottom drawer of my credenza.

He was flawless in a gray wool suit, red silk tie, and white shirt. The whole outfit looked like it cost more than my last month's rent. If I hadn't known he was a defendant, I might have mistaken him for one of the lawyers doing business in the court.

"Good morning, Mr. Carter," I said formally, shaking his hand. "Have a seat." I gestured to a bench. "I'll let the court know we're ready to proceed."

When I came back to the hall, Carter passed over one of those accordion folders that closed with a cord tied around cardboard stays. Unwinding it, I spread the folds wide.

"Everything you asked for is in there," he said. "Business license, deed to the building, some of the pay stubs and tax forms I was missing."

I peered inside the accordion folds. Looked complete. More than complete. More organized than my own business folder. Was this what bigger retainers got you: compliant clients? I'd have killed for even one of my Juvey parents to have been this organized. I don't know if it would have saved their kids from the system, but maybe it would have scared the Children and Family Services' prosecutors enough to back down in the beginnings of the cases when posturing could still make all the difference.

I shook my head clear. Water under the bridge, Juvenile Court was. Baby court was my past. I was playing with the big boys now. The stakes were much higher. If I didn't get this right, my client would be in the state penitentiary for a good long time.

"Let's go," I said. We walked into the courtroom together. Took up at the table farthest from the jurors' empty chairs. Soon enough, it would be filled with the voting citizenry of Cuyahoga County. But before that, the prosecutor and I had some motions to put before the judge. I wanted

nearly half the evidence tossed. Who knew what other sur-
prises she'd have lurking, that'd I'd have to try to get the
judge to toss as well? In my first cases, I'd found assistant
prosecuting attorneys and I didn't have the same definition
of exculpatory.

"Do you want me to ask them if they've been to a strip
bar?" I asked Carter. Normally, I didn't ask for much client
input. It wasn't useful in most cases, I'd learned. But sex
work was something about which people could have, and
probably did have, strong feelings one way or another.

"Nah," he said. Then Carter sat back in the chair. The
hand on his chin made me think he was thinking about the
question a bit more. While the court deputy got the jury
ready for their debut, I waited. "I tell you what," Carter said.
"Can you ask what church they go to?"

"Why?" To say I was hesitant to dip my toe in the swirling waters of religion was putting it mildly. Views on sex
work seemed less polarizing.

"All rise for the jury!" the bailiff called before Carter got
a chance to answer.

Twenty-four people filed in. Fourteen filled the jury box.
The deputy directed the other ten to fill the courtroom's first
rows. Mirroring Long's movements, I spread the foot and a
half wide dot matrix printout of potential jurors on the
scarred wood table. Each little square was filled. I had the
venire's names, occupations, and where they resided in
Cuyahoga County. I'd only scanned the list when I'd first
gotten it this morning, but I looked more closely now as the
judge explained how he was going to conduct *voir dire*: the
jury questioning.

Only a few were from Cleveland. I stole a peek at all the
faces, even the ones behind me. All but three were white.
The job descriptions were vague at best, even homemaker.

Seemed like a number of the housewives in my parents' church had an EBay business, Avon, or something on the side. Very few people did nothing all day. I looked at my client. Not exactly a jury of Carter's peers. Not that I'd ever heard of a jury of black eastside small business owners. I looked up when the judge started his questions.

"Juror Number one. Welcome. I'm Judge Brody and I'm going to ask you and your fellow jurors some questions this morning."

The balding man nodded. He was wearing a white short-sleeved button down shirt, slacks. Compared to everyone else, juror number one was practically in formal attire. "Good morning, Your Honor," the man from...I looked at the list, North Olmstead said.

"We're here today on a criminal matter. That means the defendant here has been accused of a crime. Have you ever been the victim of a crime?"

"Got my car broken into. Had to replace the stereo in my F150," he said.

Judge Brody gave a laugh that was somewhere between charming and fake. "That kind of thing has happened to all of us, I'm sure. Anything more serious?"

The man from North Olmstead shook his head.

"Have you ever been on a jury before?"

Juror one shook his head again. "I've never been past this part."

"Why?" Judge Brody asked.

"Because I believe anyone accused of a crime is guilty," he said. "There's a government conspiracy to jail black and brown men."

Buh-bye. He'd used the oldest tactic in the book to get out of jury duty.

"You're excused for cause." Judge Brody said.

I looked more closely at him as he gathered up a book that looked like it was penned by Carl Sagan, and a Sudoku workbook. Fuck. He would have probably been a good one. I scratched my pen through his name. I scanned the remaining folks in the box. They wouldn't be able to get away with that one. It was like a magic trick. Only worked the first time.

"Juror Two," Judge Brody continued as if nothing had happened. Jurors must flout the constitution's presumption of innocence daily. "Says here you run a delivery service. Can you be more specific?"

Juror two was a black man with more gray than black in his hair. At the judge's questioning, he sat up a little straighter, pulled down the sleeves of his long sleeved t-shirt. "I deliver newspapers for the *Plain Dealer* and *Sun*."

Judge Brody squinted as if he had to imagine how newspapers got from the printing presses. "To people's houses?"

"No." Juror two shook his head. "I pick them up from the printer, bundle them, and drop them off at distribution points."

"Got to get up early for that one," Judge Brody said with a little laugh in his voice. All fake this time.

"Yep. About three or so," the man said, nodding.

"Well, we'll try to keep you awake. Have you been the victim of a crime?" Judge Brody's tone was all serious again. I was starting to think judges and actors had a lot in common.

"I've had my wallet stolen a couple of times. My house was broken in once. Nothing more than that," the man said matter-of-factly, as if petty crime were just an everyday part of life.

"You've been on a jury before?" Judge Brody asked.

"No sir," the man said, shaking his head.

I wondered how people did it. Skipped jury service. Then I thought about it. He'd probably never been registered to vote. Maybe one of those people who got registered after the 2000 election. The Supreme Court deciding who was president had rubbed more than a few people the wrong way.

"I'm satisfied that the juror is acceptable. Ms. Long?"

Today's severe suit was steel gray. Long stood. "Juror Two, I'm going to ask you a few questions."

"Ms. Long, I hope you aren't going to state the obvious the entire trial," Judge Brody interjected.

That threw her off her game. Long visibly steadied herself and leaned forward, picking up her legal pad. "Have you ever been arrested or convicted of a crime?"

Juror two looked affronted, but his "No ma'am" answer was imbued with the right amount of respect.

"I'm satisfied," Long said.

Judge Brody looked at me expectantly. "Casey."

Showtime.

I took a deep breath. "Good morning, Mr. Hobson. Thank you for your service," I started. I asked him some questions about fairness and justice. Really filler until I got to the meat of it. For what seemed like years, but was probably seconds, I flipped a coin. Heads was strip clubs. Tails was religion. "Are you a member of any church?"

For the first time, Hobson ducked his head. "I try to attend Mount Zion from time to time, but I'm anything but a regular member," he said.

"Thank you, Mr. Hobson." To Judge Brody, I said, "If I can have a moment."

He lifted a magnanimous hand in acquiescence.

To Carter, I said, "I say yes. Seems fair. What's your take?"

He nodded. "Keeper."

"No challenge, Your Honor."

It went like that for the rest of the morning. I learned all about car break-ins, house break-ins, and the occasional assault that had visited the potential jurors. My life was starting to seem boring by comparison. At Carter's direction, I kept the churchgoers, tossed the one Muslim and the likely atheists. It wasn't until lunch recess that I finally had a moment to talk to Carter, though getting back to my office and the bathroom should have been my number one priority. Curiosity got the better of me.

"Why did you want to keep the outwardly religious?" I asked.

"Most of my customers repent on Sunday for what they did on Saturday," he said.

Carter seemed like an interesting guy, and maybe I'd have lunch with him on another day of this trial. But not this afternoon. I pointedly looked at my watch. "I'll see you back here at one o'clock. Don't go far. Don't be late."

Packing my barrister's bag, I lugged it behind me and pushed ahead to get in one of the two elevators that would let me the hell out of this place.

Ninety minutes and half a turkey sandwich later, I reversed that walk and ride to the twenty-second floor.

The best thing about a criminal trial? For the most part, it's the prosecutor's show. Nicole Long had the burden of proof. She had to convince the twelve people in the jury box that my client was guilty. And Jarrod Carter may be a lot of things, but one of them wasn't guilty.

When Long questioned the arresting vice officer, Carter looked anything other than culpable. He didn't fidget, nor sweat, nor glance around wild-eyed. He was the coolest customer I'd ever sat next to. His lack of nerves was contagious.

As I rose to cross-examine the arresting officer, I no longer felt as if the contents of my stomach would heave all over the wooden podium.

"Officer Duncan, you've testified on direct that you witnessed lap dancing in the back of The Place to Be. Is that correct?"

Duncan nodded. "Yes."

"There is no provision in the Ohio Revised Code that prohibits touching if the women are clothed, is that correct?"

"Not that I know of."

"You've also testified that you believed there was a sex for money exchange at Mr. Carter's club. Is that correct?"

"Yes. I saw several johns—"

"Your Honor!" I nearly shouted. "Please direct the witness to answer the questions asked without characterizations."

"Officer Duncan, we will not refer to the women and men in this club in derogatory terms. What they were doing is for the jury to decide."

Smiling a little for the jury, I turned back to the witness. "What is the basis for your belief that there was an exchange of sex for money?"

"As I said before, my partner and I witnessed more than one of the women enter a back room with a jo—" Officer Duncan censured himself after a peek at the judge, "a customer. The door was closed, but the sounds were clear."

"What did you actually *see*, Officer Duncan? We can't guess what went on behind a closed door."

"Nothing," Duncan mumbled.

I sat, satisfied that Long was a bit wobbly on her burden of proof.

She must have sensed it as well, because as soon as my butt hit the chair, the next words from her mouth were, "Redirect, Your Honor?"

Judge Brody nodded. Long came back to the podium for a second bite at the apple.

"Can you tell us why you thought The Place to Be was cover for prostitution?"

"One of the girls, Pearl of the Orient, said to me that I could get special treatment if I went to one of the VIP rooms with her," Duncan answered.

"Did you do so?"

"No, of course not." Duncan's affronted looks was over the top. He should have taken lessons in subtlety from Judge Brody.

"Did you give her money?" Long asked.

"I gave her one hundred fifty dollars."

"What were you promised for this one hundred fifty?"

Officer Duncan's neck turned tomato red. "A blow job."

"No further questions," she said.

"Casey?" Judge Brody asked.

I declined. In my closing argument, I'd let the jury know that asking for sex and receiving it were two different things. That maybe Duncan was a patsy and she asked for money from all the guys.

Nicole Long stood. "The state rests, Your Honor."

"Casey? Your motion?" Judge Brody asked, making no attempt to hide his boredom with procedure. Any criminal defense lawyer worth his salt made a motion to have the court dismiss the charges against the defendant at the close of the state's case. As far as I knew, the motion had probably been granted once in the history of the adversarial system. Assuming it wasn't granted, natch, I'd have to make the same motion again before the case went to the jury.

I stood, well prepared for this part. "Your Honor, pursuant to Criminal Rule twenty-nine, the defendant moves for a judgment of acquittal. There has been insufficient evidence presented by the state to satisfy the elements of the crimes charged in the indictment."

"Denied," Judge Brody said before I had a moment to take a breath. He looked at the clock behind me. So as not to appear rude to the judge or jury, I didn't follow his gaze. "It's four o'clock. Let's adjourn for the day. Casey, are you prepared to go forward tomorrow?"

"Yes, Your Honor."

"Will you be calling any witnesses?"

"Yes, Your Honor," I said, looking at the jury. The defendant was never required to testify in a criminal case. No matter how many times I've seen that explained to a jury, they didn't like it. I think jurors believed a defendant was hiding something if they didn't testify. But in our practice sessions, Carter had done exceptionally. He wasn't overly emotional. He wasn't unintelligible or an obvious liar. So we'd prepared his testimony. I was ready to go ahead.

◈-◈-◈

August 10, 2004

I skipped the Arabica on the way to court on the second day of trial because I'd actually slept more than a few hours last night. This morning, it was as if the nerves had fallen away. I was wearing a periwinkle blue suit that my neighbor Greg said complimented my eyes. I was grateful it wasn't so damned hot this summer and I wouldn't sweat through the jacket.

We cooled our heels for a while waiting for the jurors to trickle in, but by nine-thirty, the court was ready to go.

"It's your show, Casey," Judge Brody said.

"I call Jarrod Carter to the stand," I said, proud my voice didn't crack.

My client came to the witness chair, sat, smoothed his tie, and adjusted the microphone. Today, his designer suit was navy, the tie sky blue silk. The starched white shirt stood in sharp contrast to his dark skin. Cufflinks winked from his wrists. It was almost too much...almost. But he walked that line between presentable and alleged pimp very carefully.

"Can you tell us what you do for a living?" I asked after he introduced himself and told the jury he lived in Cleveland Heights.

"I run two clubs. The Place to Be and The Dive Bar."

"What kinds of clubs are these?"

"The popular term is sports bar. We're busiest during games. Most of my customers can't afford seats in the new stadiums, so they come to us to get some food, beer, and to watch the game on the big screen."

"You also have...dancing." I hated myself for that hesitation. We'd talked about what to call the strip club portion of his business and agreed on the term. But it hadn't rolled from my tongue naturally because 'stripping' and 'pole dancing' had sped through my mind before I got the right words out.

"In compliance with the law, we have provocatively dressed women serving drinks. After games, or on nights when there are no games, the servers take turns dancing on the small stage in the back."

"Do you allow the women in your establishments to perform sexual favors for patrons?"

"Absolutely not. In fact, when we hire them, our waitresses are required to sign an independent contractor agreement that outlines this prohibition."

I walked back to the defense table and pulled a two-page agreement from the stack of documents. "I'd like this marked as defense exhibit four." After giving copies to Long, the courtroom deputy, and the judge, I stepped toward Carter.

"Can you read the highlighted portion of this agreement?"

"Sexual contact in violation of the Ohio Revised Code is strictly prohibited," Carter read.

"Thank you. I have no further questions, Your Honor," I said. Carter had done good. He'd not gone off the script once. At my seat, I got ready to take notes in case my client crumbled on cross-examination and I needed to rehabilitate him.

"Ms. Long?" Judge Brody prompted the prosecutor.

"Don't you look the other way when your strippers take customers in the back?"

Carter's "No." was firm and sure.

I relaxed just a little.

"Isn't it true that you encourage men to come to your place for the sex?"

"No."

"Isn't it true that the reason your bar is more popular than any other in the neighborhood is because of the extras your customers receive?"

"No."

"No further questions."

"Casey?" Judge Brody asked after Carter made his way back to our table.

"Your Honor, I call Judith Webster to the stand."

To say that Ms. Webster sauntered to the stand would be an understatement. She was all curves and bow-chicka-bow. The tight horizontal pleated dress, though a modest white, did nothing to hide the body I'm sure attracted attention everywhere she went. I'd asked her for reserved. I should have been clearer. I'd imagined twinset, and she'd come in with a sweetheart bodice that lifted and separated her assets. I tried to hide my disappointment from the jury. But when I glanced over, I needn't have bothered. The men's eyes were bugging out of their heads. There'd be no worry they'd forget her testimony.

"Can you please tell the jury what your stage name is?"

"Pearl of the Orient."

"How long have you worked at The Place to Be?"

"About six months."

"What do you do when you're not at Mr. Carter's bar?"

"I'm a full-time nursing student at Cleveland State," Webster said. It was why I'd picked her from Carter's roster. The single moms struggling to make ends meet with baby daddies a plenty weren't ideal witnesses.

"What were you hired to do at Mr. Carter's establishment?"

"We serve drinks from the bar, food from the kitchen, and sometimes dance the late shift."

"What's involved in dancing?"

"I usually wear a short, front button dress. I dance to a couple of songs, and take it off. I always wear a bra and panties underneath."

I handed Webster defendant's exhibit four. "Did you sign this agreement?"

"Yes."

"Have you ever offered sex to any of the patrons in exchange for money?"

"No."

"Officer Duncan testified that you offered him a blow job."

Webster looked down for a long moment. "He offered me a big tip. It's not every day I get more than a few dollars shoved in my waistband. I thought he was cute, so I thought I'd repay the kindness."

I didn't look at the jury. I hadn't bought this one when we'd prepared. But Carter and Webster insisted this is what had happened. And there wasn't sound recording or video to settle the dispute between 'he said, she said.'

"I'd like this next marked as defense exhibit five," I said, pulling a single sheet from the podium.

"So marked," Judge Brody said when everyone had a copy and the paper.

I handed it to Webster. "Can you please read the line at the top of the page?"

"It says: Addendum to Independent Contractor Agreement."

"Can you read line number two?"

"If Contractor is found to be in violation of section six of the ICA, all monies earned shall be forfeited to Bang for the Buck, Limited immediately."

"What did that mean to you?"

"Some of the girls—hood rats if you ask me—will do anything for an extra buck. Soon as Sl...Mr. Carter stopped coming in every day after he opened that other place, they was turning tricks out back in the parking lot. He caught up with them and demanded all of the money. I think he figured if they couldn't get any of the money from it, they'd stop doing it."

"To your knowledge, did the other women sign the same addendum?"

Webster nodded.

"You must answer out loud for the record."

"I saw two of them sign when I was working there at night."

"Thank you, Ms. Webster."

Long came to the podium, a little unsteady on her feet. I looked down at her shoes. The three-inch heels came to a point like an arrow. It was a miracle she could stand in those things. I may not be fashionable, but I wasn't hobbled either. The last time I'd worn shoes like that had been at my ill-fated engagement party. I shook that image from my head before I went down that pothole-riddled memory lane.

Long was trying to shake Webster, but my witness held like a strong maple tree in a stiff Lake Erie wind. Nary a limb shook.

Before I knew it, Webster was off the stand and it was time for a break.

"You think the jury bought it?" Carter said to me when we were the only ones left in the courtroom except for the court reporter who was busy consulting a steno pad and typing into her machine.

"I think it's a great policy you established," I said truthfully.

"Best advice I ever got from a lawyer. It was that Brody who told me about that," Carter said.

The stomach that had been stable enough to nibble through a granola bar during our first break plummeted to my toes. "Brody?"

"Yeah, that Tom. Is this guy—" Carter pointed to the empty high backed chair at the bench, "—related to him?"

"It's his father," I pushed from my cotton-dry mouth.

"After doing one of the girls, he came out and talked to me. I nearly shit my pants when he told me he was a prosecutor. I thought for sure I was doomed. But he told me to make 'em sign something that prohibited turning tricks. Then get the money from them and log it in. I take my twenty percent off the top, and give the rest back to them in cash when I close out. Fucking brilliant, huh? Legal smarts must run in this family."

More like a thousand ways to flout the law ran in the Brody family. I wanted to head to the bathroom and toss everything in there, damned the jury listening in to my ablutions. But I didn't get a chance. Instead, I took a long drink from the water on the table and swallowed down the bile and resentment.

"Let's get closing arguments in before lunch, counselors." Judge Brody stood at the bench while the clerk got the jury back.

I stood and gathered my notes. My client was a liar. My client was a crook. My client was a pimp. My client had learned to turn the law into a pretzel from my law-flouting ex-fiancé. No Brooks Brothers suit would change any of that. But I didn't say a word of what was rattling around in my brain. I stood and delivered my memorized speech to the jury, asking them to confirm my client's innocence.

Long's argument wasn't as strong as it should have been. She mumbled through it, looking green around the gills. When she walked by, the smell of pine . . . no, gin, assailed my nose. I wondered if she were drunk. But I didn't get to think too hard about it. After the jury was excused, I fled the courtroom.

For three long hours, I stewed in my office, calling myself a million times a fool. It wasn't that my client was guilty. I'd had plenty of those. It was that I'd fallen for his innocence. I'd been another player in an elaborate drama. I was about to turn on the computer and do a search of ethics violations when a soft knock came on the door.

I nearly jumped from my seat when my assistant, Letty, came in. I'd told her I was not to be disturbed for any reason except if the jury came back.

"A verdict?" I asked.

"Yup. Judge Brody wants you back in chambers in fifteen minutes."

I shrugged on my jacket and trudged over to the Justice Center. The weather had climbed into the eighties. I willed the sweat back into my body.

When we were all assembled, Judge Brody called in the jury. No one except the jurors and the judge were permitted to sit.

There was little preamble. Brody took the slip from the foreman and gave it a glance. I think he tilted a small smile in my direction, but that may have been my imagination. I looked at the bailiff. He didn't have a hand on his gun or cuffs. I'd told Carter that if he were found guilty, the judge would have the sheriff take him into custody today right after the sentencing. I dreaded that possibility nearly as much as I dreaded acquittal. I tried not to bounce in my navy Cuban heeled shoes.

"In the matter of the State of Ohio versus Jarrod Carter. On the count of promotion prostitution, do you find the defendant guilty or not guilty?"

"Not guilty, Your Honor," the foreman said.

A hiss of a "Yessssss!" escaped Carter's lips. I glanced at him sharply in rebuke. Not that anything could happen to him now.

Judge Brody went through a long rigmarole thanking the jury for their service. It sounded like a reelection speech to me. I was one hundred percent sure when his name came up along with a lot of unfamiliar ones on the next ballot, he'd get twelve fully detached chads from this lot.

Then it was over. Long shook my hand reluctantly. Carter pumped it happily. And Judge Brody threw a compliment my way.

"Hey there," a voice said from the gallery.

Miles. "Hey there yourself. I didn't expect you to come. As a matter-of-fact, I think I asked you not to come."

"I couldn't resist. And I'm glad I did. Your neighbors may have a little bottle of champagne chilling for you back at your building."

"That's great," I said, unable to inject lightness into my flat voice.

Miles took my hand and pulled me toward him. "What's up?"

I looked over at my client who was talking to some younger black guy. He'd been in the back corner of the courtroom from time to time. I wondered what relationship he had to Carter. Then stopped wondering. "I'm tired, is all. Haven't slept much."

Miles held out an arm. "Your coach awaits. I'll drive you home."

I normally liked the anonymous time I spent on the rapid. It allowed me to decompress. But maybe a drive without hundreds of bodies pressed against mine was what I needed.

I released Miles' arm to shake my client's hand one last time. He and his friend were eyeing me in a way that made me uncomfortable. "Congratulations," I said, again.

"Thanks. I hope I'll never have to call you again," Carter said with a laugh.

17

"Did you think there was a chance you weren't coming home?" Grand, my second in command asked before he made the sharp right turn into my driveway. I wouldn't admit this to anyone, but I'd needed someone to drive me back and forth to court these last two days. I was too damned nervous to drive myself, for one. I didn't want to get into an accident on Chester where the six lane street went entirely one way or another depending on the time of day. Nor did I want Alisha to have to come get my car if they'd carted me off. I'd read up a little and some people could get bond pending appeal, but I didn't think that extended to brothers like me.

"Nah, man," I said, all bravado now. "Told you I hired a girl who was practically the judge's daughter-in-law. She followed directions and the jury saw it my way."

Before Grand could ask anything else, Alisha was out the side door like a shot. "You came back!" Normally not the least bit effusive nor demonstrative, my niece practically pulled open the passenger door and yanked me out.

Ignoring the lurch in my chest, I gave her a brief hug, then pushed her back on the asphalt.

"You got the beds?"

There was a long moment of silence. "I didn't know if you was coming back."

"I told you shit had to keep running no matter what happened to me. Go inside." I didn't discuss my business on the street. Wasn't like there was any competition up here on the leafy avenues of Cleveland Heights, but I didn't want my neighbors knowing any more than they needed to.

Grand went upstairs to have a look around. I'd told him my plans, and he needed to get the lay of the land.

Alisha put a platter of barbecued ribs on the table along with hot corn on the cob.

"This could work," Grand said, coming back down. His glance at me was a question. I nodded and he sat down, helping himself to Alisha's down home cooking. I'd nick-named the kid Grand because getting someone to work with me had brought thousands of dollars into my life.

A lot of those business books talked about delegating smaller stuff. They was right about that. Grand was good. Kept his mouth shut. Didn't dress like a hoodlum—except maybe for that diamond winking from his left ear. Had to be a half carat easily. If that was it, I'd keep my mouth shut.

"Need to stay well off the police radar," I said. No way did I want to be back in a courtroom anytime soon. This felony thing was a stupid mistake on my part. But I didn't want to tangle with the Feds. They was no joke. I heard that a prisoner could go crazy being cooped up in some Super-Max cell twenty-three hours a day."

"That was a close call last month," Grand said.

He was right about that. Some federal agents had shut down a good chunk of my business. To this day, I hadn't figured out how they'd done it. I was very careful. Part of me thought it was some grand coincidence. The more rational part of me believed that there were no coincidences. But that was probably the echo of Momma's church ladies in my ear. Those women had always been a bit superstitious.

"How are the vans working out?"

Grand put down a rib bone and wiped his hands on a checkered cloth napkin. Without a word, he walked out the pantry door and came back with a manila folder.

"There was a catering company went out of business. They had an ad in the paper. Went out to Brook Park. The guy was happy to take the cash. Think he was about to lose his house to his wife's business going under. There are six vans. Took 'em to a body shop in Lorain." He slipped a paper out of the folder. "Here's the logo for your new delivery company."

Shit. This was better than I'd thought it would be. The sheet Grand handed me had a blue globe on it with arrows pointing like they did when the weatherman was trying to tell you about a windy day. He pushed the unfinished pork away and pulled out more paper. "Here's the application for a new company with the name Intraport."

I scanned the sheets and signed my name. "When will the vans be ready?"

Grand flipped open the phone he'd laid on the table. "Three, four days. They're pulling the wall racks out. Putting blue carpet on the floor and sides."

"Let go upstairs then. We'll need to get this house ready."

18

The door to Greg's and Jason's apartment across from mine was open when Miles and I made it up to the fourth floor.

"Congratulations," came from my neighbors and my best friend Lulu Mueller. I don't know how they'd done it. But I'd walked into a little impromptu party. Only I didn't feel much like celebrating. I pushed Miles toward my friends' apartment and turned toward my own. "Let me get out of this suit and feed the cat," I said.

I heard a cork popping and the fizz of champagne before I closed the door on the revelry. Simba wove around my feet, thrilled to have me home early. The cat anticipated, rightly so, that my presence in the apartment equaled food. Before I kicked off my shoes, I reached into the cabinet below the sink and grabbed a handful of nuggets. I tossed them in the bowl. The sound of satisfied crunching followed me down the hall to my bedroom. Toeing off the pumps that I'd slipped into with confidence this morning, I kicked them into the closet. The silk suit and cotton blouse followed. I laid them on a sweater box, vowing to hang them up later.

Being thinner than I was a year ago meant I was willing to spring for better clothes. But they required more care, which I hated. I prowled my dresser for my favorite week-end sweats, then saw them peeking out of the hamper. I put on jeans instead and a t-shirt. I wasn't ready to brave shorts in public quite yet. I may be back to my college weight, but by no means did I have my college body.

I was debating between flip-flops and slippers when I heard a knock at my hall door. With a sigh, I put on the sandals and quit stalling.

"Had to feed the cat," I said to Lulu who was standing on the other side of the door when I opened it. The bling on her middle finger sparkled more than the champagne in her flute. "You started without me."

"Honey," she said and linked arms with me. "You have to catch up." I let her pull me around the steps and into my neighbors' apartment. Music was playing. Something was bubbling on the stove. Walking into Jason and Greg's apart-ment was like walking into the loving arms of your favorite family sitcom. It was warm and welcoming. Too bad my mood didn't match. I took the flute offered and drank deeply. Jason refilled it immediately, then the room qui-eted. Only the thump of bad techno-pop music filled the air.

"So," Greg leaned forward.

"So…what?" I asked.

"Tell us what it was like. Did you go all Perry Mason on the DA? How does it feel to have won your first jury trial? Is your client thrilled?"

I turned right toward my best friend, searching her face for the right response. "Don't look at me," Lulu said. "I've only been like fifteenth chair on a dispute between two in-surance companies."

I turned left toward my boyfriend. "I lost the last case even though I didn't take a single witness," Miles said.

My biggest regret at this exact moment was that I hadn't had the guts to try out for high school theater. Maybe I'd have better acting chops. I finished the second glass and put on 'the winning rookie lawyer' performance. They seemed convinced enough to move on to dinner.

We ate some kind of roast pork and onion dish while I drank more than my fair share of wine. It being a Tuesday was the only thing that saved me from passing out. Lulu had court in the morning. Jason an early meeting with a patient who was getting bad news.

Miles followed me as I wobbled over to my apartment. The wide living room door hadn't been shut more than five seconds before he got to the point like a laser. "What's wrong?"

"Sleep deprivation. Too much alcohol. Adrenaline fa-tigue." I laid out one excuse after another. Maybe he'd take one.

Miles unbuttoned his shirt about halfway, pulled off his square-toed loafers, and sat back on my futon. He didn't look convinced. I went to the bathroom, washed my hands, and came back to him by way of the kitchen, two glasses of water in hand.

Setting the glasses on the coffee table, I finally took a spot on the cushion next to him. He didn't force the issue. Gave me the gift of silence. When I slumped against him and laid my head on his chest, still Miles didn't say any-thing. He merely stroked my hair. Warm breath whispered through his lips, stirring the strands on the top of my head.

"I'm going to do something completely inappropriate," I said.

Miles shifted his hips. I'm sure he thought I meant something sexual. But what I was going to do was so far from that as to be in another universe entirely.

"My client was guilty," I said.

His even breath continued to stir my hair. "So the prosecutor failed. He'll be back. Most do come through the system more than once. It's called recidivism for a reason."

"It's not that he was guilty. I still believe every person accused has a right to a defense. That's in our constitution. It's that he totally used me."

Miles sat up suddenly, pushing me upright as well. "You're not in trouble, right? This isn't like some book where you've been roped into some ongoing criminal activity."

I laid a hand against his chest, pushing him back down. "God, no. I'm not going to end up 'Casey Cort, lawyer for the mob.' I won't be found on the bottom of Lake Erie in cement shoes." Then I started laughing. Couldn't quite stop. From Cleveland girl to mafia tool. "Who'd play me in the movie?" I said through my laughter. "Meryl Streep's too tall and too old. Probably too beautiful. But there aren't homely actresses, are there? Maybe Minnie Driver?" I swiped at the tear rolling down my cheek.

"First of all, you're lovely," Miles said. My stomach twinged at the compliment. He was probably the first person to ever call me beautiful who didn't share my DNA. "Second, I'm not really kidding. It's not that I don't trust you, but criminals are good at bringing others into their conspiracy. It's how they keep people quiet."

"It's just that I feel stupid. He wore a suit. Spoke well. In my mind, that made him innocent. I mean, who wears a

Brooks Brothers suit and pimps girls in the back of a skanky club?"

"White collar criminals," Miles said, a very serious look on his face. "Not every criminal looks like some version of me."

"Fuck. You know that's not what I mean. It's just that..." I couldn't, maybe didn't want to share how my ex had a hand in keeping this guy out of jail. "It's not like he was a mass murderer or child molester," I said, feeling better for having talked about it a little. "Prostitution is a victimless crime, anyway. The women are willing. The men are willing. The only thing that criminalizes sex between two people is the exchange of money."

"Have you thought of working for the other side?" Miles asked. His brown eyes held mine for a long moment.

"Are you kidding? My parents would kill me. They always hated those law and order families in the Parish. The county, state, and federal government are covered. Someone's gotta work for the underdog. I was just naïve."

"Come here, my naïve lady." Miles' voice was husky.

All talk of the law was done, I think.

Career doubts went away with each caress. Others surfaced. "Sorry about the jeans."

Miles lifted his head from my neck. "No need to apologize," he said, his voice muffled by my hair. A kiss somewhere on my scalp made me tingle from head to toes.

"I should do something with my hair." It was curly and not curly at the same time. It was my mother's hair and looked as messy as hers always did.

"This gentleman prefers blondes," Miles whispered in my ear, giving me the good kind of chills on a warm August night.

"It's a curly mess," I said even though I knew I should shut up.

"Back at you." Miles pulled back. He pointed at his hair which, after our time on the futon, was going every which way as well.

"I should—"

"Shh. I can't kiss you if we're talking," he whispered before capturing my lips again.

To hell with the law or my clothes. This time, I didn't ask him to go home. Suddenly, I didn't give a damn that it was Tuesday. Backing up for a moment, I wrestled the t-shirt over my head. I watched his eyes close as I moved closer and put my lips on his. God, they were both firm and soft and made me feel so good. While Miles finished unbuttoning, unbuckling, and shucking what he had on, I pushed the futon flat. Five minutes later, I forgot what in the hell I'd been so upset about.

19

I'd always hated the morning. Now, it was my salvation. Morning meant I didn't have any more visitors for at least ten or twelve hours. Like a vampire, I slept most of the day. Too damn bad I couldn't kill men at night, suck their blood.

At the rustling, I looked toward the sky. The sun filtered through the tall maple trees. The cold wind was soft on my face. All those mornings I'd lain in bed late for school unless Sydney or Momma woke me up, or Antoine came pounding at the door, came rushing back. I'd give anything to go back to high school. Sit in those dumb ass classes. Get bullied by those hood rat kids.

"This isn't a day at the lake. Get moving," Dion said, shoving me toward the back of the brick house. We'd driven from the motel to this big ass three story brick house. My guess was we were somewhere in the Heights. The yard was about five times bigger than Clark's. This was the farthest I'd been from the Sleepy Time in a long ass time. Except for maybe that one day I'd gone to some clinic where a lady had put a rod in my arm so I couldn't get pregnant. I couldn't quite put together how long it had been since I'd met Dion. Except for day and night, time didn't mean a thing.

Rubbing my hands against the goose bumps on my arms, I shuffled in behind the other girls, my shit in a dark green plastic garbage bag. I'da been happy to leave all this crap behind. Short shorts. Lace get ups. Pretending like we was on a date. I wanted to scream to these nasty ass men that a date was something I could leave. Visiting a girl in a hotel room that only had a lock on one side of the door wasn't no date I'd ever heard of.

"Don't make a sound," Dion warned, hand on his hip. I'm sure I'd seen a gun on him a time or two. Not today, but like the girls in front of me and behind me, I obeyed.

Up two flights of stairs we climbed, the first narrow, the second narrower, before we reached a hot attic room. There were four sets of bunk beds lined up under the eaves. I rushed forward and claimed a bottom bunk by a window. Lord knows it was already kind of stuffy up in here. I didn't want to dream about hitting the ceiling with my sweaty head every morning.

"Hey, I wanted that one," Shonna said.

"Don't give a shit. Take it up with Sledge," I said.

Shonna didn't say crap after that. Took her a bed closest to the bathroom. Pushing my bag under the bed, I eyed the other girls. None of them looked back my way. Assured they wasn't going to take my spot, I went over to the bathroom. There was a tub in the middle of the room. Nothing else. After crapping in a paint bucket, I wasn't complaining, but where we supposed to go in here? Then I noticed there was another room attached to it. I almost did a dance of joy. It was a real shower, and toilet, and sink. I mean I got to clean up in the motel bathroom every night depending on how busy I was, but a real bathroom nearly made me sing for joy.

"Oooh, this nice," Shonna said.

I cut her a look. "We ain't on vacation."

Dion came into the big room. Sledge pulled up right behind him. "We're changing up how we do things," Sledge said. "Got tired of that motel. You all will be living here for the time being."

"You want us to have dates up here?"

"No," Sledge said with impatience. "This here is my house. Ain't bringing none of your customers up in here."

His house? I wondered what in the hell had happened for Sledge to move us in. I don't know where I thought he went when he wasn't running girls, but this room, painted sky blue with eight matching quilts, wasn't it. I could only hope the cops was on to him. It had been a while since I'd seen some of the girls. My belly squeezed with envy wondering if they'd gotten away somehow.

"So—" Shonna started to ask what we all wanted to know.

Sledge pushed Dion forward. "Grand will explain it to you." Sledge had never been one to say much. Kept his hands on the money and free of everything else.

"We're changing things up," Dion started. I looked at my captor. His hands were shoved deep into his tan pants. He was wearing a green polo shirt today. Nothing much about Dion had changed except there was an expensive gold watch dangling from his wrist and a carat winking from one of his ears. Don't know what made him look so innocent. I'd probably buy his bullshit even if I'd met up with him now. Hopefully, I wouldn't be stupid enough to follow some guy I didn't know a second time. If only I'd stayed at home that night. If only I'd never met Clark. If only my mother had loved me like she should instead of loving men more. I closed my eyes against the 'if onlys.'

"How?" Shonna asked. That girl talked too damn much. The only reason they kept her around was because she was some kind of light-skinned Latin girl. They could probably tell the guys anything about her and they'd believe it. She had that long hair men liked to play with. Mine wasn't more than an inch long. My plastic bag was full of hot, scratchy wigs.

"We're going to take you to the clients," Dion said. He walked around the room and put a pager in each girl's hand. "When this here buzz," he explained, "you come to the door." He pointed to the entrance we'd come through. Wasn't like any of the doors I'd glanced at in the house. This one was some kind of heavy metal with two locks on the outside. Ain't nothing but smooth metal on the inside. I hoped there wasn't no fire, because I didn't think we'd survive the jump from the third floor. I turned toward the small diamond-paned windows. Shiny new-looking screws in the wood sills reflected the early morning sunlight. We'd burn to a crisp in here.

I looked at the small piece of plastic in my hand. Could it be my key to freedom? As if sensing my thoughts, Dion continued. "This work one way. It buzz, you got five minutes to get ready."

Dion looked done, so I walked to my new bed. Sat down. A paper fluttered from my hand to the bed. No one noticed it. I turned a little toward the window and looked at it. Was a receipt for fifteen of these devices. Wasn't but eight of us in this room. Not for the first time, I wondered how big Sledge's operation was. But Sledge never made the mistake of telling us more than we needed to know. To this day, I wasn't even sure of his real name.

Clouds covered the sun and I squinted to read the date. August 18, 2004. I nearly lost what little food I'd put in my belly before we left the Sleepy Time. Two thousand four. I'd been with Sledge for five damned years. High school was over. I had to be...I counted on my fingers, nineteen years old. I bit my lip hard. I wouldn't cry.

Crying hadn't gotten me jack shit. I'd cried that first night. Back when Dion had turned me over to all those men. That little thing he'd called a 'party.' He'd put an arm around me. Promised me it wouldn't happen again. Brought me pancakes with lots of syrup in apology. Bandaged the cut they'd left on my left titty.

Thought I was going home that morning. I shoulda ran out then when I had a chance, when he stepped out to argue with Sledge about some shit. I'd just wanted to sit for a spell, let the ache between my legs go away. Work up something to say to Momma that wouldn't have her going off on me. Try to figure out a way to hide the blood that was oozing through my shirt even with the pads Dion had given me.

That door had been open a good fifteen minutes. But I'd sat there like a stupid mother fucking cunt stuffing pancakes down my throat. Licking syrup off the plate to get the foul taste of dick from my mouth. If I'd have ran for my life, they probably wouldn't have chased me. I could have gone on home to Clark's house. Taken a beating for ruining her clothes. Babysat Sydney's little ones as punishment. Followed the rules of that new guy whose name I'd long forgotten.

But I'd let that door close and lock. It had only opened for Dion to bring me food or for Dion to let a new man in. How many had I been with in five years? I hadn't been bad at math when I was in school. But every time I started a calculation, my brain rebelled. I wondered if I'd done more guys than Magic Johnson had done women. I wondered if I'd die of AIDS. I crumpled that receipt and stuck it in the corner of the window and stopped thinking.

Dion went on for a bit about rules and shit, then he closed the door with a click. The lock turned. I laid down on the bed and waited for the oblivion of sleep. It was the only pleasure I had these days.

20

"There's a second container," was all I heard before I hit the button disconnecting the call. I was running down the hallway toward the elevators when I nearly knocked Chas over.

"Where are you—"

"There's a second container," I answered, jabbing frantically at the elevator button. Forget this. I ran past Chas and his open mouth.

I pushed open the exit door and started the run down the sterile staircase. We were only on the fourth floor of the twenty-three story building. For some, low floor meant low status. For me, today, it meant I could get out of here quickly and possibly solve this case. It was the break we'd all been praying for.

Valdespino was downstairs waiting, red and blue lights pulsing from the grill of the hulking SUV and at the top of the windshield. I jumped in and the agent sped off before I could latch my seat belt.

"Let me warn you, this may be a shit show. Call came in and I asked for SWAT. The higher ups got alerted, the media got involved, and who all knows who else. There will probably be a thousand cops, agents, politicians, and reporters down there."

There was the Sunrise Motel on Warrensville Center Road. Something about it looked familiar, but it was hard to place with all the activity going on. Valdespino had not exaggerated. You'd have thought we had the 9/11 terrorists in the container with the number of loaded guns, gleaming badges, and flashing lights.

Lou must have had nuts the size of soccer balls. Didn't let squat intimidate him. He grabbed the bullhorn, and control.

"This is Special Agent Lou Valdespino. We are here to help you. In a moment, an agent is going to cut open the lock. Please back away from the door and come out with your hands up."

There were enough hand gestures from Valdespino and the others to make any baseball umpire proud. But everyone moved back as a cordoned area surrounding the blue container was enlarged. He beckoned me forward and I went, only one of two people standing without a bullet-proof vest. The other was Chas, who'd somehow made it down here in record time. This must be big if the deputy chief was willing to leave his office.

Expectation hushed the crowd. A SWAT officer brandishing a lethal-looking bolt cutter approached the container. He banged loudly on the door twice. Satisfied, he opened and closed the cutters. The lock came apart like a hot knife had sliced through butter. Handing off the heavy tool, the

SWAT team member pulled a dark shield over his eyes. The crowd took a collective breath as he lifted the squeaking lever and threw the bolt.

I could practically hear the whirr of camera lenses as they focused on those doors. Two SWAT team agents, flash-lights poised, stormed through the metal doors. The clomp of their boots rang out as they stomped across the thin floor-ing.

I held my breath, waiting for women to stream from the container. Nothing. Were they as hesitant as the last bunch, I wondered. But the SWAT backed out empty handed. A quick conference with Valdespino. I stepped forward, my curiosity getting the better of me. Protocol be damned.

"It's empty," an agent said. Lifting his visor, he repeated, "It's empty."

Valdespino took the flashlight the guy proffered and pointed the laser-bright beam into the blue corrugated dark-ness. His eyes met mine and I stepped forward again. My eyes followed his beam, touching every one of the far cor-ners, sweeping the floor.

It was indeed empty, or nearly so. There was some detri-tus, a nearly flat pillow, a plastic water bottle, a paint bucket. But the women who may have occupied it were long gone.

While Valdespino shook his head, the SWAT team leader spoke into a transmitter and waved his hands over his head. The men ran through the weed-choked lot and swarmed the hotel.

In less than a minute, guests spilled from the occupied rooms. I walked across the lot to get a closer look. A fat man in tent-like boxers, a half-dressed woman, a couple doing their best to wrap themselves in skimpy towels, all stood looking scared out of their wits.

An agent went into the check-in area and he came back frog-marching a middle-eastern man.

An agent without a visor approached the hotel manager.

"Where are the women?"

"I don't know what you're talking about," the hotel employee said, a pleading tone in his voice. He wiggled the fingers behind his back, uncomfortable in the trussed position.

"Did you sell them to Saddam?" an agent spit in his face.

The man stepped back as best he could while the other agent held his cuffed hands.

"Son, you know exactly what I'm talking about. There's someone running through Cuyahoga County pimping out women and children to the highest bidder. And here you are with a container in your backyard. When we pick up that container, and don't think we won't, we're going to vacuum every last hair and fiber out of there. I'm gonna bet your sand nigger ass that you're all wrapped up in this thing here. I'll personally ship you back to where you came from."

Valdespino approached the cursing agent. "That's enough."

"That's not our property," the guy said.

"What?"

"That property back there. It isn't ours. The motel property line stops at those bushes."

I looked at the parking lot again. There were some scraggly hedges that may have been boxwood. But they'd been cut down short, starved for water, and trod on so many times that without a plot map, it would be difficult to tell one pothole-riddled lot from another.

"Robinson," Valdespino called. "Check the property lines."

Everyone stayed in place for the five minutes Robinson disappeared into a van. He came back with a printout. Four or five agents huddled together. A few seconds in, I saw Valdespino's crewcut head pop up from the group and scan the crowd. Spotting me, he waved me over.

"What's up?" I asked the group of middle-aged agents.

"Lou said you were on the job," a guy threw at me.

I nodded, validating something because the group relaxed, if only a bit. "What kind of search can we do here?" one agent asked. "Can we detain the hotel employee?" another asked.

Maybe this is why Chas had disappeared from the front lines into the passenger seat of one of the cop cars. Not only would he stay out of the possible line of fire, he wouldn't be on the hook for what went down. For the briefest second, I considered calling him over. Putting *his* ass on the line.

"Question everyone as quick as possible. Take the guy out of handcuffs, question him. But you're gonna have to let them go after that."

"Can we search the hotel rooms?"

"Yes, no, and maybe," I answered.

"Better to ask forgiveness…" one agent muttered.

"Look," I acquiesced. "Take a quick look for the girls. Ask any women if they're here involuntarily. If it looks kosher, you'll need to leave it alone for now," I said. Unfortunately, there wasn't a good answer to the search question. Courts were all over the place with Fourth Amendment searches. For the most part, the government had to stay the hell out of your house. But a room you rent for a few hours or a few days? It depended on so many different factors that I couldn't even begin to explain now.

But I had a case not to fuck up. And I didn't want to blow any good evidence on improper searches. That was for sure.

So I hoped they took my advice and kept the room to room minimal.

I backed out of the huddle when talk turned to logistics. Taking a page from Chas' playbook, I took myself to Valdespino's car to wait. During the next hour, things got quieter and quieter until a crane and flatbed truck barreled through the connected lots. In less time than it takes to get a fast food burger, the container was lifted into the air and up on the truck.

"Where they taking it?" I asked when Valdespino stuck his head in the truck.

"Virginia."

The FBI crime lab would have a field day with that. I wondered how long it would be before any usable information came from the forensic investigation.

"Hotel clerk say anything else?"

"He doesn't know a thing. And if he did, he isn't saying shit. He's still smarting from Agent Wheeler's remarks."

"Fuck."

"Yeah, well. This terrorism shit gets some people's panties tied in a knot."

"What next?"

"Go home. I'll let you know if anything pops up. But I think this was another dead end." Valdespino banged on the hood in frustration. "Sledge is always one step ahead of us."

21

"Where are we going?" I asked Valdespino as I slipped into the passenger seat of the unmarked black Chevy Suburban.

"Sleepy Time," he said, shifting the SUV into drive and pulling out of the lot.

The Northfield Center Road motel didn't look any better than the last time I'd seen it. As a matter of fact, daylight didn't do it any favors. The stucco was flaking off in places. The part remaining was either gray, blue, or beige, like it couldn't decide. I looked around the neighborhood by the highway that I didn't frequent.

From the looks of it, I could cash my paycheck, rent to own furniture, and get chicken fried steak all without driving more than a half mile in any direction. Valdespino pulled into the far side of the parking lot and cut the engine.

There was a sole worker at the wide check-in desk. Valdespino flashed the gold shield. Introduced us.

"Mani Emad," the man said in slightly accented English. "How can I help you?" I didn't understand if his reserve was cultural propriety or fear of authority. I'd seen it before in illegal immigrants and people who'd been harassed by the police. I wondered into which category he fell.

"We're here to ask you about that container found in the parking lot a few months ago," was Valdespino's opening line.

"That's not our lot," Emad said. He pointed out the plate glass window. "See those concrete dividers?" he asked.

I looked where he was pointing, then back at him. Valdespino did the same, nodded, spoke. "What about them?"

"That's where the motel ends. That container was in that other lot. Not ours." I looked at Valdespino, but his face showed no hint of recognition. The story was achingly familiar to me though. This Sledge guy did not make mistakes. There were rarely coincidences in investigative work, I reminding myself. I pulled my mind back to the task at hand. Valdespino was peppering the guy with questions.

"Now that you've had some time to think about it, you see anything out of the ordinary? Girls coming and going? Did you smell anything? Had to be a pretty foul odor coming out of there when it was opened to get food in."

Emad shook his head, gestured toward his computer screen. "We stay pretty busy here. Got hooked up with a few internet booking sites, so I have to monitor that along with our native reservation system."

I looked around again. There weren't any flowers, water, complimentary coffee. There didn't even seem to be a room to have a free breakfast. I couldn't imagine he was beating away potential lodgers with a stick.

"You have full occupancy?" I asked.

Emad hesitated. "We have industry standard occupancy rates," he said. The phone bleeped. He pressed a button, the sound stopped.

"Thanks," Valdespino said. We stepped outside.

"You knew that container was on a different parcel of land, right?"

"That's why we couldn't get a warrant for the hotel. Crime didn't happen on their turf."

"And that first time the girls were in the container, so there was no going looking for them." Not like the night last month. "So why are we here?"

"Because I've been keeping an eye on the place and nothing is happening."

"So he runs a shitty business," I said.

"You heard him talk," Valdespino said. "He sounds like he's got a college degree in engineering or marketing. You think he's been there nearly ten years running a shitty business?"

I took a long look at Valdespino. Lifted my shoulder, dropped it. "What's the story?"

"Our man over there, Mani Emad, came to the U.S. from Egypt in the mid-nineties on a Student Visa. Dropped out of some Ohio State graduate program. Put himself into hock to buy this motel. He went from an apartment in Warrensville Heights, to a house in Richmond Heights. He paid cash for the house."

"So maybe he's got some other criminal activity. Sledge is running girls in one lot. Emad runs drugs or something in this one."

"Then we have that other guy at Sunrise. Remember him?"

I shrugged. "He was from the middle east too. Big region. Lots of countries with Arabic speakers."

Valdespino pulled a small leather notebook from his pocket. "Mostafa Tarik. Also from Egypt. Got a loan from the same bank to buy their hotels a year apart."

"You're reaching," I said. "My mother's family came to Philadelphia from rural Virginia. Everyone from AME Bethel in Virginia moved to the same neighborhood. Borrowed money from the same bank to buy their houses. It's how communities grow," I said. I was sure Casey's family had a similar story as did millions of others.

"But you're forgetting Occam's Razor," Valdespino said. "The likelihood that Emad and Tarik are running two completely unrelated businesses is small. You've got involuntary prostitutes. You've got a hotel with beds and plenty of parking. You have vacant lots with containers."

I nodded, seeing his logic. "So what you're saying is that it's no coincidence that Sledge took up with these guys. They have complimentary businesses."

"Bingo." Valdespino pointed an imaginary gun.

"So what, you're going down to the local Mosque. Poke around. Even if some guy in a kufi says that a guy fitting Sledge's description came by, that's still not enough to get a warrant. And we found the containers; unless Sledge is a complete and utter idiot, he's not coming back here. And *if* we had a warrant to poke around Tarik and Emad's bank accounts, I doubt they're funneling cash through there. That would be idiotic."

"So what's Emad doing for money?" Valdespino's look told me what *he* thought.

"Hooking up with Internet reservation systems and keeping his fingers crossed?" I answered. I didn't have a clue how Emad was doing what he was doing. I didn't know anything about the numbers of the downscale motel business.

But Lou seemed to have a clue. He said, "But he's gotta be losing money. The house is paid off. But this motel isn't. He's got taxes coming due. The eastside isn't cheap."

"So what's the plan, no warrant man?"

"We've got to find the weak spot," Valdespino said.

I turned, looking through the plate glass window again. A girl, not more than sixteen, was on her knees scraping something from the floor. A mop and bucket were next to her.

"Who's the girl?" I asked.

I could see Valdespino flipping through his mental file. If eyes could light up, his did. "Our weak spot."

22

Jarrod "Sledge Hammer" Carter
September 20, 2004

"What are you gonna do about Sleepy Time?" Grand asked, flipping his hand back and forth on the dining room table. He wasn't a fidgety mofo by any stretch so it took no more than a moment to realize *Dion* had some new bling on his hand living up to his nickname.

"Don't know. What they asking?" I held my tongue about running around looking like a gangster and kept the talk about work.

"That we keep up the payments."

"But we moved clear out," I said. "Ain't been there for two months by my count."

One thing I'd read in the business books I borrowed from the Cleveland Heights Library was that a man could hold on to a bad business model too damned long. The Sleepy Time, the Sunrise, and those containers had been a damned mistake. One that was going to continue to cost me if I didn't figure something out.

Maybe it hadn't been a bad idea in the beginning when I was getting things up and running. Expanding beyond the bars. When I was learning the ropes of management. But after that?

The delivery trucks were a damned stroke of genius. I should have done that or bought some cheap ass property in the hood to do my business. I'd kept those motel people in my business too damned long.

First off, they'd cost me a pretty penny. Nearly ten percent off the top had gone to them. Room rent, they'd called it. Room rent, my ass. Both Mani and Tarik had been running a seedy by-the-hour operation when I'd started there. That's why I'd picked them. About a mile apart so I could go back and forth, I'd kept them rooms filled in the way they never did.

I made sure we kept the drug dealers and other lowlifes away. Didn't bother them too much about cleaning. But once they'd talked down at the Mosque or whatever they church was, they'd gone in together. Hiked up the payments. Took my money without blinking.

"Mani say if we don't pay, he may not be so inclined not to speak to the feds sniffing around," Grand said, jerking me out of my thoughts.

I rubbed at the middle of my forehead, willing my new headache to go away.

"Chicken and dumplings," Alisha said, slapping two bowls down on the table.

"What happened to the meat?" Grand asked, holding the spoon she had set down between his fingers like it was used toilet paper. He'd gotten too used to fried chicken, ribs, and the fried catfish Alisha usually served.

"Meat is for one or two people," Alisha said. "I'm feeding Sledge's momma and ten more people besides? This I can make for any size group."

Grand didn't say anymore. Stuck his spoon in and ate like he was a starving man.

I dipped my own spoon in. It was good. Better and cheaper than what the girls had been eating. They'd been living on fast food value meals for quite a while. "Maybe they'll fatten up. The customers like them healthy," I said. Once the girls had moved in, I hadn't exactly told Alisha what I was up to, but I wasn't hiding it either. My only rule was keeping Momma safe and sane and in the dark. She'd have kicked my ass with her one good leg if she knew I'd expanded beyond the bars.

"So what are we to do about Sleepy Time?" Grand asked again. First the bling, then this. I held back from taking him to task about his lack of initiative. Seemed like he was having an off week. And it *was* my business to run.

Delegate. Delegate. Delegate. That was the lesson, right? That thought fought with: You want something done right, you do it yourself.

"Lemme think on it," I said, kicking myself for what I knew was bad management. Decisions should always be made in the first instance. Waiting around always made problems worse. I picked up a dumpling, chewed, and swallowed, pushing aside the thoughts for now. "The vans were genius," I said, practically patting myself on the back again.

A small smile snuck around the side of Grand's mouth. "The customers sure are happy. Plus we've expanded our base beyond mofos willing to come to the east side."

"That's the most important," I said. No matter what the business, customer service was always something a manager should strive to improve. Most businesses weren't doing that anymore, but I still thought it was important. "Are there any downsides we're not working out?"

"Not that I can see," Grand said. For a moment, I thought I saw his eyes shift. "Girls stay up in your attic room. They get in the vans. One of the guys escorts them to they house or The Place to Be. Then we get on to the next location."

"How's the new system working out?"

"A-ight," Grand said. "I'm trying to teach the drivers to keep it all in their heads."

Another thing to add to the list of shit that I was worried about. The lists. Changing up how we did business hadn't been easy for all my guys. Instead of taking calls and pages and moving men between the rooms at the Sleepy Time or Sunrise, we were moving the girls around.

But ain't like no one who did well in school is working for me. So I'd found out the guys were writing shit down. And not even in some kind of code. It was like they'd never seen *Goodfellas* or *The Godfather* or any fucking mob movie. Keeping notes always took an organization down. That's why Oliver North was at the shredder. If no one can prove you did shit, then you ain't done shit.

"You using the shredder I bought?" I'd taken a page from the disgraced lieutenant colonel.

"Every night," Grand said, nodding.

Crossed that worry off my list. Dion had been as good as his word the last six years with almost no fuck-ups. "Eat up. You got a long night ahead."

23

"Can I see one of your rooms?" Valdespino asked Emad, following our impromptu script we'd worked out ten minutes ago in the nearly empty parking lot.

The clerk looked from the quiet phones, to the computer screen, out the window and back. Making some kind of decision, he nodded. Emad pulled a key from a hook and took the FBI agent out the front door.

I paced, then 'accidentally' kicked at the bucket the girl had been moving around occasionally. "I'm so sorry," I apologized, righting the plastic.

"I've got it," the girl said softly. With a quick swipe, she cleaned up the spill, then got back to scraping at the unrecognizable substance from the floor.

I squatted, getting eye-level. "I'm Miles Siegel." I held out my hand. She didn't take the cue, kept on scrubbing.

With a sound of satisfaction, she scraped the gummed material into a paper towel, stood, and threw it in the trash on the housekeeping cart.

"How old are you?" I asked, standing to meet her eyes. She was a tall girl, probably five foot seven at least. Dark, dark brown her eyes were. They were a perfect match with her nearly jet black hair. In comparison, her skin was pale, with the hint of a tan. If I didn't have the curly hair, we could have passed for brother and sister.

"Sixteen," she said, her voice gaining volume.

"Why aren't you in school?"

"One of the cleaners didn't come today," she said.

Her voice was kind of lilting. She wasn't from Ohio, or America for sure, and her first language wasn't English. Not by a long shot. "I grew up in Philadelphia," I volunteered. "I kind of find Ohio different. What do you think?"

The girl stopped stacking paper cups for a long moment. "I think the food is weird," she confided. "The *hummus bi tahina* and *aish baladi* they have in the market here are awful."

"Cleveland isn't known for its..." I made like I was taking a shot in the dark, "Egyptian food."

"How did you know I was from Egypt? Most people guess Iraq, or Israel."

"I went to Egypt with my parents when I was about ten or eleven," I said, grateful for my wanderlust parents. We'd gone to Turkey on that trip, as well. I think I'd whined about the heat for days. Thank goodness they'd pressed on, ignoring my protests.

"What did you think of my country?"

I tossed the honest response about yet *another* damned place with colonial colorism from my mind. This wasn't wine bar chat with a group of fellow students. "I liked the

Pyramids. They were more awesome than in pictures. The food was great as well. *Kibda* and *mahshi* were my favorites.

"I love *kibda*," the girl exclaimed. "But everyone here says liver is disgusting."

"I didn't catch your name," I tried again.

"Rida," she said. Her voice had gone from loud to soft, from excited to calm. The contrast was odd.

"How long have you been in Ohio?"

Rida's eyes darted away. "Two years. I came after my parents died."

"I'm sorry for your loss," I said automatically. Immediately, I regretted the pat phrase. But I'd said it so often when I was on the force that I forgot the impact of death. Rida's eyes shifted back to the cart full of toilet paper and industrial spray bottles of blue and green liquids, like it was calling her name.

"I gotta get back to work," she said.

Between her skittishness and Valdespino's stall, I was running out of time.

"Have you ever heard of a guy named Sledge?"

Rida tittered behind her hand. "Is that a real name?"

"No. Nickname. We think he's responsible for the girls in the containers, and we're looking for him."

"See that stone line out there?" Rida gestured much like her brother, cousin, or uncle had.

"We know. Not your land. I understand. Just wondering if you ever saw anyone coming or going from back there? Maybe they crossed your parking lot? Asked to use the bathroom? Used your soda machine?"

Rida held my eyes as long as she could. I think she knew something. But a force bigger than the FBI, the US Attorney's Office, and compassion for those women kept her silent. Eventually, she slowly shook her head. "Sorry."

"What are you sorry for, Rida?" Emad and Valdespino came back in through a door I hadn't noticed to the left of the front desk.

I threw my hands in the air in apology. "It was my fault. I kicked the bucket." Not a laugh out of a single one of them. "That's what dry cleaners are for, right?" I pretended to swat at my pant leg.

Valdespino and I hustled our way out of there. Wasn't much reason to hang around. The FBI agent led the way to the lot where we'd started this investigation in July. The crime scene tape was long gone. Nothing remained but a few scrapes in the cracked, weedy pavement where the container had been. The heavy blue metal had gouged the earth when the crane had lifted it onto the flatbed truck like it would do later for its mate.

It had been dusted, sprayed, and vacuumed for evidence. There were hair and fibers galore. Some had belonged to the women and girls. Others, probably the johns. But no database hits so far. Nothing yet for the second container.

"What did you see?" I turned to Valdespino, shading my eyes to read his.

"Shitty hotel rooms. Old bedspreads. Sticky carpet. The whole thing stinks, literally and figuratively," he said.

"I think the girl knows something."

Blue eyes shifted toward mine. "Her visa is long expired. I assumed Emad was living alone."

"Is she in school?"

"I'll check Richmond Heights and connected districts."

"Gonna pull her in for status violation, aren't you?"

"She's the weak link in the chain. It's time to get out the pry bar."

24

I swear to God, this was like slavery without the chains. Dion locked me in the back of the van with a click of the lock and a jingle of keys. I hugged my knees, tucking into the crease of blue carpet where floor and wall met. I squeezed my eyes shut. These rides were making me dizzy as hell. I wanted to throw up more times than not when I was back here. I'd tried eating, not eating, eyes open, eyes shut—none of it made me feel better during the zig zag rides through town.

"Got six tonight," Dion threw back behind the driver's seat. Said like that was supposed to be a relief. In the hotel, we sometimes did eight or ten. Some guys were so quick you could do two in an hour. But for the most part, it was first guy around eight, last guy around three or four. Sunrise came, we were allowed to sleep.

The drive was long, so I knew we'd be starting on the westside. I hated westside guys. Parma guys especially. There was a certain type of white guy who wanted to fuck a black girl, but hated himself for wanting to, and hated the girl more. I braced myself, not only for the jostle of the van as we made enough turns to let me know we were in some-one's neighborhood. But I braced myself for whoever was coming out to the van. More likely than not, I was in for a couple hours of rough play and probably a slap or two. Even when I knew a hand or fist was coming at me, the hit still surprised me every time.

When I heard the other girls whispering to each other at night over the last few months, I knew some of them got better guys than me. The light-skinned ones, the white ones, got guys who treated them like it was a date. I got guys who treated me like a dirty little secret they couldn't wait to get rid of when it was over.

The minute the van stopped moving, I went far away. When the door opened and slammed, I was long gone. I went to Antoine's aunt's house in my mind. Maybe one day, I could move in with him. If his aunt let him live there and he was gay, surely she wouldn't judge me. We could go to school together. Be best friends like we used to—us against the world. We'd talk about what we wanted to be when we grew up. I wondered if he still wanted to be a singer. I expected him to turn up on *American Idol* at any moment. He had been that good.

Maybe we could get an apartment in New York. I could draw, maybe get a job at a newspaper or something drawing the funnies while he was singing at night. I was in an apart-ment in Harlem with Antoine painting big pretty flowers on our dingy living room wall when a painful twist of one of my nipples brought me back to the present.

"Ouch!" I cried out. I wasn't supposed to say anything unless I was asked to say anything. But pain had a way of making me break Sledge's rules.

"I was talking to you, cunt," the man spit in my face.

I turned my face aside, but a vise-like grip brought it back. "I'm paying for you to give me what I ask for," the man said. "Tell me how much you want to suck my cock," he said, pulling it from inside me.

Shit. He was gonna be one of those nasty ones. The words I'd learned to keep things moving fell from my numbed lips. When you didn't give them what they asked for, you could be in there for a long time waiting for them to get off. By the time he got out of the van, Antoine and I had finished painting and were making a list of second-hand furniture we thought we could afford.

"You're fucking bleeding," Dion said.

"There ain't no water in these vans," I said. That was something the hotel had over this. You could take as many showers as you wanted and nobody said a thing. Now Sledge had a one shower a day per girl rule. Wasn't nobody allowed to use that pretty bathtub.

Giving me a disgusted look, Dion slammed the door with so much force, I nearly fell off my butt. Another long drive. Back on the eastside. Gimme a black man over some nasty white guy any day. Can't believe I thought that after Clark. But live and learn, right?

The first time a half-bald, red-faced white man had come into my motel room, I'd sent up a prayer to a God I no longer believed in. I thought he was going to be the savior. Meek, mild, was how he looked. But that man was anything but a mouse. He thought I was a fast food restaurant and had to do things his way. Second one was that way too. Maybe not all were like that, but I kept my expectations real low after that and had never been disappointed.

The van bumped along what was probably a cracked up driveway. Definitely east side if not East Cleveland. I wiped away the crusting blood, cleaning up as best I could with a wet rag I kept in the corner. Dion opened the door. Taking huge gulps of fresh air, I tried to get my dizzy head straight. The fumes from the new carpet in these vans was the second worse thing about Sledge's new home delivery service.

"Out or in?" I asked.

"In," Dion said, jerking his head back. The big ass diamond I'd probably paid for winked at me.

I scooted on my butt to the end of the van and jumped out, making sure not to twist my ankle on the weed-choked cement under my four-inch heels.

"Where?" I looked around for a door cracked open, trying to find a brown fist curled around a doorknob, nervous eyes beckoning me. But all the doors I could see were locked up tight.

This house looked a lot like the one Momma and I had lived in with Clark. But that house had a big hole in the driveway pavement, a piece of iron had stuck out. That shit had driven Clark crazy, but even he didn't have the right tools to fix it. Every patch he'd ever smoothed over had crumpled up and sunken in. Nothing ever seemed to fill that hole. I shuffled toward the door, kicking something. I looked down. Rebar?

"Is this Clark's house?" I asked Dion, violating one of Sledge's rules about asking questions.

"I don't know who Clark is. But your momma's still living here," Dion said.

"And what, her newest man has ordered in a girl?" I said, shaking my head. That would be just the kind of man

Momma would hook up with. They never had been worth a damn. Except maybe for Syd's father—

"I'm bringing you home," Dion said, breaking into my thoughts.

"Home?" I looked at the East Eighty-Eighth Street house. It had been blue. But this flaking off paint was white, or nearly so. I picked at a chip on the wood siding near the back door. I took my other hand and peeled the thin, flaking strip into two. A sliver of blue showed between the chalk and some brownish color on the back.

"Hurry," Dion said, giving me one mighty shove toward the door. "I got to figure out something to tell Sledge."

"Where am I supposed to go?" I said, utterly confused. Had the new owners of Clark's house ordered me like a pizza?

"Home," Dion said, his movements jerky and impatient. "I'm gonna tell Sledge that the last guy took you out of the van and never brought you back."

Freedom loomed large and scary.

I'd dreamt of it a thousand times. Maybe a million. It had mixed in with dreams of a life with Antoine. It had mixed in with nightmares of grabbing hands and open mouths. But I'd never thought I'd be back here. Exactly the place I'd walked out of on that night.

"Momma still live here?" I asked, amazed that she'd have been able to stay in Clark's house all this time.

Dion nodded. "She's married. Her name is Mary Dixon now. Go on. Get."

I turned to ask more about what I was walking into, but Dion had already shut the back door, moved around to the front, and started the van. It scooted out the driveway, then took a right. I watched the blue and white delivery truck go with a pang. He may have been shit, but the only friend I'd had for the last five years had walked, no, driven right out of my life.

A man opened the kitchen door, nearly knocking me off my step. "We didn't order..." When he got a load of me, he backed up a foot. "What in the hell we got here?"

25

Jarrod

September 23, 2004

I would never admit to another human being that I'd been in that damned store in Tower City Mall that sold shit with inspirational quotes on it. But when I'd moved my office from the club to Momma's house, I'd picked up one of those engraved rocks. It read, "Never put off till tomorrow what you can do today."

After the girls made it downstairs, and the vans had their routes planned out, I made sure Alisha had everything she needed to keep Momma settled for the night. I left them watching some Tyler Perry play on DVD and eating some kind of low carb veggie chips.

I got my car from the garage and made one last drive over to the Sleepy Time. Mani was there, same as ever. Having been gone for a few weeks, I gave the lobby the once over.

"You cleaning up?"

"New paint job," Mani said. "Trying to aim for a better clientele."

"My clientele may not have been upscale, but we paid our tab," I said.

"You got today's rent?"

"About that," I started. Then Rida came into the room. She was Mani's Achilles heel, and until now, I hadn't needed to use it. "The way I see it, you owe me. Grand's been paying, but we ain't been occupying. The way I see it, you're collecting double. Some from us, the rest from whoever staying in this shithole—"

"It ain't—"

"The way I see it, is I'mma let you keep the money you already got. We call it even."

"The FBI was here today," Mani said like it was a threat.

"And they ain't found nothing, otherwise I wouldn't be here," I said, trying not to twitch in fear. They was getting way too close to me. And I didn't have no backup plan.

"Guy left his card," Mani boasted. "I could call this Lou Valdespino. Solve the Tragic Case of the Women in the Container for him," he said like he was sitting an anchor desk with a microphone in his ear.

"But you won't," I said, extending out our long game of chicken.

"'Cause you're going to pay me?" he said with a hint of weakness.

"'Cause if I'm going down, you're going with me," I said, poking at his fear. Then I amplified what was probably his biggest worry. "You think they're going to let you off with less than a felony? You don't think they'll send your ass right back to the Middle East? I'm sure a couple of federal charges will derail your 'path to citizenship.' You think on that."

Having made my point, I stalked from the lobby. Mofo think he can threaten me? He think he's better than me? He think he can put my ass under the jail and walk away scot free? Nuh uh. I drove across the street and got me some sausage gravy, biscuits, and coffee. I looked out one plate glass window and through another. My opportunity would come soon.

26

"I'm . . . Destiny," I said.

"Destiny?" The man looked me up and down, slowly, carefully taking in everything about me. "You must be at the wrong house. We don't need anything you're selling." The way he said that last made me feel even dirtier than usual. He made a move to close the door. I stuck my foot in the hinge of the screen door.

"Not Destiny," I said quickly. Destiny is the name Sledge had picked for me. I'd kind of liked it because it was the name of a girl who used to make fun of Antoine and me. Every time a man hit me or did something I didn't like, I pretended he was doing it to her. She'd gotten hers in the last years. "My name is Stefanie," I paused. My tongue was so unused to that combination of letters. "Wells." I took another minute to figure the best way past this man. "Mary Higgins. I'm here to see her."

"Her name Mary Dixon now. Are you some kind of kin? Seems like her kinfolk would already know that." He tried pushing the door closed again, like I was handing out Jehovah pamphlets.

"Who are you?" It was rude, but I was past caring. I wanted to see my momma.

"John Dixon. I'm her husband. We've been married two years. This here is our house. Now—"

"I'm her daughter. Stephanie. I...haven't been around."

The man stepped back. It wasn't an invitation, but I took what I could and put one foot into the small room behind the kitchen. "Are you the one that ran away?"

"Is my momma home?" I asked. I ducked my head, taking in my stupid heels. If this man didn't let me past, I was going to cry. The last thing I wanted to do was let him see me with tears on my face.

"Mary! There's a girl here claiming to be Stephanie."

He let me into the kitchen. It was different. The fake brick walls were painted white as were the cabinets. There was a pot of something cooking on the back of the stove. Smelled kind of like ham hocks and black eyed peas. I wasn't always sure of the days or months, but knew it wasn't New Year's either.

The sound of feet pounding distracted me from the sights and smells of the kitchen. First, Sydney burst through the door, then Momma.

I put my arms around Momma and held on for dear life. She felt the same as I remembered. Soft flesh squeezed under my fingers. Her hair smelled like that hair oil in the pink and yellow bottle I knew was in the bathroom. Tears blocked my vision. Snot clogged my nose.

Momma.

I was home.

❧—❧—❧

Momma kept pulling me forward and pushing me back. Looking at me through puffy watery eyes, then squeezing me in tighter and tighter embraces.

Letting me go, Momma shook me, hard. "Where in the hell have you been?"

"Around," I said.

"Why did you run away?" Syd asked, her arms crossed.

"I don't know," I answered.

"You don't know. Do you know how much we worried about you? We tried star six nining your boyfriend, but it never went anywhere. Have you been with him the entire time? Right here in Cleveland?"

Without invitation, I scraped a chair across the kitchen floor and sank into it. There hadn't been enough time between stepping out the van and getting to my momma's house to figure out what in the hell I was going to tell them. The truth wasn't an option.

"Where Sheron and Jaylen?" I asked. I tried not to remember a time when babysitting them had been the worst thing someone would ask me to do in a night.

"My friend took them for burgers," Sydney answered.

"What grade they in?" I tried to work out the math, but my head wouldn't cooperate.

"Sheron in second—"

"Do you have any idea how worried Mary has been?" Dixon said.

I turned my head toward where he stood by the back door. He was big like Momma liked them. My dad had been small, wiry in the pictures I'd seen. But Sydney's dad and on down the line had been like John Dixon here. All looked like they could play football if'n they wanted. Clark certainly had been big enough to hold me down. I turned away.

Why couldn't I have come back when Momma was single? If I never saw another man again, it wouldn't be too soon.

"I'm sorry," I whispered. And I was. Sorry that I'd ever believed Dion was my friend.

"Where do you live?" Momma asked.

"Nowhere." Unless Sledge found me and dragged me back to his house.

"Where you been stayin?" That was Sydney.

"Around." I took in the kitchen, tried to twist my head to see the family room. Everyone was quiet, tense looking at me. "Can I stay here? I ain't got nowhere to go." My voice cracked. My nose itched. But I held back the tears.

"Jaylen in your old room," Syd said. "Sheron in the attic room. Only thing left is the basement."

Was that a little smile playing around her lips because she finally got her way?

"That's fine." I looked at the woman I'd known longer than anyone. "Momma?"

Momma looked at Dixon.

"Temporarily," he said. I ducked my head, trying to work out what that meant. Temporary until they could toss me out. Temporary until I could move upstairs. "Where's your stuff?"

I'm guessing he didn't mean my collection of high heels, short skirts, and wigs. "I got nothing," I mumbled.

"Extra clothes?" Momma asked.

"Only this," I said, pointed at myself.

"You got a bruise coming up." Momma leaned across from her seat at the table and laid a hand on the area above my eye—still tender from that westsider. "Your boyfriend knock you around? That why you come back?"

My hand flew to my face where she'd pressed a little too hard. I drew in breath, my hiss filling the room. Latching on to that little bit of story, I said, "Yeah. Got out with the first shoes I could grab. Can't go back. I think he'll kill me."

"You want some black eyed peas?" Momma asked, pushing herself up from the table.

I nodded. I'd figure out the rest of my life—after I ate something.

27

"Do you really want to go to this happy hour thing?" I asked Miles while flipping through my closet. It was full of fat clothes, skinny clothes, but nothing I wanted to wear.

"It's where we had our first real conversation," Miles said. He was laying back against my headboard, his head and arm propped on pillows. His three-button sport coat was casually tossed on the foot of the bed. But black socks poked out from dress pants held up by a less-than-casual belt. "If you don't have a problem being seen with me, I'd like to go."

He slipped it in so offhandedly, I may have missed that tiny hint of insecurity while looking for something that didn't make my hips look big.

"Oh, God. That's not it at all," I said.

"Are you sure you're not worried about running into Tom?" Miles asked as coolly as he'd thrown out the last.

I turned from the closet this time so we could talk face to face. "No. No. Do you really think I'm worried about being seen with you? What people might think?" I was horrified that he could think I could care about race in that way.

Miles' crook of the head was nearly imperceptible. He lifted a palm, then dropped it. "It's happened before. I haven't even met your parents and they live in town."

"I don't care that you're black," I said, putting my naked foot right into my mouth. I was surprised I hadn't choked to death on it in that moment. "That's not what I meant. I like you for who you are," I said, sitting down on the bed. "My parents would love you." At least, I think they would. They'd never talked about race in a city where there was talk about almost nothing but.

They'd hated my very Irish ex-fiancé. But that may have been because he was rich, or because he'd dumped me, or because his parents had treated mine like the red-headed bastard step-children when we'd talked up wedding plans. But I don't know how they'd feel about Miles. I'm not sure his law enforcement background would go down well. Especially after the last prosecutor in my life.

I stood and pulled a sleeveless black and white halter dress from the closet. "I'll change and then we can go," I said, not at all addressing the issue of my parents.

Miles was silent on the Rapid. But maybe that was because the metal wheels on metal tracks made such a racket that talk was impossible. He helped me down from the tram when we got to the Flats, but didn't let go of my hand.

I bathed in the little zing of pleasure that rippled through me. I liked having a boyfriend. A guaranteed date. Someone who I knew was going to take me home tonight and not rush off to someone or somewhere else. I shook my head, surprised that the insecurity my cheating ex-fiancé had inspired still had a hold on me.

"You thinking about the case with your guilty client?" Miles asked as we walked closer to Lake Erie and the young lawyers' gathering.

"I've let that go," I said. It was almost true. "If I'm going to be a defense lawyer, guilt will come with the territory." Our hands swung as we turned down St. Clair. "How's your case going?" He hadn't talked about it much. Cracking open criminal conspiracies was more difficult that it looked on TV, I suspected.

"We have a moniker for the guy in charge, as well as his second in command. Sledge and Grand," he said, laughing. I had to laugh as well at the idiocy of street names. The Cleveland Police Department had an entire database dedicated to known aliases.

"My clients have silly names as well. But sometimes, there's something to the names," I added.

"I remember from my cop days," Miles said. And there went the insecurity again. I paused as we neared the door. I could already see the place was populated with about a hundred people I'd rather not see.

"What's up?" Miles asked.

"It's not you," I said again. "I'm kind of dreading spending the next hour trying to talk myself up."

"Why? You're great," he said, his voice and eyes full of sincerity.

"Says you who went to Swarthmore and Penn. The five year Philly Police Department veteran who's a federal prosecutor. In the game of one upmanship, you'll win against nearly everyone in Cleveland."

"Ah, none of that really matters," he said.

I wasn't going to convince him that his and his parents' Ivy League legacies were a whole different kettle of fish from my background. Not in the ten seconds before we had to go in the door. Turning, I sighed and pulled open the door.

I found a table while Miles went to get us something to drink. Despite my wine-savvy neighbors, I still hadn't learned much about grapes, fermentation, or picking the right color. White was usually good, so I was grateful for the tall glass Miles brought to the table. I saw he'd chosen red for himself. It was another way that we were different. His parents had a basement full of wine they collected from their travels around the world. My parents weren't operating in that stratosphere at all.

"I got us lobster mac and cheese," he said while sitting in a chair across the tiny four-person table. "It's supposed to be good."

"It's gotta be better than the stuff I had last time," I said, thinking about the bacon-wrapped dates and other so-called delicacies Tom had ordered.

Speaking of last time, I thought as I watched Tom Brody, my ex-fiancé, stride over. I looked at my watch. We hadn't even been in here ten minutes, and already this was hard. After Tom and I cancelled our engagement, I'd kept my side of our bargain, keeping his secret about his little habit of visiting prostitutes. Which I guess wouldn't have been as big a problem if he hadn't been a Cuyahoga County prosecutor—a man whose job it was to enforce the law, not break it.

"Hey there, Casey," he said, leaning down to buss me on both cheeks. Right then, he broke his end of the deal—the part where he was never supposed to speak to me ever again.

"Tom."

My ex-fiancé flipped an empty chair around and sat ass backwards on the thing, careful to tuck his tie behind the rungs. "Been a media blitz on the Container Case," he said. "Seems like we can't go a night without speculation on how such a horrific crime can remain unsolved." Tom waved to a couple of semi-familiar faces. "People keep asking me why the Cleveland Police or anyone in our office can't find the culprits. But I throw up my hands—" and Tom did just that, acting out the scenario, "—and say it's not us, it's the Feds. Take it up with them."

"It's a hard one to crack," I said, rushing to Miles' and the FBI's defense. "It's not like the guy behind this is just going to turn himself in and face life in prison if not the death penalty."

"You on this one?" Tom said to Miles, his voice dripping with innocence.

"Yeah. We're working the case hard," Miles said.

"So...why can't you find him...or her? Someone who keeps women and children in a container and sells them for sex is among the worst of the worst."

I wondered if my head was going to explode. Of all the...the audacity...that...he. My brain couldn't grasp what I was hearing. Some of those women in the containers had no doubt been with Tom. He probably knew *exactly* who the ringleader was.

"I think I see your deputy chief over there," I said to Tom, pointing toward a thick knot of people.

"Gotta go," my brown-nosing ex said, standing abruptly.

I gulped at my wine in his wake while I did the mental gymnastics necessary to get at what was fluttering in the back of my mind. I waited until two servings of mac and cheese appeared and the waitress disappeared before I spoke.

"I think Tom Brody knows who runs the ring," I announced.

"What?" Miles said distractedly, moving food around on his plate.

"Did you just see what happened?" I probed.

"What? Your ex coming over here and rubbing my nose in my shitty record?" Miles said, looking aggrieved. Men. I needed to get him refocused on what I was trying to say and off his damned ego.

"Your win rate is high," I placated.

"Not with the cases that matter. His uncle got off on my watch. And the sex trafficking mogul is about to do the same."

I wanted to shake Miles. Instead, I gripped his forearm hard enough for him to feel my fingers through his starched button-down. "Yeah, he was probably taunting you. *That's* not what I'm saying."

"What *are* you saying?"

I took a gulp of the tap water on the table, trying to clear my head. "Remember that night I asked you to follow Tom over to that motel?"

"Yes." Miles nodded.

"Do you remember him going into some room with a young girl on his arm?"

"That was so fucking wrong of him to cheat on you," Miles said, aggrieved again, this time on my behalf.

I gripped his arm again. "Look, that's not the point. I didn't marry him. The point is that he was seeing a girl in that same motel where the container was found. The point is that he had to make arrangements with someone to hire that prostitute." I took a long pause while Miles got away from his own ego long enough to hear what I was saying. "The point is, Miles, that he probably knows or has a good idea of who the guy behind the containers is."

"Shit. I never thought of that. I've been worried about your rep—"

"Your chivalry is noted. Besmirchment gone."

"Besmirchment," Miles let out a hearty laugh. "Is that even a word?"

"No, probably not. I'd lose at Scrabble." I shook my head. When I glanced at Miles again, I had to laugh too. It probably took us a good two minutes to get it under control.

The stuffed shirts trying to network their way to cases, jobs, career paths were looking at us none too kindly. I didn't care anymore. I'd been humiliated in the worst ways already. There wasn't much more that could happen to me. Miles felt the same, I imagine, as he was in the Federal ivory tower. Local Cleveland politics weren't going to make or break his career.

After a long moment, Miles sobered and looked me straight in the eye. "You're probably right about Tom."

"And?" I scooted forward on my seat, waiting for my schadenfreude moment. I was ready for vindication. I was ready to hear how the U.S. Attorney's office would finally take someone in the Brody family down.

Miles finally spoke, "And...if the Judge Eamon Brody case taught me anything, there isn't a damn thing I can do about it."

I'd practically handed my current boyfriend my ex-boyfriend's head on a platter and he was looking away. I took a drink of wine trying to hide my disappointment. No one was perfect. Miles maybe knew things I didn't. I grabbed his hand under the table. At least I wasn't in this alone anymore.

28

"What do you mean she got away?" I wanted to slam the wall with my fist. But I didn't want to go to the hospital and have to try to explain why my knuckles were busted. Plaster was a lot stronger than drywall. Back when Cleveland Heights was young, good building materials had been important. I hated the cheap paperboard shit that sectioned off the back rooms of The Place to Be, but I could use the satisfaction of putting a big ol' hole in something right now.

"He said he had a fantasy about chasing a girl through the woods and catching her like she was a runaway slave or some shit," Grand was saying when I tuned him back in.

"So, how that work?" I didn't really need the details. I needed to know if Grand was lying. Because something about this shit weren't right.

"He say he let his dog go out there all the time. That he knew the woods like the back of his hand. Took Destiny's shoes and told her to run. She checked with me, then did what he said. But when he went after her, he couldn't find her nowhere."

"Did *you* look?" I caught his eyes and didn't look away.

"'Course I did." He pointed at his muddy shoes. Personally, I thought he was more upset about ruining his kicks than losing one of my most productive assets. "But it was dark out there. I don't know nothing about them parks. You wanna go back and look with me?"

No, I didn't want to be running around no damned park. A black man in a park at night was just asking to be arrested. "What's this guy's name?"

Grand shifted a little in his chair. "Put it through the shredder already." He leaned forward, real earnest. "You told us to make sure we got rid of shit."

"I think it was *you* who told me that," I said. "Where did her momma used to live?"

Grand sat back. Took a drink of the beer he'd asked Alisha for. Tried to remember the last time I'd seen him with alcohol. Couldn't. This mofo was guilty or lying or something. But after years of loyalty and not fucking up anything, I was warring between disbelief and letting it go. "Been a minute," he finally said. Eyes was rolled up in his head like he was thinking hard. "East nineties, I think. Right by MLK in the park."

"Think she went back there?" I asked. I half rose out of my seat like I was gonna get the truck keys and haul ass out that way.

"Wouldn't think so," Grand said around a huge mouthful of beer. His arms waved me back down in my seat. "Her momma was living on borrowed time. House wasn't hers and she couldn't pay the rent back then."

"Either way, make sure you go by there first thing tomorrow morning. Check around." Grand nodded readily. "You don't find her. You gotta replace her. She was getting kind of old. Maybe you'll get another kid the age she was when you met her. Young ones make more."

For a long second, I thought Grand was going to say no. His eye twitched something awful. "I hear you."

"Your envelope gonna be real light this week," I warned. His fault or not, I wasn't taking the hit on this. I had bills to pay.

"I'll scope out the wannabes at the club," he said.

Wasn't exactly what I was going for, but I let him take the easy way out. There wasn't no shortage of girls who wanted to shake they titties and asses at the men in Cleveland. In no time, they was ready to do an extra favor or two when they realized the pockets of out of work men was thin for tipping. But I'd never met a guy who couldn't come up with some cash when guaranteed pussy was involved.

"Alright," I said, leaning my elbows on the table. I ignored Alisha's stare that said my manners wasn't shit. "From now on, this is how we're gonna do things." I handed him a slip of paper. "Memorize this. Alisha's going to take orders on this central number. Write down what they want, plan out the route. Either they come out to the van or you escort the girls in. No more outside runaway slave fantasies. I ain't running a paintball park or fast food restaurant. They can't get things their way. You make sure the girls ain't running out the back door. Make sure the customers don't think they gonna get to keep them. You got it," I finished.

Grand nodded. "The motel was easier."

"It was," I agreed. But I wasn't buying no motel. Not now when places like that were probably under heavy surveillance. That would be like painting a target on my back. "The thing you gotta make sure everyone understand is that we got to keep this shit low key. I ain't stupid enough to think the feds found a container full of girls and walked away. They're looking for me something hard, I know."

"I'm paying Mani regular as clock work," Grand put in.

"Right now, they're our greatest liability. They talk and it only matter of hours before we all locked up under the jail. I watch the news. They making me out to be the worst thing since Saddam Hussein cause of that underage girl. They should see the hundreds of girls working out here who ain't eighteen." I stopped myself before I got on a rant.

"Look, I ain't willing to put my business on hold while things quiet down. But we got to stay low. I think the trucks do that for us. But we can't have girls running away. Especially since they living at my house and could lead the cops here like Hansel and Gretel. So I don't know how much muscle you gonna need or how you gonna do it. But your number one job is protecting our assets. My job will be protecting all our asses so we can all keep making money." Grand kept up nodding. "You feel me? Pussy ain't never going to go out of style."

Grand got up to leave. It was damned near midnight and I was tired as hell. That buzz from that diner coffee had long wore off. "Wait." Dion stopped in his tracks. "Get the keys to that van Destiny was using. It's time to get us some leverage."

29

I was dotting my 'i's' and crossing my 't's' when the hollow wood door that stood between me and my colleagues flew open.

"She's gone!" Valdespino barged in, slamming the door behind him.

Adrenaline flooded my veins. Had someone kidnapped Casey? But that wild-eyed look on the FBI agent's face wasn't directed at me. I got my breath again. "Who's gone?"

"Rida Emad."

"The hotel girl?"

"The very same one."

I looked at the huge dry erase board opposite my desk. Despite the computerized docketing system, I kept important dates on that calendar. My eyes swiveled through the days. It was the twenty-seventh, four days after our visit to the Sleepy Time and Emad.

"Where is she?" I asked, wondering where we'd have to go to question her.

"Well, isn't that the fucking question?" Valdespino huffed.

"We were there last Thursday, right?" I asked.

"Between then and now, she's disappeared."

"I thought you were going to follow up on Friday."

"The terror alert went from yellow to orange to red."

There was a big placard in the building lobby with alerts, but I'd long ago learned to ignore it. The color-coded sign didn't tell you shit, but raised your blood pressure nonetheless. "What was the threat?"

"Some fucking chatter out of Iran about nukes. But it was all hands on deck," he said derisively. I knew his frustration. Terrorist threats trumped everything. A lot of hot leads grew cold while agents were sifting through intelligence. Drug dealers and domestic terrorists went right about their business under our collective noses while we tried to figure out if Osama bin Laden was making plans.

"So, Rida?"

"When I got off terror duty, I got back to my desk. She's enrolled in the Richmond Heights Secondary School."

"What's the school say?"

"Not much of anything. Turned out to be hell getting her enrolled there, probably. The school requires a student have a social security number. Federal law requires public schools enroll any student regardless of immigration status."

"So?"

"So she sat home half of the last school year while Emad jumped through hoops getting the school to take her. They finally did. But her attendance has been spotty already this year. When she didn't show up, either they figured she dropped out or went back to Egypt. I can't find anyone who looked too closely to see why the girl wasn't coming to school."

"She wasn't in school on Thursday. I think she said something about subbing in for a cleaner who called off," I added. It wasn't just the school that was lax, but Emad as well.

"First Kelly Tucker. Then this girl. I swear to God it's too damned easy to disappear a kid in this country," Valdespino said, his frustration boiling up to the top.

"What does Emad say?"

"Nothing. He said he needs a lawyer. Won't even admit that he has a sister. And since she barely existed in any system..."

"Do you think he's hiding her?" I asked. "Maybe he figured what we did, that she's the weak spot and didn't want to be vulnerable."

Valdespino shook his head. "Nope, he was too damn nervous-looking. I have a sneaking suspicion Sledge is behind this."

"You think he took the girl?" I asked. This was chess, checkers, and dominoes combined. Everyone had a strategy, but different aims.

"If we thought she was the weak link, then he probably did too. I think Sledge wanted to silence the little Emad family. I say he threatened to turn that little girl out. If Emad saw even ten percent of what went on inside those rooms, I say he's going to be as quiet as a church mouse from now on."

The creak of my brand-new office chair was the only sound in the room. "Fucking A. He's protecting his enterprise no matter what. We gotta find that girl or another way in."

It took five hours for me to wind down from Valdespino's visit. I needed some time away from this office and this case.

Fortunately, Casey had been up for a distraction. Dinner had been good. The wine better. Sex has been the best. Instead of turning over and going to sleep, which probably would have been the best move I could have made, I was complicating things.

"My parents are coming into town," I said as nonchalantly as I could muster, which wasn't all that nonchalant.

"Why?" Casey asked. I could feel her tensing up just a little on her side of the bed.

"My mother loves festivals. Apple cider and fried dough at the Big E. Watching horse racing down in Virginia. She'll travel anywhere for local food and Clydesdales," I answered.

"They're coming for Oktoberfest?"

"Yep. Does your family go? She was hoping to meet your parents, maybe buy them a beer."

"Of course," she said. "Like clockwork. It's a time to mingle with some friends they only see once a year."

I'd suspected as much. Given how authentic her mother's strudel was, I'd assumed there was some love of the old country. When I'd mentioned Casey's mom was German, my mother had probably bought tickets that day. She loved my dad, but was suspicious of all other white people as far as I could tell. She wanted to come here and look Casey in the eye. See if my girlfriend cared about me despite my race, or because of it. I'd never quite put a finger on what my mother was looking for in girlfriends who weren't black.

Though my mother had one agenda, I had another. I wanted Mom and Dad to know that I cared deeply about

Casey. Oktoberfest was my mother's flimsy excuse. But she wasn't wrong in her instincts. I was starting to really like Casey. A lot. Maybe love her. So much so that I felt bad, really bad about how I'd treated my last girlfriend. The one I'd still had when I'd met Casey.

She'd been a single mom who wanted to get married. I'd been…a guy.

"How's the investigation?" Casey asked. I knew she was deflecting the stuff between us, but I let her.

"Our guy has disappeared."

"What do you mean disappeared?"

"It's like he never existed. We finally found what we think was the second container. Got a warrant. Got a SWAT team. Fifty men. Enough firepower to start a small war."

Casey sat up, pulling the sheet up to her neck. One day, when we weren't naked, I'd tell her just how much I liked her body. The nudge from her foot let me know she'd noticed my distraction. "I saw it on the news. They said it was empty as Al Capone's vault. Was that true?" Her question was leading.

"And nothing. The container was empty. Our guy had probably moved those girls weeks ago when we came upon the first one."

"What about that motel? You were with me when we saw Tom go in there."

"Manager says he's never allowed any illegal activity there. Runs a family motel. Got him to give us a look at his books. They're clean as a whistle."

"So maybe he or she closed up shop. If you took a drug dealer's stash and patrolled his corner every few minutes, he'd be out of business."

"Chas is leaning that way. Lou doesn't buy it. If it weren't for the twenty-four/seven news harping on this story every few days, it would probably have gone away much sooner. Chas says not everyone's a mobster. Small fries sometimes get scared out of business."

"Do you think someone who'd lock women and children in a container is a small fry? That seems very calculated."

"That's what I said. But then where did he go? If his regular customers came to the Sleepy Time or Sunrise, they haven't been back. Not a one. How did he contact them all? Where did they move? Cuyahoga County isn't that big. We've visited hotels, motels, big and small."

"Maybe he moved to a house, and he's running it like a Madam."

"Then it's the proverbial needle in the haystack. He's got the Fourth Amendment on his side."

"Well, we should all be safe from unwarranted search and seizure."

"It would be a damned bit easier *if* we could do a door to door search. I keep thinking of that girl. That there are other children out there."

"It's a good thing that we can't," Casey said. "It's already over the line that felons on probation are subject to warrantless searches." She paused for long time. "Have you figured out a way to call Tom Brody in for questioning?"

"Do you still think he's somehow involved in this?"

Casey gave me a look like I'd flunked kindergarten. "That Sunrise Motel I saw on the news looked an awful lot like the place we saw Tom."

"Look, I like my job. I want to stay here in Cleveland right now, so no." I could hear my own voice get quieter. How embarrassing was it that I'd put my own career ahead of exploited women. But Casey had to know better than anyone that crossing the line with the Brodys was tantamount to putting a noose around my own neck.

"Funny how you thought nothing of having me hang myself out to dry, to try to convict Eeamon Brody, but now you're all about self-preservation," she said her voice getting tighter.

The pot had met the kettle. She was right, but I didn't have anything more to go on than what I saw when we'd chased him down. I wasn't ready to burn that bridge quite yet.

"So, Oktoberfest?" Changing the subject seemed like a better idea than going down the Brody corruption road. "Do you want our parents to meet there or should we schedule a dinner? Maybe at Charley's Crab? Or if there's an equivalent on the westside."

"I'll have to ask them if they're busy," Casey muttered. I could tell she was hedging.

If talking about my case hadn't already killed the post-coital, post-wine buzz, her hesitation made it fade away in a heartbeat. "You've told your mom that you have a new boyfriend, right?"

"We're boyfriend and girlfriend?" Casey deflected.

"I'm not seeing anyone else. Since we're together whenever we're not working, I assume you're not seeing anyone else either. Is that a safe assumption to make?"

"Of course."

"But you haven't said anything to your parents?"

"I'm not fifteen, Miles," Casey said on a sigh. "Plus there's the little matter of my recent broken engagement. I mean, they're not conservative. But they are Catholic. I don't exactly want to throw in their face that I was sleeping with you when I was supposed to be engaged to someone else."

"Did you tell them why you broke it off with Tom?"

"Hell, no. It's private anyway. My inadequacy isn't something I want to wave like a geek flag for everyone to see."

"There's nothing wrong with you. Do you think there's something wrong with me for being with you? Do you think a black guy is the best you can do?"

"Oh, God, Miles. No. You're mixing up about a million issues."

"Straighten them out for me."

"One. I like you a lot. Two. I...I'll talk to my parents about us and about getting together with your parents. Three. You have to understand. I wasn't some belle of the ball in high school. I went to all-girls St. Joseph. I didn't date much. I was too busy trying to live up to my parents' expectations. They wanted for me what they didn't have and I wanted to give that to them. I didn't party at a party school. Then I met Tom and thought we'd get married. That's it. I'm not some mythical siren with men dropping at my feet. So it's awkward. This conversation about dating. It's like announcing to my parents that I have sex."

I was quiet for a minute. I'd gotten my back up over my *own* sense of inadequacy. "Sorry, my parents were a lot different. There wasn't anything we *didn't* talk about. Sex. Money. Politics. Religion. Nothing was off limits."

"Even now?" she asked. I heard the subtext. I was in my thirties. Some things should be private.

"Even now," I conceded. "Maybe I'll think about that going forward. But they know about us, so..."

Without another word, Casey slipped from her bed into a robe and left the room. A minute later, I heard her murmuring into the phone positioned in the hallway nook. I found my boxers wrapped up in the sheets, put them on, then came down the hall. Casey was already putting the phone back in the cradle when I slipped my arms around her waist.

"So we're all set for next weekend."

That wasn't exactly joy I heard in her voice.

"It'll be fun," I said, mentally crossing my fingers that my mother didn't bring up sex, money, politics, or religion. I might want to marry this woman and hoped my mother got things off to a good start. The fact that my mind was steering toward marriage nearly knocked me off my feet. Rather than say something stupid, I kissed Casey instead. Sometimes, lawyers used too many words, and not enough actions. I wanted to break that cycle.

30

Stephanie
October 7, 2004

"You haven't left this house for two weeks," Momma said.

"Where am I gonna go?" I asked, pulling my eyes from the TV. John—he'd asked me to call him that—liked his TV sharp as a tack. A huge Sony Trinitron had replaced the mega-sized, ugly ass projection thing Clark had in here. The screen was smaller, but the picture was a whole lot better. I could see the holes in people's skin, which was kind of gross.

Until we'd moved to Sledge's house, the one pleasure in my life had been TV. The reception in the hotel was as shitty as the TV sets, but when I got up in the afternoon, I'd watch some of those dumb ass court shows you knew were fake. Make believe or not, I liked to see people get theirs. And Oprah. I never missed it. She'd survived her cousin or uncle or whoever and look at her now. Gave me hope for whatever in the hell came after Dion and Sledge. If I'd survived and made it through that, maybe....

Momma stared at me hard like my brains had fallen out of my head. "I don't know. Back to school? Get a job?"

"What would I do? I don't know how to do anything." Except lay on my back, put a condom on with my mouth, smile, and pretend I'm having a good time even after a hard slap in the face.

Momma muted *Divorce Court*. I tried not to snatch the remote. I really wanted to know if the husband had cleaned out the bank account and had taken the kids' savings bonds like the wife claimed.

"You still ain't told me at all where you been for five goddamn years. All I can guess is you been laying up in some man's house for a long time. I was as mad as hell in the beginning. I know bringing Tyson in right after Clark probably wasn't great. But I was getting lonely and I needed someone to help me with the bills. Sydney ain't never been one to hold down a job. And you was too young to work.

"John is a good man, though. You could have called. I ain't moved or changed the number." My momma ran out of steam. I didn't mention that she hadn't been exactly looking for me. Sometimes, Sledge had to disappear other girls when the police came knocking, looking around the motel for missing and runaway kids. My name ain't never come up like that. I pulled my mind from going in that direction.

The only person who'd ever wanted me was Dion. Late at night since I'd been back with Momma, I kind of even thought of trying to stay at his house. I even got so far as putting on my clothes in the middle of last night and tiptoeing upstairs. John prowling around in the kitchen and thoughts of Sledge made me walk my ass right back down to my newest prison cell.

"You ain't said nothing." Momma's voice intruded into my thoughts.

I was way too shamed to tell her the absolute truth. So I added a little to the story I'd decided was going to be my new truth going forward. "I was mad, Mamma, I ain't gonna lie. So I ran to Dion. He was so nice, and clean, and everything," I said, starting with the truth. "But he was like one of those men you only hear about on Oprah. He didn't want me talking to no one. Having no friends. He locked me in when he went to work at night." That was only half a lie. They locked me up all night, all right. But it was in a hotel room with whatever man had paid them enough for my body.

"So why he let you go?" Momma asked. It was a good question. I still didn't quite understand it. One minute, I was under some nasty assed westside man. The next minute, I was in Momma's driveway knocking at the back door. When nobody was watching me, I was still peeping out the windows waiting for Sledge to come get me. Never met a man who clung tighter to a dollar. Momma was looking at me strangely. Then I remembered she'd asked me something.

"Found a new girl. Someone as young as I had been," I said. That could be true, sure enough. I'd seen them bring in the new ones. Fresh-looking and clueless. They cost a lot more because that innocence didn't last all that long. Sledge could only sell virginity three or four times.

"That shit is illegal all up and down. You want me to call the police? He shouldn't be doing this kind of thing to underage girls. Some other mother done lost her child," she said, tut-tutting and shaking her head.

I unmuted the TV and turned it loud enough to drown out my thoughts. It was a commercial for a chairlift in your own home. I wondered if that would be fun or would you get tired of going upstairs so slow.

Momma jabbed at the red button on the upper right corner, turning off the set completely.

"You lost all your home training?" Her voice wasn't soft or nice like it had been the last couple of weeks. I guess the vacation was over. This was the momma I knew best. I tried to think what in the hell I should say. If'n she put me out, I have nowhere to go.

"Why you bagging on Dion?" I asked. Wasn't that what women did? Protect their abusers. I'd seen that on Ricki Lake more than once.

"He practically stole you when you was fourteen and kept you hostage for years. Now you saying he doing that to another girl. Someone should stop him."

"You wasn't this mad about Clark," I whispered. I couldn't believe my mother was riled up on some guy she didn't know messing around with young girls when Clark had been doing that same damned thing right up under her nose.

I bit my bottom lip hard. It was how I'd kept myself from crying over the past years. Shonna had taught me that little trick. Mens thought you were hot for whatever shit they was doing. But it kept you from ruining they good time. Except for the ones that liked crying. I felt my body start to shake. That was a whole different kind of monster.

"I ain't say this to you back then 'cause you wasn't ready to hear it. But what happened with Clark ain't nothing new. Most girls I know had the same thing happen with their father or uncle or cousin. You wouldn't have understood it back then, but you got to keep on keeping on. Women take they knocks and get back up. Someone gotta wash the floors, cook the food, take care of the kids. We can't lay down and go woe is me like white women do. It's not how sistas roll."

I didn't want to wash floors, though. I wanted to chain myself to the pipe in the basement and die. Kind of funny that my worst nightmare was now my greatest wish. "I hear you," I said, hoping she'd walk away and leave me to drowning out my thoughts with talk shows.

Momma dug in the pocket of her too tight jeans. She tossed a Benjamin my way. I scooped it up, glad I didn't have to hand it over to Dion or Sledge. "Thanks."

"That ain't no Christmas gift. Get yourself something presentable to wear and get a job. I'm real sorry that you got mixed up with Dion. But at least you don't got three or four kids. You lucky that way. You got until next month to start bringing in some money. Otherwise...."

She didn't need to say more. Otherwise, I was on my own. Otherwise, I needed to get the hell up outta here. Otherwise, otherwise, otherwise. I stuffed the money in my own pocket and poked at the little plastic rods under the skin of my arm. Sledge had made sure I didn't have no kids. Yeah, lucky.

When Momma didn't move except to give me hard looks, I went back down to the basement. Took a minute to get fortified. Twenty minutes later, I'd pulled on the clothes Momma had let me borrow and hopped the bus over to Shaker Square. They had a new Gap there. Flipped through the sale rack and bought some khaki pants and a couple of tops. Wasn't till I walked up outta that store that I realized I was going to look like Dion when I got dressed. Should have tried something else, but I had no idea what I should look like. And clearance items couldn't be returned.

I wandered up and down the square, wondering what to do with the last ten bucks in my pocket. It wasn't too hard a choice. I'd been a little shaky the first couple of nights I'd been home. But the upside of the basement is that John kept his beer stash down there. Two or three a night and I could get to sleep without too many dreams. Sledge may not have given us much, but he kept us in alcohol. My favorite was a shot of Mad Dog. It was sweet and kept me buzzed right good. But John didn't have that crap downstairs.

Plus John had noticed some were missing. I ain't copped to nothing, but I couldn't keep drinking up his shit. With this money in my pocket, I could get something I liked a little better than that bitter, foul-tasting shit he liked.

I prowled the little grocery store for something. I was in luck. There was a special for margarita flavored beers. Ten for ten bucks. I plunked them on the conveyor belt. When it was my turn the cashier looked me up and down.

"ID?"

ID? I'd been drinking five years and ain't no one asked for ID. The men who visited me certainly didn't want me to be twenty-one. I nearly laughed in her face. "I ain't got no ID," I said.

She squinted, then ran the cans through the scanner. I passed over my money and she bagged them up. I'd looked in the mirror since I'd been home. With my short hair and a couple of scars, I didn't look like a young 'un anymore. Maybe that's why Dion had brought me home. I hadn't been much to look at to begin with. Now, I looked like the crack hoes I saw on the street. No matter. I snatched up my beer and started the long ass walk home. Didn't have no money for a bus ride back. When the men hollered out the window, I ain't say shit to them. And they moved on. Couldn't imagine I'd ever get in another man's car again.

Halfway home, I saw a white van with blue lettering parked on Buckeye and nearly dropped my shit. I glanced all around. Dion and Sledge had never been out before dark, and it certainly wasn't dark now. I looked everywhere, but there wasn't nowhere to hide. I hated this about Cleveland. Wasn't like New York City with lots of building doorways or dark alleys to duck into. We had nothing but open space here. City liked to knock down buildings and leave weeds in they place. I started to turn back the other way, when I saw people line up at the van.

Sledge ain't never had no line. The cops would have gotten on him for that, for sure. My heartbeat came back to normal. Was probably some kind of food for the homeless kind of thing. I pulled my shit together and kept on stepping. When I got closer, though, I noticed most of the people lined up to get shit was women. Then I got closer still. Knew better, but I still couldn't pull my eyes away. The blue logo I thought was Sledge's was really some kind of cross. There were a bunch of churches on this stretch of road. Probably some ministry outreach shit.

Suckers.

Rich people got money. Poor people got God. Some of the girls used to fall down on their knees and pray to God to get them away from Sledge. I'd looked in the eyes of enough men to know there weren't no God left in this world.

A skinny white man jumped from the back of the van and walked my way.

"Can I help you?" he said like I was walking into a store and not down Buckeye.

I pulled my bags close. "No, I don't think so," I said, stepping just a little bit faster.

"I'm sorry. I think we can help you. We give out condoms to working women. We also have a group you can join if you're ready to give up the life," he said, trying to shove some kind of shiny pamphlet in my face.

Careless of the heavy bags I was carrying, I put out my palms and shoved him squarely in the chest.

"I ain't no whore," I yelled, then took off running. Made it a couple of blocks before I had to stop and suck in air. I let the tears come then. It was too dark for anyone to see them. I ain't no whore, I repeated to myself with each step home. But flashes of memories flickered in my brain like channels flipping by when I had the remote control in my hand.

I wasn't nothing *but* a whore.

31

Lettie snagged me by the door to the reception area before I could take off my overcoat and hang it on the coat rack.

"There's a client here to see you," she whispered.

Great. I looked down at my jeans and long sleeved t-shirt. I was planning what I called a churning day. My best friend Lulu had told me years ago that her firm made an effort once a month to churn through files as a way to bill hours, but also as a way to make sure nothing got forgotten on a case because even big firms could made mistakes.

Now that my clients were more well-heeled than they'd been a couple of years ago, I'd taken on the churning idea. But the dust from hundreds of pieces of paper and the cardboard file holders killed my wallet with a fat dry cleaning bill.

So in preparation for the monthly review, I'd dressed down, and had purposefully made *no* client appointments. To maintain professionalism, I tried to only let clients see me in a suit or at least a dress or skirt, and some makeup, and my hair in…well…something less than disarray.

"Who is it?" I asked, wondering which one of my clients would just show up without an appointment. The answer was actually ninety-nine percent of them. Because they were going through a crisis, they were oblivious to everyone else.

Clients had a way of calling and showing up whenever they perceived an emergency. I'd even made the mistake of giving out my home number in those first years. I'd had to change it because I couldn't finish a meal without the phone ringing.

"That Jarrod Carter guy," Lettie whispered while I looked through my bag for the hair clip I used on humid or rainy days when the frizz was out of control.

I dropped my bag at the mention of his name. Lip balm and moisturizer rolled to far corners of the waiting room. I'd never told Lettie that I'd found out he was guilty. When she'd brought me my favorite Presti's cannoli to celebrate the victory, I'd played along with the fiction that I'd saved another innocent man from the jaws of the system.

I lifted the clip from the carpet and gripped my innocent hair tight in the jaws of the plastic tortoise accessory. "Did you tell him I wasn't seeing clients today?" I hissed. Then I got on hands and knees and scrambled to put everything else in my bag.

Lettie's eyes skittered away. She knew she'd violated my strict rule about letting clients get their way. Especially after hours. I'd put a stop to that with an angry cop client in a contentious divorce case. Me alone, pissed off guy with a gun, bad equation. Nothing happened, thank goodness, but I'd never do anything that stupid again.

"He's kind of scary," she said.

I may have half-agreed with her, but my back went up immediately. Dating Miles had made me more sensitive to any perceived racial slight than I'd ever been before. I hated the idea of someone judging my sweet, smart boyfriend because he was half-black.

"Why would you say that?"

"He's a big...guy," she said. I could see her mentally backpedaling, having purposefully left out the word black.

"Fine," I snapped. I didn't know why I was arguing with her. Nothing I could say here in the waiting room would make Carter disappear. Best to get it over with. He was probably in trouble again or needed help with the city. I'd listen to his problem, turn him down, and get back to work. Easy enough.

Carter was standing by the radiator cum window sill, looking through my wall of windows that gave a beautiful view of Lake Erie, when I pushed through the door.

"Good morning!" I tried to put cheer into my voice. "We don't seem to have an appointment. Can we reschedule for another day?" Putting off a client today usually guaranteed they'd find other counsel. I'd found that out the hard way, much to my detriment, years ago. But Carter finding another lawyer would be a gift.

"I really need to talk to you now," he said. His tone was inflexible.

"Are you facing charges?" I asked. He looked as cool as a cucumber to me. Not like a man under a second indictment in as many months.

"I might be," he said.

I dropped the pretense of innocence. "Is it for the same thing? Prostituting girls out of the back of your club?" I moved away from the window and sat in my high-backed leather chair. My clothes may not be professional, but I hoped the chair lent some kind of dignity to my position. That and the huge framed diplomas behind me.

"Is what I tell you confidential?" Carter asked, following my cues and taking one of the two seats on the other side of my desk.

I closed my eyes in contemplation. Then I pulled a legal pad and pencil from my desk. "Let me explain confidentiality," I said, doing my lawyerly duty. I took a deep breath and plunged into the speech I'd heard my first year Crim Law professor give during one of his first lectures. "If you killed someone, robbed a bank, or ate your neighbor for lunch, then come to tell me about it. I'm bound by my duty of confidentiality. I can't tell most people about it."

"Most people?" Carter cocked his head.

"I can tell Lettie, my assistant. Or if I hired an investigator I could tell them about what you'd done. But that's about it. I can tell no one else, ever."

"I think I'm—" Carter started.

I held up my hand. "I'm not finished. There are some instances when I'm not required to keep what you tell me a secret," I said.

"Like when?" he asked before sitting back and rubbing at his clean shaven chin.

"If you come in here and tell me you're going to murder someone, going to rob a bank, or are going to kill and eat your neighbor for lunch, I'm required to call the police and tell them to save the people or bank from harm. You got it?"

Carter nodded, sagely. He appeared to get in a few minutes what had taken me weeks to wrap my brain around. In my limited experience, I'd concluded there were dumb criminals and smart criminals. The former was the guy who snatched your purse in broad daylight under a CCTV sign. The smart criminal cased your house, opened the one window with a broken latch, and took an unused credit card from the bottom of a desk drawer. Carter was clearly in the latter group.

"So do we have something to discuss, or do you need to collect your bag and jacket and walk out the door?" I prayed silently to a God I didn't much believe in that he'd do just that. I toyed with the communion crucifix hanging around my neck for good measure.

"I think you need to clear your schedule, because we have some talking to do."

"Excuse me," I said. I turned to the computer on my credenza and woke it up. I shot Lettie a quick ICQ message, letting her know to hold my calls.

"So you know how I run The Place to Be and The Dive Bar?" he said before I could even sit down and pull my pad to me.

"Yes, I'm familiar with both establishments," I said, clicking out the ball point and jotting down the name of both nonetheless. Mainly for something to do with my hands than for information.

"In addition to dancing, the girls perform tricks for the customers who ask," he said matter-of-factly. Like that hadn't been the single issue the jury had to decide in his case. Like he hadn't walked out of court a guilty man who'd beaten the system.

"You mean you don't fine them for breaking the rules?" I asked a little too sarcastically.

"Yeah, well, sorry about that," Carter said. "I couldn't lay out the whole defense or you wouldn't have followed my lead. I do remember your earlier explanation about how you didn't want to know if I committed the crime."

"Well then, I'd made my own bed, I guess." I tried not to let the guilt and ick feeling from that case ooze through my veins. "How can I help you?"

"I think I'm being investigated by the FBI," he said.

My heart beat sped up. My not so recent bashing in federal court came to mind. I was a baby lawyer. That place was for grown-ups.

"What makes you think that?" I asked, trying to look as placid as Lake Erie. "Did you receive a target letter?" I had no idea what in the hell a target letter was or would look like, but my very smart criminal client probably did.

"No, it's more complicated than that," he said. "I've looked at this from all sides, and I think they stumbled upon my extended operation."

Stumbled. Extended operation? Maybe I didn't get enough sleep, or needed a better relationship with caffeine, because I felt like I was drowning on those deceptively calm waters of the Great Lake outside the window. "How do you mean?" is what I asked.

Carter took a deep breath and looked as if he were deciding something. "Do you watch the news?"

"Sometimes," I said. Had he done something newsworthy? I'd quit watching the news as much after the whole Brody thing. It had infuriated me how often reporters got it wrong. How often they didn't have a fucking clue what they were talking about. I must have tuned Carter out because what he was saying wasn't computing.

"Can you repeat that?"

"The women in the container," he said. "That was nearly half of my business, right there. It was a huge blow to my income. They was right about relying on any one thing for much of your income. I'll be working on diversification more in the future. But right now, I need the feds out of my business."

My brain was having a hell of a time reconciling what I'd just heard. Had Carter admitted to masterminding Cleveland's crime of the year? Or was he talking about a stock portfolio?

"You were keeping women and children in a container?" And before I could censor myself I blurted out, "Oh my God. I was there when the FBI found that!"

"You?" Carter asked. Silent in my embarrassment, I studied him.

"I was passing by on my way back from dinner," I hedged.

"Those girls might talk. That's the core of the issue. I don't think they have much to tell. I had very little interaction with them, but who knows what they learned. I need to stay out of jail."

"Why?"

"Why, what?"

"Why do you think you get to stay out of jail? Sometimes, criminals go to jail."

"I need to take care of my mother. She's got the sugar. Lost a leg. I'm the only one working in my family to support her. My sister's a hood rat, doing God knows what, God knows where. So I have to pay my niece to watch her full time while I work. Money like that don't grow on trees. I don't want her to lose her house to Medicare."

Sick mother. Drug addict sister. Niece. I tried to sort through all the stuff he was throwing at me. I went back to the crime. "The container didn't put you out of business. What happened to the girls who *weren't* in the second container?" I said out of morbid curiosity. Then held up my hand. "No. Don't answer that."

"Nah, that's why I have diversification like I was saying. I've moved the other girls to a safe place," he said.

I held my hand up. "Stop there. If you're still engaging in this criminal enterprise of pimping women and children, I can't hear anything about it."

"Understood."

"You're not facing charges, so what do you need from me?" I was stupidly entertaining the hope that he'd get up and walk out after admitting he was the Midwest's most notorious sex trafficker.

"T—another lawyer advised me that it would be best if I bought a lawyer like the big companies do."

"Why didn't you hire *him*?" I asked, realizing I was still trying to talk Carter out of hiring *me*.

"He doesn't take on clients. Works for the government."

Would Tom Brody's shit never get off my shoes? My motel visiting, law evading, ex-fiancé had to be the 'government' lawyer he was talking about. When Tom and I had agreed to walk away from that disaster of a reunion/engagement, I'd promised to keep his nighttime proclivities a secret and he'd promised referrals. But now, I felt like he was wrapping me up tighter in the Brody web of lies and deception. The money kept me bound with the Brodys. Without them, I'd be back eating my cat's food.

Unaware of my mental gymnastics, Carter pushed at the metal clasp on his bag and the three-ring binder emerged. Without asking for an amount, he penned a check with a flourish.

My hand automatically extended, grasping at the crisp paper. I let the check flutter to my blotter. Fifty thousand dollars was about to separate me from my common sense.

32

"Very nice office," my mother said absently, rubbing the back of my office chair. I'd finally moved from my temporary quarters to a space recently vacated by someone higher up the seniority chain.

"Do you want me to get your diplomas framed?" Dad asked. I'd left those big parchment scrolls in my parents' house in a closet somewhere. Achievements that had seemed so all-fire important: this degree, that diploma, had faded in the background when I was out solving cases and putting real criminals in jail. But Dad had his in his study, the big sturdy frames dwarfing the tiny Latin diplomas. I'm sure he'd imagined the same for me since I was born.

"Nah." I shook my head, turning down his perennial offer. There wasn't anyone to impress here with all that parchment paper. My client was the United States and like a wife, she'd already married me and knew what she was getting. My mind swerved to Casey and thoughts of marriage. I needed to keep those premature thoughts to myself.

"We better get going if we're going to meet the Corts," I said, coaxing my parents toward the exit.

"You seem pretty serious," my mother said on the way down to my Jeep. I guess I wasn't putting a thing past her. "How did Claire take your break up?"

Momentary guilt flooded me. I'd really messed up with Claire. "In all honesty, I probably shouldn't have dated a single mom," I said. What I didn't say is that a cute woman with nice lips had blinded me to the reality that she was daddy shopping. And I had no intentions of being anyone's daddy in the near future. Thoughts of a pale child with unruly hair and tanned skin scooted into my mind. I pushed it away.

"Does this Casey know you just broke up with someone?" my mom asked. I put the truck into gear and took in my dad's silence. He was sitting in the back seat, looking out the window. I'm sure I'd hear his thoughts later. But he liked to have all the information before saying anything. I'd have to sit through dinner and dessert before he put his thoughts into words.

"I think Claire's back with her baby's daddy," I offered. Left out Casey's representation of Claire and all that awkwardness. "Casey though, just got out of a relationship with her fiancé. So we're both on the rebound." My intended laugh came out like a bark. I refocused on the traffic before me.

"Well, now, that's all very interesting," my mother said, her voice up an octave on the last word.

I hoped my mother wouldn't ask Casey about any of that.

I regretted saying anything. Now it sounded like we were two people well past adolescence and without the judgment our parents gave us. But this wasn't a rebound for me. And I didn't think it was for Casey either. I didn't think she'd really loved Tom the second time around. And I knew my time with Claire had been more about hormones than heart.

"I haven't met her folks," I said, prepping my mother. She did not like to go into situations cold. Probably due to her time as a political activist. Preparation had always been her ace in the hole.

"Do her parents know you're black?" my mother asked in a way that was meant to sound offhand, but totally wasn't.

My stomach fell to the floor of my truck. Leave it to my mother to go right for the anxiety jugular.

"Maybe they're not like you, Linda," my dad said. "Maybe it doesn't matter to them that his *mother* is black."

"You've lived with me for more than thirty years," my mother parried. "You know race *always* matters."

I shifted my eyes out the windshield and kept them glued there. My parents would argue about this all the way to Middleburg Heights. Which took the heat off me and my own anxiety about the forthcoming meeting.

After I parked the Jeep and steered my parents through the crowded parking lot, I spotted my girlfriend right away. My heart sped up a little—okay, a lot—when I saw her. Casey was smart, pretty, and kind of unaware of it. She was comfortable in her own skin in a way that made me feel like being with her was coming home. Two older people sat on either side of her, a heavyset woman with the same frizzy hair Casey had, but with a bit more gray. The man sitting across from her was leaning forward earnestly, trying to explain or convince her of something.

Trying to catch her eye, I raised my arm in a half wave, half salute. Nothing.

As we got closer to the table, I heard Casey's dad say, "This was supposed to be your wedding day, *lieb*. Are you sure you're up to this?"

Out of the corner of my eye, I saw my mother clutch my father's arm and look at him with alarm. That, I didn't know. They'd set a date. I mostly disregarded Tom because he was an ass from the privileged Brody family. The Brodys acted as if they could get away with anything—which they mostly did. But in an instant, her dad's comment brought me back to the fact that the woman I thought I wanted to marry had been all set to marry a certain law-breaking asshole—today.

Clearing my throat, I said, "Hey, Casey." I put a hand on her shoulder. Rather than rise and kiss me, she turned her head and held my gaze for a long moment. I wasn't sure what I was supposed to see in that.

"Miles, these are my parents, Birgit and Peter Cort."

I stood speechless. My own parents, fortunately, were self-possessed enough to introduce themselves. I heard my mother say, "I'm Linda Ramsey. This is my husband, Emmanuel Siegel." My mother had held fast to her last name. She'd gotten married in the heyday of feminism. People calling her Mrs. Siegel drove her around the bend, so she always led with Ramsey. The Corts made room for my mom and dad on the roughhewn bench. I didn't sit. I was jumping out of my skin far too much for that.

"I'll get something for you," I volunteered. I'd stand in line. Work out how I was gonna approach this. "Casey?" She stood quickly, wobbling the bench. I was offering to get her something. Not have her join me. But she missed that cue and came to stand with me at the end of a long queue for bratwurst, sauerkraut, and pierogies. "You were going to get married today?"

Casey shrugged. "It's October sixteenth, the day the Brodys reserved at Lakewood Country Club," she said, fiddling with meal tickets in her hand. She tore at a perforation and handed me three.

"Did your parents ask about us?" I said, sounding too damned insecure and needy. I wanted to pull it back, but I couldn't seem to get a handle on my emotions right now.

"Obviously, Miles. I wouldn't spring you and your parents on them at Oktoberfest over beer and sausage."

Casey didn't elaborate. The line inched forward.

"Are they upset with you dating right after Tom?" I couldn't stop myself from asking.

"A little. Maybe." Casey shrugged. "But they're worried about me. I didn't tell them everything, or anything. Just that we decided to call it quits. So they think I'm more heartbroken than I am, I guess." She fiddled with the tickets some more. "I'm not sixteen, though, and playing the same sad song a million times in my room."

We were at the head of the line. I got large plates for me and my father, and mostly vegetables for my mother who flirted with vegetarianism from time to time. "Can I carry something for you?" I offered even though my arms were full and I'd never waited tables so had no idea how I could carry more.

"I've got it," Casey said, loaded down with her own family's dinner.

When I came back to the bench, my mother was comparing notes with Casey's parents on Germany. My parents had traveled quite a bit and were familiar with lots of different places, Germany among them. I watched the back and forth.

My mom was on her best behavior. Pleasant. She could be...difficult. Usually, she liked to challenge people's assumptions. And I knew from having been to Germany with them when I was ten that much of her focus on that trip had been visits to former concentration camps and Holocaust museums. My father the Jew had preferred Heidelberg castle and other medieval structures.

When my dad saw my mom about to take a conversational left turn, he brought up the castles. Good move. Aristocracy was more palatable than genocide, at least over a meal.

With our parents engaged in food and chit-chat, I turned to Casey and a neutral topic. "How's work? Anything new coming in?" Her practice was far more varied and interesting than mine. She got to work on whatever she liked and wasn't constantly bucking against a hierarchy and endless dues paying. Crack cocaine possession was the misdemeanor of the federal criminal court.

She shrugged and played with her food. One thing I liked about Casey was that she wasn't shy about eating. I hated to think our parents getting together made her that nervous. "I think I'm going to get a beer flight," she announced and rose.

I dropped my fork and followed her this time. Even though she looked like she needed time alone, I wanted to convince her that things were going just fine. My mom was being nice. Her dad, despite her warning about his penchant for silence in awkward situations, was actually talking.

"What's wrong?" I caught her wrist and moved my fingers down to intertwine with hers.

She paused, looking at our joined hands, then at my face for long seconds. She pulled away and her hands rested against her forehead as she shaded her eyes from the sun and tilted her head up. She shook her head and looked down. I could barely hear the words coming from her mouth as she spoke to my chest. But it sounded like she was murmuring "…going to get disbarred for this. But I…"

"What?"

"I know who your criminal mastermind is. I know who's behind the girls in the container."

My heart leapt to my throat. "Tom? Did he fess up to you?" Was she seeing her ex again? Would she pass along a break in the case that would send my career soaring? I didn't know if I wanted to shake her for seeing that lying, cheating, scumbag again, or kiss her for possibly being the best girlfriend ever. I did neither.

"Nope. Wasn't Tom. Not at all. The guy you call the Mastermind, he's now my client."

Behind us, an Abba tribute band started up. 'Dancing Queen' blared through speakers. At the same time, a woman pouring small cups of beer glared at us. We were at the front of the line again, not ordering a thing.

"Sorry," I said and pulled Casey away from the noise to a quiet corner behind a wooden booth.

"Did you say the Container Girls guy is your client?"

Casey's eyes shifted from right to left. "I've already said too much, I think."

"Too much? You haven't said enough. Can you get him— damn, I assume it's a him—to turn himself in? Take a plea?"

My girlfriend looked at me like I'd asked her to dance naked on the Oktoberfest stage. "You've got to be kidding me. I'm not walking my client into the death penalty. May as well turn in my defense bar card right now if I did something that stupid."

"But you were there with me." How could she not remember our wonderful-awful first date? "There was a child in that container."

"Okay. Maybe we should get back to the table. If my dad's talking and there's beer, he may go off on the Judge Brody situation and I don't want to have to explain any of that to your parents."

I didn't move. "You drop this bomb. Now you want to walk away?"

"I shouldn't have said anything in the first place." Casey no longer looked at me. Her hands had dropped to her sides and she seemed very interested in her white leather sneakers.

"But you did," I whispered. She looked at me again. I squinted, trying to glean something from her eyes. But hazel irises stared back at me. "Why?"

"Because you're working so damned hard to find the person. I don't know. I kind of needed you to know that the whole thing wasn't a figment of your imagination. You and Lou keep going around in circles."

"And that's it."

"Miles, I have an ethical obligation."

"And that trumps the continued violation of dozens of women."

"I have no evidence of continuing crimes."

"Of course you don't. I'm sure you stopped the conversation right there. Heard the dirt, took a check, and put your fingers in your ears. Because *that*, you'd have to report."

I could tell from Casey's flinch that I'd hit the nail right on the head. "Don't mock me. I did something I shouldn't have because I love you. Now...we can never talk about it again."

It was like standing in the middle of a thunderstorm. The cold wind of crime battled against the warm current of emotion causing turbulent thought. "You love me?" I blurted out the question.

"I think maybe." She closed her eyes, shook her head. When she opened them again, her gaze was focused, unwavering. "Not maybe. I do. I'm falling in love with you, Miles Siegel."

This was not at all how I saw this playing out. Not at all. I had hoped for wine. Maybe candlelight. Not beer and parents and prostitution. I wanted to say "I love you too," that I'd been holding back because I was worried about it being too soon. That I wanted to start to map out a future. But two monsters, Sledge and Grand and one victim, Kelly, were holding me back. "I would never tell anyone that I got the information from you," I said instead.

"I'm not playing at my job, Miles. I take it very seriously. Defendants need all the help they can get."

Part of me wanted to agree with her. The part that saw non-violent criminals sent away to maximum security prisons. But the part of me that had heard Kelly's story and had seen pictures of how those women were stored when not being used and abused vehemently disagreed. "*This* defendant?"

"Isn't charged with a crime. Is innocent until proven guilty. Is constitutionally entitled to a vigorous defense. And most of all: isn't a defendant." She ticked off on her fingers.

"Yet."

Casey shrugged. Lifted and dropped her shoulders while Sledge was walking around pimping out girls one at a time. She started walking back toward our parents. I didn't follow. I stood there for a long moment wondering if love could withstand our legal adversarial system.

33

I wasn't ever any good at lying. So when Momma's harassment didn't stop, I started walking the streets of Cleveland.
Shit had gotten better in the last five years. A bunch of new
houses had gone up. They looked all nice and clean and shit.
I couldn't imagine where in the hell anyone had gotten
money in Cleveland. But the strip of Buckeye closer to home
remained pretty much the same. I walked it today to the
grocery store to get my beers and back. Of course on the
way home, the rain started falling. I almost laughed at my
first impulse which was to run to Dion's house.

Instead, I looked at one church, then another as water
dripped from my hair. I wondered if I could run into one of
them for a bit. I could sit in the back and pretend to believe
in God and they could ignore me. I picked the one with the

white bird in the blue background from the van and ducked toward it.

Fortunately, the door was open. When I was a kid, I used to see people coming and going from churches all times of day and night. But when the neighborhood got bad with people stealing from anyone who didn't have they shit locked down, the doors stayed closed except on Sunday and nightimes at night for the drunks and druggies.

New Day Sanctuary looked like it had gotten more than a new coat of paint. Even the entryway smelled new. The blue circle was painted on the wall and New Day Sanctuary was in big ass letters. The word church was so small, I practically had to squint to see it. I guess God wasn't winning any popularity contests.

"Can I help you?" a woman asked before I'd even closed the door right against the rain. She had some big ass titties. I could only imagine the amount of attention men gave her over those. On top of them, she had a black shirt with gold lettering. "Church Girls Rock," it read. Ooh-kay. That was about a million miles from the stiff dresses I'd had to wear the one or two times my grandma had made me sit through church with her.

"It's raining," I said. "Um, I thought I'd sit here and pray a little while I wait for it to stop."

I must still suck at lying, 'cause she didn't look like she believed a word I said.

"Welcome to New Day Sanctuary," she said. "I'm not sure the Lord takes advice on the weather."

I tried to cover my laugh with a cough. "New Day, huh?"

I wondered if she was high, because she didn't purse her lips at me or look like she was ready to run me out of there.

"Well…you *can* sit in the auditorium but it's kinda cold in there. We're all down in the Welcome Lounge anyway."

I wanted to back the hell out of this place and get on steppin' home. But the girl looked nice enough and I was kind of cold. "Sure," I said, keeping a tight hold on my bag.

"You can bring that down here, but we don't allow drinking inside the church."

I could feel my face heat. It wasn't like I was going to crack open a six pack and get started in here. "Gotcha," I said through clenched teeth and turned around. I'd maybe get less harassment at home. Especially if Momma and John were out.

"I ain't saying you ain't welcome," the woman said, putting a hand on my shoulder. "Just c'mon down. Maisie made some of her barbecue chicken and cornbread. She can cook the hell out of a kitchen."

Just the mention of some good food made my stomach grumble. We both had to laugh at that.

I followed her down some linoleum stairs to a wood door. She pushed it open. "Hey there, we got one more for supper."

"What's her name?" a girl asked.

"Damn, sorry. Manners never was my thing." She turned and stretched out her hand to my free one. "I'm Paulette."

"Destiny," I said without thinking. Before I could fix it, though, Paulette was telling me everyone else's names. None of them stuck. I was too busy being surprised that everyone else wasn't black. There were a couple of girls that was probably mixed. And a couple of white girls. There was even some Asian girl. I wondered how they'd found their way to east Cleveland. I ain't never seen many white people 'round here that wasn't cops, social workers, or men looking for drugs or pussy.

I took a plate one of the girls offered me. It was full up with a chicken thigh, beans, greens, and cornbread that wasn't shy on butter. Momma had been cooking for John some, but she gave me the evil eye if I even thought about seconds.

Sydney and her kids could get as much as they liked, but me, I was supposed to be grateful for whatever I got. Not much had changed there. Plus Momma was extra mad at me for what she called my 'disappearing act.' Maybe she thought if she starved me, I'd disappear again.

Put a group of women together and they can't keep they mouths shut. I only half listened as the women talked; too busy thinking about when I could get home and have a drink or two. I'd run out two nights ago and was feeling a little edgy. Memories of some of the worst johns was starting to creep in. I needed to keep that shit away.

"I'm not really fit for any job," one of the white girls said. "Plus there are no men that want me now. I'm not sure *what* I'm supposed to do with the rest of my life."

I wanted to raise my arm in the air and shout, "Amen, sister," but I knew better than that. What she'd said had the ring of truth though. I looked at the girl closely while trying not to look like I was looking. She was pretty enough, I guess, probably a little older than me. Other than a piece of cornbread she was picking at with her fingers, she didn't have much on her plate.

There was one of those white blackboards behind her. 'HOOK' in all capital letters was written on there. The markers were the same blue as the church name on the front door. I kind of wondered if they special ordered that kind of thing.

"What HOOK stand for?" I whispered to the girl next to me. But I must have been too loud because everyone in the room got silent.

"Aw shit," someone said.

"We're a support group for former sex workers," the white girl said. Her voice was all proper, so it took me a good minute. I finished chewing and laid my chicken bone down real slow. But I couldn't swallow the sweet, tangy meat in my mouth. Then there was a flood of water behind the food pushing it out. I put my hands up and ran out, frantically looking for a bathroom. I barely made it to the toilet before all that food came up.

Wasn't a few seconds before someone was knocking on the stall door. I ain't closed it. Swung in and hit my back. She pulled it back open and came in behind me.

"Destiny, you okay?" Paulette said, rubbing my back. "Maybe Maisie's food wasn't so good today."

More crap heaved from my stomach. I spit out the bitter until I couldn't spit anymore. Paulette rubbed my back again. Then she was gone, the slam of the bathroom door let me know she'd left. I flushed a couple of times, then used up a bunch of paper towels trying to get that sick smell out my mouth and off my hands.

The door swung open again. I wondered who'd come to laugh at me. But it was Paulette with a big mouthwash bottle in her hands and a thin plastic cup.

I poured a healthy amount and swallowed it.

"That one, I ain't seen in a long time," Paulette said, snatching the bottle from me.

After some of the girls passed out, ruining the 'customer experience,' Sledge had cut back on the amount of alcohol we could have. But he ain't never limit the mouthwash, so I'd watched girls get drunk on that blue shit for years. I'd never done it, though. Dion always kept me topped up.

"I didn't mean to," I said. I wasn't sure if I was telling the truth.

"Uh, huh." Paulette looked me up and down. I followed her eyes. My shirt was wet. Momma's jeans too. Damn. I had to get home quick. Get myself together. Get this shit clean. And a few of those sweet beers would help—a lot.

"I think I need to get on home," I said, grabbing a shit-load of paper towels and rubbing at my clothes.

"Here, let me," Paulette said. Before I could stop her, she had my shirt over my head. Without a thought, I jerked my hands back and covered the scar.

"Where you get that?" she asked, jabbing her finger right at the spot I was trying to hide.

I didn't answer. It was my souvenir from that first night. Five minutes before Dion came back in, one of the guys thought it would be funny to carve his initials in my tittie. Don't remember his name. Don't know if I ever knew it. But "D.H." was roaming around Cleveland somewhere. "Can I get my shirt?"

For a long time, Paulette was quietly staring at me. I wanted to run out of there, but I wasn't doing it in a dingy gray bra. Then she lifted her own shirt. I was about to come at her, telling her I wasn't interested in no lesbian bullshit. During the last few years, I found out I didn't like women no better than men.

But instead of coming out my mouth with that, I stared. She threw "Church Girls Rock" over the door of the stall. Then she unhooked her bra. Them huge ass titties fell out. But that wasn't what I noticed the most. It was that she had almost exactly the same scar, in exactly the same place. I knew it was rude as hell to stare, but I couldn't pull my eyes away.

Paulette watched me watch her a good long time. "The thing is, I think you need to stay."

34

I have to say I hadn't expected to hear from Hami Emad ever again. I figured what in the hell ever Sledge was giving him, or threatening him with, was greater than his worry about federal prison. Or he wasn't involved at all and two containers being near two hotels was merely a coincidence.

There were quite a few vacant industrial lots out that way and a lot of motels. I mean, it wasn't like we were assuming girls were serving johns from the back of the rent-to-own furniture stores, or the local diners. I stuck that in the back of my mind as a possible line of investigation to mention to Valdespino. Maybe the net hadn't been cast wide enough. Maybe not. That was back in needle-in-the-haystack territory and I didn't want to go there if I didn't have to.

Shelving all that in my mind, I pushed open the door to the FBI interview room. The Egyptian man was sitting at the little table in there, visibly agitated.

Valdespino acknowledged me with a nod.

"Mr. Emad, you remember Miles Siegel." The hotel owner's red-rimmed eyes met mine. He nodded. "Again, I'm going to ask if you'd like a glass of water, coffee, pop?"

Emad's head shake was emphatic. "It's Ramadan."

Valdespino shrugged as if to say, 'It's your religion.'

"Why have you contacted the FBI?" Lou asked.

"As I told you on the phone, my sister Rida is missing."

Valdespino flipped through a notebook. "On September twenty-seventh, I visited you at work regarding your sister. Do you recall that visit?"

"Yes."

"I recall you saying—" Lou flicked up his index finger, "—one, you didn't have a sister." He raised his middle finger. "And two, if we had any more questions or wanted to make any more visits, we needed to contact your lawyer. Do you remember any of that?" Emad nodded. "Are you admitting now that sixteen year old Rida Emad is your sister?"

"Yes, yes of course. She's always been my sister. Always," Emad said with so much regret my heart twisted for him.

"Where do *you* think she is?" I asked my first question, pushing away the empathy.

I could have recited Shakespeare's longest sonnet, *The Rape of Lucrece*, in the silence that followed the question. But Emad had come to the FBI, not the other way. So I sat. Valdespino sat. We waited him out.

"I think Sledge has her," Emad admitted in a tone so forlorn, I'd have thought he'd signed his own death warrant.

Valdespino had been right that the sister was the weak spot. But Sledge had gotten there before us. My ungodly ass prayed for two things. That Rida was all right, and that this was the break we needed.

I pulled a legal pad from my briefcase, uncapped a brand new government-issue Paper Mate pen, and looked at Emad. "Let's start at the beginning."

For nearly an hour, Emad led us down the path of over-staying his student visa, to dropping out of school in the hopes of getting a job and helping his family back home, to meeting Mostafa Tarik at the eastside Islamic Center. I had to give it to Valdespino. He was right on the mark about Emad's background.

"He had just bought a motel. It was impressive," Emad said of Tarik.

"And you wanted to emulate him?" I asked.

"Yes. Everyone knows that with American business ownership, the sky is the limit. Look at Warren Buffett."

I wanted to point out that the streets were littered with failed businesses and ruined families. But this wasn't my show or one of my mother's political rallies. "So you bought the Sleepy Time?"

"The Islamic Center put together a fund for business lending. They helped me with the down payment."

"But..."

"But it was hard going. We cleaned out the trashy people, and bought a 'under new management' sign, but that didn't work. These new Internet...Web ratings stay forever. So if Joe Smith had a bad night two years ago and gives a one star rating, every new Joe Smith stays away. And if the owner comments, then we get shouted down."

"So what did you do?"

"The bank notes come due every month. I was also re-paying the Mosque. I didn't want to default. Sledge came by one day. Said he'd noticed that I'd cleaned up the place. And he had a proposition."

I couldn't help but lean forward. It wasn't quite the missing link, but it was close. I glanced a look at Valdespino. He'd pitched his bristly head forward as well.

Emad looked between us. "I have forty-five rooms. He said that he'd take twenty. Pay me five percent of his take."

"And did he?"

"What?"

"Pay you?"

Head nod. "It was enough to cover the payments."

I looked at Valdespino out of the corner of my eye. Houses weren't priced like San Francisco or New York here; still, buying a home outright was outside most people's reach. "About how much?"

The long hesitation could be covered with three letters: I.R.S.

"We're here to shut down this sex trafficking operation. Not turn you over to the tax man," I said. I hadn't played this role in a while: lying cop—fast and loose with the truth. Lou and I and probably Emad all knew that if push came to shove, we'd have the IRS all over him in a matter of minutes. If that was the wedge between him and the truth, I'd shove it in—hard.

"Maybe a thousand a day."

In my head, I doubled then tripled the amount he was reporting. Law enforcement was the wrong business unless you did forfeitures.

"Did he always pay you?" Valdespino asked. Not because he wanted to know about Emad's bank account, but because, I assumed, it gave him a good idea of the size of the operation.

"Yes. He or that guy he worked with."

"Can you describe the other guy?" Lou's question came before mine could.

"Maybe my size. Those braids Africans sometimes wear."

"What was his name?" I asked, pen poised and ready.

"Sledge called him Grand. But in the beginning something different. I can't remember it that well now."

Made a note of that. We'd have to pound on that one later, like a hammer chiseling out the important bits. I'd be willing to get a hypnotist in here if that's what it took.

"How long was he using the Sleepy Time?"

"About five years, maybe close to six," Emad answered.

"When did the containers come?"

"I told him it wasn't necessary," Emad said as if he were the nice guy in the situation and not an accomplice to kidnapping and exploitation. "I told him that changing the locks so they opened only from the outside was enough. But a couple of girls left and never came back. So he started putting them in the container at night."

"Do you know if he uses another hotel?"

"Other than me and Tarik's Sunrise?"

"Yes, other than those two."

Long pause. Head shake. "I do not think so. Because he was here so often. I'd think he would have been here less hours if he had yet another place to be."

"Do you think he's still operating even though the containers are gone?"

"Probably. It's why I'm worried about Rida. Sometimes, the new girls were young. And they were very popular. And can you please find Rida? Those other girls, I don't know, they probably came from bad families or something. But

Rida is pure. She prays *salat*. The men who came and went don't care about my sister's devotion to Allah."

"Where else could he possibly have them? Any ideas?" I probed.

"That why I'm here. If I could figure it out, I'd be there right now banging on his door. But I just don't know."

"Where did he live? Did he stay at the hotel?"

"Not most nights. Maybe once in a while when he partied with the customers."

"Did that happen often?" I asked. Maybe he had his own demons, a dealer he paid to make them go away. Another person who maybe knew who this guy really was.

"No. He was pretty clean. I think he lived on this side of the Cuyahoga, though."

"Why?" I asked, only half paying attention. It wasn't exactly a revelation that he lived on this side of town. Most blacks did. And it would be hell running a business driving across town twice a day. People did it who lived on the westside and worked for Cleveland Clinic. And eastsiders who worked at American Greetings did it. But for someone who worked for himself, it didn't seem like the best idea. "Say that again," I demanded when my brain tuned Emad back in.

"I said I think his mom was sick."

"Cancer? Something else?" I never wished anyone ill, but I was hoping for kidney failure. Combing through dialysis patients would be cake. Or a rare form of cancer subject to a federally funded trial.

"Sledge called it...the sugar. Is that diabetes? She was housebound for some reason. He made a lot of calls about that."

"Calls? Did he use your phone?"

"No, he always had a different cell."

We'd pull phone records anyway. Witnesses didn't always have the best memories. But everyone had heard of burners after that first season of *The Wire*. No criminal worth his salt would ever use a traceable phone again. That show had made law enforcement all the harder where smart criminals were involved.

"Do you have that number?"

"I didn't want his number. I didn't want to be connected to him or his business in any way. I want my sister back."

35

"He kidnapped a girl," Miles said after the waitress had walked away.

Though I was hungry enough to eat a bear, I'd been good and ordered the fish instead of a big plate of pasta. But my ravenousness of a minute ago went away like a puff of smoke. If the boyfriend diet had gotten me thin, the defender of the guilty food plan would keep me that way.

"Who?" Maybe this conversation wasn't going where I thought. Maybe someone other than Jarrod Carter was guilty of kidnapping.

"Sledge," Miles said, bursting that tiny bubble of hope. Gone were my thoughts of a nice dinner at Aldo's. The Italian restaurant was the one my parents had brought me to when I thought I was all grown up at ten in a stiff dress and stiffer shoes. Aldo's is where I went after high school graduation, and college graduation.

I'd drowned my sorrows in too much Chianti but not enough garlic bread to ward off a hangover. And instead of me probing him on the hints his mom dropped to my mom about our future together, it was going to be wall-to-wall Sledge. For a very long minute, I debated calling my parents and ending this night right here. No way was this evening going to go well.

"Why are you telling me this?" I asked instead, trying to be mature. I was in my thirties and *not* going to go crying to my parents.

"Because I want you to re-consider." Miles' voice was earnest.

"What?"

"Tell me who Sledge is."

I thrust my hands in front of me. They hovered over Miles' bread plate. "Cuff me now. Call Lou. Call Tom. Call the cops. That's one hundred percent against the law. And you of all people asking me that…" I shook my head.

"Get him to turn himself in, then," Miles said like it was a compromise. Like we were on an episode of some legal drama. Turn your client in, trial montage, we share wine and a single joke at the end, credits roll. But that was TV. This job, this career, these legal and ethical obligations were my reality.

I pulled my napkin from my lap and laid it on the table. I was actually going to have to get up and leave this dinner. I stood, grabbed for my purse, and walked from the restaurant. Long minutes passed while I watched the red, white, and green glow turn my skin mutant alien colors under that stupid neon flag.

Resolved to being alone, at least for the very near future, I crossed the middle of the street, ignoring the honking, and stood in a neatly mowed area in Veteran's Memorial Park, in stiff tall leather boots that I thought would entice Miles to my apartment. Now my aching heels made me wish for a bench.

It seemed like ten long minutes before Miles did his own jaywalk and joined me. He reached for my hand. We walked through the park and found that bench. My feet were grateful, if not the rest of me. I took my hand from his and rubbed my arms. Autumn was just about done. It wasn't much above fifty. The knee-length cardigan I'd chosen wasn't much protection from the chill. I'd only imagined I'd be warmed tonight by wine, by Miles....

"I love you, Casey," Miles said matter-of-factly.

How I'd longed for those three words. But the tone did not bring joy to my heart. I fiddled with the cross nestled in my cleavage. The gold sent tiny pinpricks of cold through my fingers.

"I love you, too," I parroted back.

"I think I want to marry you someday," he said. But he was no longer looking at me, rather into the growing darkness. The shadows from the few trees made long dark streaks on the ground.

Why hadn't that almost proposal felt better? Why had I made that single mistake of disclosure? I wanted a life less complicated by worries about money, and clients, and prosecutor boyfriends, not more.

"But I want Rida to be able to get married too, if that's what she wants," Miles was saying into the silence between us. A small puff of condensation left his mouth, then disappeared into the night.

"Who's Rida?"

"Sledge ran his girls through two different motels. The one you saw Tom at, and the one where the first container was found. I'm not sure whether the hotel owner tried to blackmail your guy, or if we're breathing down his neck even if we didn't know it, but just when we were getting close, the motel owner's sister disappeared." The mouth that had kissed me so thoroughly only hours ago was forming those words about blackmail and abduction. But all the softness was gone. Miles' shoulders hunched forward. The cords in his neck strained.

I turned my head away, watching an off-leash Dalmatian chase something his owner threw. "How old is she?"

"Sixteen."

I really tried to control my chest, my belly, stop the swift intake of breath. But I couldn't. My imagination got away from me. When I was sixteen, I wasn't ready for life outside my parents' house, much less being hired out as an unwilling prostitute. I put a leash and muzzle on my straying thoughts.

"Do you think there's a possibility she ran away? I mean a brother who's in deep with a pimp doesn't sound like the world's greatest role model. What kind of relationship does she have with her parents?" I asked Miles, mentally unloading responsibility on him.

"They're dead," was Miles non-responsibility accepting, matter-of-fact answer.

"Who?" The loudness of my voice must have scared the dog, because he let out a startled bark and ran back toward his owner, his black and white tail no longer wagging.

"Rida's parents. They died in a train accident two years ago. She moved from Cairo to live with her brother. He was doing well. So her family thought she'd have the best chances here."

"I guess he didn't tell them it was money from illegal activity," I said. Jarrod wasn't the only culpable person here. The most to blame, probably. But not the only one.

"So," Miles huffed, "Rida's been missing since September."

Carter didn't mention it when he came to see me. I had absolutely no idea if he had the girl. Not that it would have made a difference if I knew. I still couldn't and wouldn't say a word.

"Are you serious about marriage?" I asked. A tiny thrill ran through me at the words. Even though I'd been engaged just a year ago. The idea of marriage, and kids, and settling down, still held appeal. I wanted that dream so much I could taste it. With Miles doing the parental bumrush, I thought he was on the same track. But there was hesitancy in his voice. If I learned only a single thing in the last year, it was to see all the signs, not only what I wanted to see.

"Yes…" Miles hesitated for a beat too long.

"But," I added for him. It was obvious that the mere idea of spending a life with me needed to clear one giant obstacle. I waited to find out if it was insurmountable.

"What did you think of my mom, Linda?" Miles asked instead. It was like he was taking me on a Socratic dialog. Bravely, I put one foot into the verbal minefield.

"She was…opinionated," I said. Like Linda, I wasn't winning any diplomacy awards. I was usually better at tact, but this whole thing was lowering my inhibitions.

"Look. My mom is difficult. There's really no other way to put it. I love her dearly, don't get me wrong. But she doesn't do things to make anyone like her. She has no filter. She's nosy, and doesn't always respect people's boundaries. But there's one thing that she does unfailingly."

"What's that?"

"She supports my father—one thousand percent."

"There's only one hundred in a percent," was my snarky reply. How had we so quickly come to the 'you can't compare to my sainted mother' part of the relationship? I thought a woman had to wait at least two years for that.

Miles ignored me. "My mother didn't bend on much. For ninety-nine percent of our life, it was her way or the highway. But when it came to my father's career, she'd do anything. Put on the country club dress, go to the dinner, make nice."

"She sounds like Tabitha or Samantha—you know the lady married to two Darrens on *Bewitched*."

"Minus the vacuum running by itself, it kind of was like that," Miles admitted.

"That's kind of interesting, all that about your parents and their relationship," I prefaced. "But what does that have to do with you and me?"

"In order for this to work. This...us. I need to know that you're on my side."

"Of course I'm on your side," I said, not doing anything to disguise the hurt in my voice. "I want you to succeed, win cases, climb your way up the government ladder— whatever your goals."

I'd been nothing but supportive, I thought. I listened to him talk about work, gave him wine and the occasional blow job. And he'd done the same for me, minus the blow job. We'd fallen into the kind of partnership and relationship I thought most professional couples aspired to. Worked for Greg and Jason. I thought it had worked for us so far, too.

"I want to believe you. But first there was your hesitancy with Judge Brody. And now Sledge."

I looked around the park to make sure it wasn't filled with crack dealers. Because Miles had to be high.

"I may not be as heavy as I was this time last year. But let me fill you in on something. I like to eat. Nearly every day. I like a roof over my head. I like not having to jaywalk across Memphis Avenue barefoot." I gestured to my new boots. "I have been on the wrong end of the Brody stick. Never again. And this case is different anyway. This time, I have a legal obligation which I violated by telling you that the guy really existed. I'll regret that to my dying day. But my feelings for you and desire to let you know that you weren't tilting at windmills got in the way of my common sense. That will not happen again. It may not look like it with a practice I've cobbled together out of spit and string, but I'm proud of what I do. I take it and my clients seriously."

"So that's it?" the law and order prosecutor in Miles said.

My stomach took a dive. I didn't know if he was breaking up with me, but I had a sudden urge to see my own mom and dad who only had to love each other and not follow any rigid rules.

"Good night, Miles," I said as I walked to the other side of the park. I waited until I was done crying before I flipped open my phone and called my dad to come pick me up.

36

"I want to go home," that damn girl wailed.

"When your brother promises to keep quiet," I said. I was playing a game of chicken that had gone on too damn long. If I gave the girl back, I'd have no leverage over Hami. I wasn't sure if I did anyway. I was in big trouble and didn't know how to get myself out of this one.

"Why don't you shut the fuck up?" Shonna yelled at the girl. "You don't have to do no work. Act like a princess around here. We all started working on day one. You been here I don't know how many weeks, cryin' and moanin' and belly achin'. If it was up to me, I'd give you a little something to cry about. My third guy last night would have tore you right up." Shonna turned her light eyes on me. "When you gonna put *her* in a van? Huh? She too good because she pretty and talk all funny?"

I closed the steel-reinforced door to the attic and left the problem of the girl on the other side of it. She was like a splinter in my palm. If I didn't make some kind of decision, Shonna or one of the other ones would cut her up for sure. I'd never played favorites. All girls were initiated. All girls worked.

Sighing, I went down the stairs, careful to tiptoe past Momma's room. But from the sound of the *Price is Right* blaring, she couldn't hear a thing. A big loud TV was covering up the sin of bringing my business into my house.

Grand was in the kitchen, sweet-talking food out of Alisha. The man acted like he never ate. He needed to get him a good woman at home and get the hell out of mine.

I pulled him to a corner of the dining room. "What was your plan when you snatched that girl?" I asked for probably the hundredth time, hoping for a different answer every time.

"Let Hami know who was in charge. Keep him from going to the police."

"And where did he go?" I asked, though I knew I was going over the same old ground. I just wanted a different answer, was all.

"The FBI," said Grand, giving me the same answer as before.

"Do you think he kept quiet?" I asked him and myself. "How long was he in that office?"

"Our guy say five hours tops."

"So now we have a kidnapped girl. A snitching hotel guy. And the possibility that the Feds are breathing down my neck." My stomach churned as the smell of food came our way. At any moment, I expected a battering ram and SWAT at my door. Every day they didn't come was partially a relief. But it also made me nervous as hell that the next day would bring them in.

"But they haven't caught on to the delivery service. That was genius," Grand said.

It was the only way I was limping along. Momma's health insurance was my biggest monthly nut. But if I cancelled it, we'd never get it back. She was the poster woman for pre-existing conditions. Then there was the mortgage my sister had convinced her to take out after I'd paid off the damned house. Didn't transfer it into my name because Momma had been so proud to own a home in Cleveland Heights. Then that hood rat sister of mine had come along, talking about some get rich quick scheme with her dumb ass boyfriend. Momma had invested in my sister like she was Warren Buffet and my sister was Google.

Ain't seen my sister since. Instead of the twenty thousand I'd paid off, Momma was in one hundred thousand at eleven point seven five percent. Red line loans, I thought of them. Add on the leases on the club and it was a lot to keep this boat afloat. I didn't have time for Hami's ten off the top. I didn't have time for the FBI to shut down a quarter or half of my business.

"Let's go," I said, pulling Grand away from the fried chicken Alisha had just put in front of him.

"But I was about to eat. Alisha's is way better than Mama Joyce's," Grand complained.

"You can eat later." I pulled the remote from the breakfront. The garage door creaked open. I replaced the remote and pulled out the keys instead. "Drive."

"Where we going?"

"Downtown. I'm paying a lawyer. Time to get some advice."

That lawyer's secretary looked twice as startled as last time. Maybe because I had another guy with me. "We gotta see Ms. Cort," I announced.

"Do...do you have an appointment?" she stammered.

"Nah. She busy?"

"Have...have a seat. Let me check," she said, scurrying off. Grand and I made ourselves comfortable on the waiting room chairs. I stretched out my legs. Two white guys came in joking and laughing like an Eddie Murphy routine. Came up short when they encountered my legs.

I was guessing that I wasn't the usual guest. Probably a bunch of suits suing each other or a bunch of women crying over leaving their good-for-nothing husbands. Grand was messing with his phone and didn't look up. But I gave them a two finger salute, sending them running down the hall.

"Mr. Carter, how can I help you today?" my lawyer asked. She wasn't wearing jeans today. But what she was wearing didn't help her none. White people ran the whole damned country. I always wondered why they didn't look any better. Give me a poor black woman any day and she'd have her shit more together than the average white woman. I half wanted to give her Judith's number. My girls knew how to look good. Maybe we could barter or something. Clearing my mind of that stupid mess, I stood and shook the lawyer's outstretched hand. I prodded Grand to rise. He took my lead and copied me.

"Can we talk to you?"

"I think first, we need to discuss protocol," she said, not budging an inch. For a moment, I was kind of flustered. In my business, girls never talked back to me unless they were high, drunk, or plain stupid.

"What does that mean?" I asked, coming back to myself and making an effort to keep my right hand at my side.

"You can't just show up in my office. 'On retainer' doesn't mean I'm at your beck and call. Are we clear?"

"Crystal."

"At any time, I can return your unused retainer and our relationship is terminated," she said, not blinking. She didn't even move back when Grand stepped forward in the way he did when girls got mouthy.

Then the woman didn't say a word. Looked at me straight in the eye like she could see into my soul and didn't much like the view.

"Can we talk?" I asked. Grand's look told me all I needed to know. I looked like a pussy for deferring to this woman. I'd tell him later that sometimes, you had to play one game with white people, another with everyone else.

She actually huffed. It was quiet, but I heard it. "Let's go to my office."

Grand and I walked toward the door. But she didn't open it.

"Do you remember the discussion we had about attorney client privilege?" she asked, turning back to look at us. Her green-brown eyes pierced me.

I nodded. I wasn't planning to give her my business plans. I'd heard that part loud and clear.

"Attorney-client is a two-way street. There aren't any detours. If your friend comes into the office with me, nothing you say is privileged," she explained.

"Can you represent him too?" I asked, looking for a way to keep Grand in the loop and out of jail.

She shook her head. "Doesn't work that way. If he were to snitch on you, I couldn't represent you both. And if I represented Bang for the Buck, then I could talk to both of you, but would have to choose the business before the two of you if it came down to it. So no, he can't come into the office. And no, I can't represent him."

I motioned to Grand. He could stay in the waiting room, scaring the hell out of white people. I nodded my understanding and the lawyer finally opened her door. She walked behind her desk, leaning her bare arms on the desk. I noticed she didn't wear a ring of any kind. Funny, she didn't seem like the single type, though.

"So what did you need that was so urgent you couldn't call the phone number on the card I gave you and make an appointment?" she asked all brisk and business like. I guess she wasn't talking down to me. It wasn't like we were the chit-chat types anyway.

"We need to know what to do with a girl," I said.

The lawyer sat back in her big leather chair. Made her look small, not important. I think she was probably going for important. "What girl?"

"The owner of Sleepy Time said he'd go to the police if we didn't continue paying even though we'd cleared out of the hotel. I don't believe in paying protection money. It's not how I do business. So I took his sister. Thought that would get him to shut up," I explained.

"But he went to the FBI anyway."

She didn't look like she was guessing. She looked like she knew this for certain. I was sure her guy or ex-guy had been in the local prosecutor's office, not with the feds. "I hear he spent at least five hours talking to them," I said anyway. "I'm guessing they know a lot more about my operation than I'd like."

"So, back to the girl," she said, leaning forward, elbows on desk.

"Rida."

"How long have you had...her in your...custody?" she asked, tiptoeing around shit she didn't want to know.

"Three weeks," I answered. Something was off. She wasn't surprised about anything I told her. It was like she already knew that, too. I rubbed at the dampness that appeared on my upper lip. I flipped through her long ass explanation of attorney-client in my mind. There was no way she could tell anybody what I was doing. I was for sure that's what she'd said.

"Is she...unharmed?"

"She airight. Complains about the food. She says the room is too hot and noisy. The other girls hate her. But she's fine. We only threatened to sell her out. Wasn't planning to do it."

"What would be your perfect solution?" she asked.

"For Grand never to have taken her. But I can't go back. So for her to go home. For Hami to leave me alone. Call a truce."

"If you drop her back home with her brother, what do you think would happen?"

"The cops would grab me."

"Are they watching Hami?"

"Think so. They'd be idiots not to. I'm sure they assume he's more involved than he's letting on." She looked out the window. "What are you thinking?"

"The best way to accomplish your objective. You want to return a girl you admittedly kidnapped. You want to do it outside of police surveillance. You want Hami to leave you alone. You want to...I'm guessing...continue to operate your business without repercussions."

"Yeah. That's it."

"Well, I fucking want a million dollars. Unless a big sack of money falls out of the sky, that's not going to happen. That…would be a miracle. But I don't perform miracles."

"Can you make a deal?" I asked. On TV, there were always deals.

"What kind of deal?"

"I don't know. What do you think the prosecutor wants?"

"I talked to him yesterday. He doesn't know who you are, how to find you, or how put you in jail. There's no deal without you going to prison."

"Seriously?" I had to sit back in my own chair. Kind of wanted an hour to think on that one. She knew the guy who was looking for me? How in the hell did she manage that? Was she going rat me out? I'd've asked if that confidentiality thing ran both ways, but didn't want to show that she'd scared me. "How do you know so many prosecutors?" I asked, really curious about the answer.

She squinted like she was in pain. "Small world, Cleveland."

"So…"

"So if you get some random third person to drop her off at the hotel, what's the worst that could happen?" she asked. I'd come in here to get answers, not more questions, but I kept my anger to myself and answered her stupid question.

"She could tell them where I keep my girls. And who in the hell knows what the girls have said to her about my business?"

"If she were to go home, I think none of these things would be a problem," she said like it was a fucking riddle.

"What? Richmond Heights?" I asked.

She shook her head.

"From what I understand, she came to the U.S. because her parents died. But I'm sure she has other relatives. If she were to go all the way home. Given the limited resources of the United States outside of terrorism, I can't imagine they'd fly her back should they ever need her to testify."

"So I what? Drive her to the airport?"

The lawyer shrugged.

I stood and walked out of the office without so much as a goodbye. "Grand, get the car. We've got a long drive ahead of us."

37

Two boyfriends in two years and the only thing left in my belly was dread. I couldn't remember the last meal I'd had, but I wasn't hungry. On top of that, I had no idea what I should wear. Miles had e-mailed and invited me to dinner at the Chinese restaurant right here on Shaker Square. Not a phone call. Not an impromptu visit. E-mail. I almost called my ex-client and his ex-girlfriend to see what the deal was, though I was kind of sure I knew.

The last week hadn't been the same heady rush of dating as before. Everything had felt infinitely harder. I didn't talk about work and neither did he. The one thing we had in common and liked talking about the most was—by unspoken truce—out the window.

I was waiting for Miles in front of the building door. I gave him my biggest smile and my best *faire la bise*. A kiss on both cheeks was both intimate and not, at the same time.

"Let's walk," I said. "Unless you're really hungry."

Miles shook his head, so instead of turning right outside my door, we went left. We didn't talk all the way to Larchmere. Or where North Moreland morphed into Fairhill. I stopped when we got to the tiny brook that fed into Shaker Lake. Without the crunch of leaves under our feet or cars rushing by, there was nothing but silence. Wood smoke from the big old houses set so far back from the road I could barely see their lights tickled my nose.

"What do you want to tell me?" I asked. I turned to him—finally. I could only make out parts of his face in the falling dusk and shadows from the few colored leaves clinging to the trees.

"How did you know—"

I hadn't known until just that moment. "Intuition," I threw out glibly. Tried to keep my voice light. I may have been failing.

"I've been temporarily assigned to Toledo," he said. Which explained where he'd been last weekend. Relief that he hadn't been avoiding me battled with surprise that he'd now be so far away without me knowing.

"Is that even in the Northern District?"

"It is. Northern doesn't mean northeastern. I'll keep my apartment here, but the government will put me up at some hotel there during the week."

"What about your cases?" I asked, when I really wanted to say, 'What about us?' I started spinning out scenarios for making a long distance relationship work in spite of the mounting evidence that *we* didn't work.

"They'll be reassigned," he said. My thoughts and plans ground to a halt.

"So...we could see each other on weekends. I could drive out sometimes. I could save you the time. Do you want me to get your mail?" I stopped talking when I realized, no, he didn't want any of that. Not from me, at least. I stopped when I realized I was one step from *Dreamgirls'* Effie.

Miles' inhale took forever. "I think we should take a break," he finally exhaled.

"You mean, we should break up," I said, infinitely proud of myself for finally getting the truth out.

"I'm not saying that." He gathered my cold hands in his. They'd been in his very expensive-looking overcoat pockets and were very warm.

"No, Miles, it's exactly what you're saying." Ten years ago, I'd have twiddled my thumbs by the phone waiting for the 'break' to end. I wasn't that girl anymore. I wasn't even the woman I'd been a year ago: the doormat so grateful for any attention that I put up with anything.

"I care about you a lot," he said.

Care, not love, nailed the coffin shut. I turned toward the water, watching the tiny dam make a bubbling brook. A boat, turned upside down, showed wear in the paint chipping from its hull. I squinted. Think it was a rowboat. There were canoes too. Didn't seem like a big enough lake for boating. The spot was terribly romantic.

The irony wasn't lost on me. Deep breaths were all I could do to keep from crying. In those breaths, I tried to figure out what in the hell was wrong with me. Why no one wanted me for me. Last year, I was a beard. This year, I was supposed to be a carbon copy of a soon-to-be mother-in-law. I dreaded 2005.

"Why Toledo?" I tried to add pep to that voice. I still sounded far away to my own ears, though.

"Three of the lawyers are caught up in a long-term prosecution and they need someone to pick up the slack. It's an excellent opportunity to broaden the kinds of cases I'm working on."

"What about the Container Case?" Miles' look of sad resignation that greeted the question made me regret asking it.

"Lou and his guys are doing the heavy lifting. Sifting through motel phone records. Looking for johns. Following up on the leads from the women we freed. It may take weeks to get a break unless your client slips up. But they'll get him. Rachel is happy to take over the case. It should have been hers from the beginning, right?"

I wished it had been hers. Really wished it—hard. Then my soon-to-be ex-boyfriend may not be so ex. I would haven't made a stupid decision based on a false moral dilemma.

"Right," was all I said.

"Casey, look at me," Miles said.

"Why?" I asked even as I did what he'd commanded.

"It's just not our time. I need to get a firm foothold in the U.S. Attorney's office. I'm a new lawyer, and I want to build a career on a solid foundation. Being a cop probably got me in the door. But convictions are going to keep me there. I can't pass up an opportunity to work on the kinds of cases that go to trial, that matter to the safety and security of Americans."

"Will it ever be our time?" I couldn't help asking. I wanted to kick myself for how needy I sounded. But I needed to know if I had to close the door forever, or if there was even a crack of hope. Because a girl could live on her mother's strudel and hope.

"Never say never," Miles said. Then he leaned in and kissed me full on the lips. My belly fluttered, betraying my feelings. But when he pulled back, I knew for Miles the kiss meant goodbye.

38

"You *could* get a GED," John said.

"You certainly can't expect to sit in my house all day, eating up my food, doing nothing," Momma huffed. She slapped the rest of dinner in a Tupperware, jammed the lid on, and slammed the refrigerator door after putting it in. She didn't really need the emphasis. I got it.

"You can get a job while you're studying. I saw that the pizza place around the corner is looking for someone to do take-out orders," John said, all reasonably and mild-like. "You could do that while taking your classes."

"Then what?" I yelled. I'd had up to my neck with this shit. Every few days, we went through this same damn thing.

"You bring some money into this house. Ain't no one living for free."

"What money Sydney bring in?" From what I could see, my sister had her hair done, her nails done, and some nice clothes. Ain't never heard nothing about her working or schooling or anything much other than laying up under mens, for that matter.

"She's got two kids," Momma said.

"So if I have some babies, you'll stop bugging me?"

"Don't you even think of bringing some little rugrats up in here. You managed not to get pregnant while you were gone, so you know how birth control works. Keep it that way."

"So—"

Momma shushed me as she turned up the TV.

"It's been more than four months since the FBI came upon the girls in the container. Our crime reporter Victoria Greenlee followed up with the FBI yesterday to see if there are any leads in the case that dominated the news this summer."

The anchor disappeared from the screen. The picture switched to another reporter, Victoria whatever. She stood outside a brick building, holding a microphone to a woman's mouth. "We continue to aggressively pursue all leads at this time. We won't rest until the men or women behind this criminal ring are brought to justice."

I didn't hear what they was saying, because I couldn't believe what I was seeing. Some of the girls I knew were coming out of a container. The lights on them were bright, but I knew who they was. I'd wondered why Sledge and Dion had moved us to a nicer place. The police were looking for him, not because they wanted what was good for us like Dion had said. Lies and truth jumbled in my head. Momma sucked disapproval through her teeth, then turned the sound back down.

"Maybe tomorrow I can carry you over to Tri-C and get you signed up for the GED," John offered.

Then what? I wanted to yell at them again. Then what? I was going to what, go to college? Or was I going to be one of those people wearing a dress to work? The only thing I knew was how to take off a dress. But I didn't say anything. If I kept my big mouth shut for ten or twenty minutes, Momma would huff and puff, John would rub her back, then they'd toss me ten or twenty bucks and be out of the house for a while. I'd watch some TV, walk to get my beers, and be down in the basement when everyone got home.

"Well, I gotta get to work," John said, lifting himself out of the kitchen chair and picking up his keys. Momma stomped upstairs, coming back down a minute later in dark blue scrubs. John pulled some wrinkled bills from his pocket and left them on the counter. Then they was out the door and I had the house to myself.

Peace—at last.

❀—❀—❀

Ten seconds after I woke up, I was face down in an old paint bucket. Every time I took a breath, something new came out of my belly. I kept on coughing and puking until my stomach stopped heaving. I looked at the pink, green, and yellow slime in the bucket and dug my fingers and heels into the air mattress, pulling myself as far as possible from the mess, so I didn't start up again.

I closed my eyes and took a deep breath, trying to remember why my stomach was churning like it was. Then it hit me. Momma and John had gotten on me about getting a GED.

From what I could figure out, I'd have to sit in some room and take a bunch of tests, a bunch of classes, and a bunch more tests. And add on top of that a job, and I wanted to close myself in the basement and never come out. What in the hell would I have in common with anyone working behind a counter or sitting behind a desk?

After I'd run out of my sweet beers last night, I'd broken my own rule and had a few of John's beers. I tried to keep the number down to four or five beers a day because getting more than a little bit of money out of Momma was hard as hell. But the nightmare that woke me up wouldn't go away.

In my dreams, I went to the FBI and told them everything I knew about Sledge and Dion. Then Sledge found out and locked me in a hotel room. When I looked out the window, the line of men through the parking lot was as long as people lining up for tickets to Beyoncé.

Even after I turned on all the lights, jammed earphones into my ears, and blasted some Alicia Keys from Sydney's old iPod, I couldn't put the pictures out of my head. So I'd drank until I couldn't think any more.

When I could stand upright, I took the bucket out back and poured it behind the rotting shed. Filled it with the hose a couple of times to get the nastiness out. The dogs behind the fence barked like they hated me. I gave them the finger. Fuck 'em. Their owners made they lives nicer than Sledge had made mine. If waking up early was their biggest problem, they needed to check theyselves.

"What are you doing in the back?" John said, standing at the back door. I jumped back. Man nearly scared the living daylights out of me. Couldn't be more than five in the morning.

"I was just talking to the dogs back there," I said, gesturing to those same damned animals I was cursing before.

"Sounded like you were throwing up and trying to hide the evidence," John said, putting a meaty hand on his hip.

"What business is it of yours what I'm doing?" I threw back. "You may be fucking my mother, but you isn't my father."

"I think you need something else," he said, shaking his head.

"Motherfucker. You want some of Destiny. Thought you were nice. You ain't no different than any other man. So if I don't do what you ask, will you what—tell my momma I came on to you—get her to throw me out of the house?" I yelled. Then realizing how stupid I was, I whispered, "I ain't got nowhere to go, man."

John backed up the two steps. I followed him. "What you like?" Forming my fingers into a loose fist, I made the universal symbol for a BJ. "Or you one of those freaks who like it in the butt? Destiny do what you need."

I put on the pout the girls had taught me. I got up real close like and whispered some dirty shit in his ear, so I didn't see the shove or the slap coming. God damn it. He was going to be one of those rough motherfuckers. But I could take it. I'd made it this far.

"I don't want anything of the kind from you. You need some kind of serious help," he said, shaking his head again like I was shit on his shoe. He went back into the house somewhere.

I took my ass back down to the basement and had a couple more of his beers. Didn't care that it was morning.

It was kind of dark when I woke up again. My mouth tasted like ass. I could barely get my eyes open enough to figure out where in the hell I was. Then it hit me: Clark's basement. A phone buzzed near me. Sydney's throwaway phone. She had a shiny new phone with a color screen and didn't need this one anymore even though it was still under contract.

So Momma said I could use it as long as I didn't run up no bills. Run up bills? Who in the hell was I gonna call? The only number I knew was Dion's. I fought hard with myself everyday not to dial him. Ask him to take me out of this hell. Because I knew he'd only put be back in a different kind of hell.

I looked at the thing and let it ring. There wasn't a single person I needed to talk to.

I have no idea how long it was, but someone was banging on the basement door. "What you need?" I called up.

"Someone here for you," Sheron yelled down. Still freaked me out that she was a big girl now. The toddler I'd babysat was long gone. It was like the little girl who'd curled up in my lap and watched movies with me and eat all the good pieces of popcorn had disappeared into thin air. Sometimes, I wanted that little girl back.

I didn't say nothing. In a minute, I heard the door open and saw the big old chest with the church symbol on it before I saw the light-skinned girl and her thick cornrows behind them come down the stairs. "Where you been?"

"What you mean?" I asked, my tongue thick.

"You ain't been to New Day in a couple of weeks."

"You know I ain't no god worshipper. I was just stopping in to keep dry on my way home."

Sheron was standing there, hand over her wide open mouth, hanging on every word. Paulette turned to her. "Can you give us a minute? I'm sure you've got something better to do."

My niece beat it out of there. I musta smelled like shit for her not to nag me about sticking around. Sheron mighta kept her mouth shut on the way out, but nosy assed girl denied her ten minutes of drama slammed the door—hard.

"Tell me about your scar." The way Paulette said that all bold like, I didn't think she'd take no for an answer.

"You really want to know." When she nodded, I said, "Don't say I didn't warn you." Then I told her minute by minute what had happened to me that night. Starting with Dion asking me out, and ending with that man pulling out his pocket knife and carving his initials on my chest.

I told her things I had made myself forget. I didn't cry, or throw up, or blink. I waited for her to get up and walk away. Instead, she did the very thing I never expected. She hugged me. I couldn't help myself. I cried then. I started crying and couldn't stop for a long time.

"I'm sorry I got snot on your nice shirt," I said. Paulette, who smelled like perfume and sunshine, didn't say nothing. Reached behind her and unwrapped some squares from the toilet paper I kept by the bed. I wiped my face best I could with the wad she handed me.

"Damn near same thing happened to me," Paulette said, looking directly at me.

"You worked for Sledge?" I asked. I wanted to turn away from her, but I kept my eyes steady. If I looked at her, I didn't have to think about me.

"Hell, no. I didn't have no pimp. My boyfriend turned me out. He said if I loved him, I'd do this for him. Just a few of his friends and we'd have enough money for an apartment. Enough so I could leave my aunt and uncle's house."

"Did you move out? Did he marry you?" I said, wondering if she looked so joyful because she got happy ever after like Cinderella and Snow White.

"He was lying. I turned tricks for two years before I got saved. He had me out on every damn street corner on Lorain Avenue. He had dudes do me in his car, in hotels. Anywhere."

"How did you get away?" I asked. But I wanted to know *why* she wanted to get away. The other men may have been shit, but I wondered why she'd want to leave a boyfriend who loved her. It didn't take me too long to figure out Dion didn't love me. If he had, he'd have at least let me stay with him, and not let Sledge carry me any damned place. But maybe him sending me home did prove that he loved me. My head hurt trying to figure it all out.

"I walked up to one of those New Day vans," Paulette was saying. "They found me a place to stay that night. I ain't been back since."

"What about your aunt and uncle?" I asked. At least she had people who loved her. A place she could go that probably wasn't a basement.

"Those pious church-going mofos couldn't forgive me my trespasses."

"As we forgive those who trespass against us," I murmured. "And lead us not into temptation, but deliver us from evil." Antoine had sometimes taken me to a Catholic church. The prayer had just been words I'd heard everyone mumble. But this time, it kinda meant something.

"I haven't told my momma the truth," I said. "I don't know if her and John would throw me out. They halfway going to kick me out anyway unless I get a job."

"Are you drunk?" Paulette asked.

"I'm not feeling too high right now," I said. But even I could hear the slur in my voice. My throat hadn't caught up to my brain which was stone cold sober.

Her sigh was long. She leaned forward, making me look her in the eye again. "Here's the deal. I can get you a place to stay. You'll get three squares a day. But you have to agree to come to meetings and talk to a counselor. And there's no drinking."

"Sound like jail."

"No more jail than the hell you're living in. Look. It's an inpatient treatment program for recovering sex workers." She held up her hand. "Nah, nah, nah, before you say something, hear me out. You're dying in here. You look like you weigh about ninety pounds. You smell like you're drinking your breakfast, lunch, and dinner. You're not in school. You're not working.

"I don't want to get a call that you cut your wrists and bled out down here. I ain't saying it's easy. But if you want to live, you've got to get the hell out of here and find out who you are."

My eyes burned with tears because the idea of laying down and never waking up sounded perfect and horrible all at the same time. Through the tears blurring my eyes, I looked Paulette in the eye and nodded.

"Tell me what I have to do. I'm ready to go."

39

Jarrod
November 26, 2004

"Where are you taking me?" Rida asked from the back of the car for about the hundredth time. I swear she was worse than a noisy ass child.

I wanted to shove a fist in her face, shutting her up for good. But that would only draw attention to us. And we needed as little of that as possible. I looked at the dashboard, then looked at the signs outside the windshield. We were almost there. A couple of hours and this whole ordeal would be over and done with.

"Park in long term," I said to Grand as he steered around the airport.

When he found a place to put the Lexus and that was safe from possible damage, Grand turned off the car.

"Look. You have two choices," I started, turning my whole body so the Rida girl could see me full on. "You can go back to Egypt."

In the silence, Rida looked out the window toward the air control tower. "What's the other option?"

I gave her the hardest stare I could. It didn't take her too long to figure it out.

"Fine," she said.

I held out a burner. "Call your family. You'll be on KLM flight five fifty-three. You'll land…" I checked the paper in my hand. "At two fifteen in the afternoon."

She gingerly grasped at the phone. I carefully watched her dial. Making sure it was a lot more than ten numbers. "Put it on speaker," I demanded. Rida fiddled a little, but she did it. The ring sounded like a beep, so I figured it wasn't Ohio she was calling. Rapid Arabic filled the cab of the truck. Five minutes in, I tapped her thigh—hard. Taking the hint, she said her goodbyes and hung up.

"Grand here has a ticket on the same flight from Detroit to Amsterdam. He'll make sure you get where you're going," I said. I gave them both their tickets.

9/11 made the wait good and long. But I kept myself busy driving around Detroit. It was nice being in a city full of black folks. The white folks done cleared the hell out of this place. They were still hanging on to what was left of the good jobs in Cleveland.

Found a fish joint. Watched the folks go wild when the Pistons won. Richard Hamilton hit it with less than two seconds left on the clock. Then LeBron blocked a shot, making the Cavs win. It was going to be a very good day. I couldn't wait to check the cash from the bars.

Games equaled drinking. And winning meant they spent more money on girls. Once Rida was gone, it was going to be smooth sailing. I needed to start thinking on legit ways to expand.

"She get on?" I asked Grand when he opened the passenger door in front of Departures.

"Yep," he said when I hopped out my side and we switched.

"Think she's gonna bail in Amsterdam or wherever she's changing?"

"I don't think any middle-eastern girl could safely get off a flight and roam around. She probably won't chance it."

When some police started giving us the evil eye, I flicked him the keys and he started the car. It would be a good twenty-four hours before I was sure she was safe. I'd be holding on to this burner until then. One ring from her and I'd toss it in the Cuyahoga River. I never carried around a phone that had anything incriminating on it, but I'd make this one exception. I opened the glove box and popped it in.

"What in the hell is this?" I asked, pulling out a handful of something that felt like broken glass. I pulled out at least a handful of yellow meth crystals

"Aw, shit," Grand said, sounding like a kid caught stealing from his mama's purse. "I promised I'd do Iceman a favor."

"Iceman?" I said to myself more than Grand. "Don't you tell me Derek has been dealing from our vans?"

Grand didn't say a word. I shoved him hard, not giving a shit that we were on the highway. Grand couldn't keep the damned truck straight. Nearly hit some shitbox. Fortunately, he was able to save my truck from damage.

"What in the hell are you thinking? I'm running a misdemeanor operation here. Maybe a low-level felony like they tried to lay on me a few months ago. But this here is fucking stupid," I said, throwing a few rocks at him. "I don't do federal crime. In less than twenty-four hours, Rida will be out of the picture, then there's *nothing* linking me to the container or hard time. Not a damn thing. But this shit here," I said, shaking my hand again. "This shit is just stupid. You know better than this."

"I told him I'd drop it off and pick up the cash in Toledo. It's a low risk operation. I didn't think you'd mind too much." Grand was talking as fast as a drug commercial.

"Didn't think I'd mind, or didn't think I'd find out?"

"Look, it was stupid. But now that we have the shit, let's just drop it off and be done with it."

I didn't say a damn thing to him for a half hour. But I had to wonder if I could trust him anymore. Did he call the feds on the first container? Did he let Destiny go on purpose? Was he dealing drugs outta the vans paid for by me and in my company name? One stupid ass thing had me wondering if I could really trust him on anything. If the feds ever did find me, would he turn on me?

"Here," Grand said, pulling up to some shit house. The street sign laying halfway near the ground said LaGrange.

"What's the plan?" I asked.

"I'm to call this number," he said, turning over his arm, "and we're going to do the trade."

He popped open the glove box and pulled out the phone, putting in the blue ink digits. I heard the faint sound of ringing, even though the phone was up to Grand's ear. It stopped and he listened for a bit. "Yeah, we got your stuff. Come to the passenger side."

I pulled out the folded paper bag from between my knees. A brother with jeans and Timberlands came around the side. My neck unkinked in relief. Wasn't no hinky white cops going to bust me tonight. I'd decide on the ride home what I'd have to do with Grand. Fire him or make sure he ended up in the river with this phone. I hadn't had to get rid of anyone since Dashanique.

"What you got for me?" he said.

"Package from Iceman." I dropped the sack in his hand. "What you got for *me*?" 'Cause I'd taken a little off the top of Iceman's delivery. I'd give it to a few johns or something. And when these Detroit folks found their package a little light, Iceman would learn him a lesson about doing stupid shit.

Guy pawed through the bag. I was glad he didn't weigh it. I didn't want to get shot over this shit—but Derek needed to be taught a lesson. Couldn't wait to watch that play out. Flipped a plastic zipper storage bag into my lap full of cash. "Good looking out," I said. Grand pulled down the street.

"Easy peasy, lemon squeezy," he said like he was in grade school or some shit.

"Whatever. Pull over here to this burger joint and let get me a little something for the road." Rida was gone. Iceman's stupid errand was done. I was ready to relax with some fries and a pop. I'd be glad to use a couple a Iceman's bills to pay the tab.

Grand pulled in and went to get my standard order. Quarter pound of meat, fries, and a Mello Yellow. I was peeling off a few bills when something hit the truck. "Shit!" I yelled and looked out the window expecting to see some drunk or doped up fiend in a hoopty. But when I turned, my worst nightmare came to life. My truck was surrounded by police vehicles all suited up in armor like I was Bin Laden or some shit. The thud came again, like a battering ram.

"Get out!" came one shout. The door opened and a cop yanked me from the seat.

"Grand! Dion!" I yelled. But no relief came from the strong arms holding me or the shock of electricity that made me piss myself.

"Get down now!" someone else yelled. Then my head hit the pavement and all went black.

40

The Lucas County Jail could have been a carbon copy of Cuyahoga County. The walk from the public parking lot to the tall imposing building had done me a world of good. Driving for two and a half hours during Thanksgiving weekend had to be at the bottom of my life's wish list. The circulation had only returned to my butt when I got to the courthouse steps.

I wasn't sure my parents didn't think I was crazy. I'd finally worked up the courage to tell them that it was off with Miles, but before I could get more than three words in, my phone rang. Ten phone calls later, I was approved to visit with my client Jarrod Carter in the Toledo jail.

While most jails promised nearly round the clock attorney visits, the reality was very different. I pressed the buzzer on the locked side door for a good ten minutes before a sheriff younger than my oldest jeans answered the door.

"Ma'am."

"Attorney Cort here for visitation," I said officiously.

"It's Thanksgiving weekend," the teenage deputy responded.

My cold fingers fiddled with the stiff leather pocket of my briefcase. "Here's the fax." I jammed the blurry pages at his chest.

The text may not have been too clear, but the county seal was. He backed away from the door and let me in. Most jails were nice. This one wasn't. While there's nothing nice about incarceration, jails were usually spotless, smelled strongly of disinfectant, and didn't make you think of virulent strains of bacteria. This one made me want to wash my hands even though I hadn't touched anything.

When the deputy offered me a chair, I elected to stand. Brown rusty spots dotted cracks in the floor, walls, and ceiling. Cold air blew from a vent that I was sure was supposed to be heat.

Jarrod Carter would hate this.

Nearly an hour later, I got to sit with Carter in a tiny attorney room.

"This is some bullshit," he started before I could even get comfortable in the metal chair on my side of the table. He sounded more like my regular clients than the Brook Brothers-wearing business man I was used to.

"How'd you get the bruise on the side of your head?" I asked. He looked like shit. Gone were the nice clothes, good manners, and expensive leather messenger bag. In its place was crusted blood and jail-issued coveralls.

"How you think? A boot hit my head. My head hit the ground."

"Do you want to file a complaint?"

"No. I want out of here," he answered.

I collected my thoughts and pulled a pen from my purse "Meth? You told me you weren't in the drug trade."

"I'm not. It was Grand's idea."

"Where is Grand?" I asked. I was sure he'd be pestering me to represent his weasly little accomplice. Had my speech already in place about conflicts of interest.

"Don't know," he said.

"What do you mean, you don't know? Wasn't he arrested with you?"

"He wasn't booked with me. When I asked around, ain't nobody heard of Grand or Dion Fortune."

"So what you're telling me is that one day out of the blue, your long-time deputy decides to do a drug deal. But somehow, you end up with the drugs and money while all he's holding is a burger and fries?"

Jarrod Carter had the wherewithal to stop and think on that a second. I didn't want to sign Mr. Fortune's death warrant or anything, but something didn't smell right, and it wasn't only the jail. I wanted to hip my client to the possibility that either Grand was working with the Feds or maybe needed my client out of the way to take over their little organization.

"Or maybe it was one big fuck up," I said. In reality, it didn't matter what in the hell had happened. We had to think about the indictment that would be coming from the county prosecutors as soon as they got back from their turkeys. "From the initial police report, you're looking at a first degree felony. Three to eleven years with prison mandatory. I've never been before Lucas County judges so I don't know the likelihood of the full sentence."

"So the judge ain't going to be your future father-in-law, huh?" Carter said with what was either a smirk or a grimace.

Fuck me. Somehow, he'd known about Tom or the Brodys or something. He'd hired me because he thought the judge would play nice. Not because of my legendary legal skill. He'd been right, though. Played the whole justice system like a violin. As quick as I could, I made sure to mask the butt hurt from that comment. I pulled up my big girl panties and leaned forward to get to the heart of why I was here in person and not eating my mother's strudel.

"Your biggest problem is that the feds are sniffing around. They could take this case over in a heartbeat. I don't have a lick of influence over anyone there." I left anymore from that sentence.

41

She'd fucked him.

Those were the first words that came to my mind sitting in this sterile little room with my lawyer. Casey had stiffly shaken the prosecutor's hand. But neither one of them said their names. I cleared my throat. Then they remembered they manners.

"Miles...Mr. Siegel, this is my client Jarrod Carter. Mr. Carter. This is Assistant U.S. Attorney Miles Siegel."

I stood and shook hands with the light-skinned brother. He had a nice watch on the other hand. Ain't never met a brother with a thing for watches. That was a white man's hobby. This guy wasn't going to have an ounce of sympathy for me. Probably one of those niggers thought he was above a guy like me.

"Why am I here?" I asked. That was the question that was squeezing my heart and making me dizzy. I wouldn't tell this shit to anyone, but while I'd been laying on that musty cot in the common room—overflow accommodation, they called it—I'd barely been able to sleep.

Prison had never been in my plans. That little charge from a few months ago was like swatting away a gnat. State court was a cake walk. There was always some way out of that system. Anyone with half a brain could beat a county charge.

But Federal. I never wanted nothing to do with this shit. It's why I stuck to girls and stayed the hell away from crack.

Meth. I ain't never had nothing to do with that shit. That was for those gap-toothed ofays.

"We're hoping you can assist with our investigation," the federal attorney said.

I started to say something, but Casey's fingers squeezed my arm. It was the universal sign for shut-the-hell-up. I took it.

"Which investigation might that be?" Casey asked. Did her voice shake? Maybe her voice was just like that. She'd been kind of weird during the beginning of the trial. In her office, I thought she was all brass balls.

"Methamphetamine transport from Summit to Lucas and from Hamilton on up."

"My client isn't in the drug business," Casey said, looking relieved.

"Why did he have," the guy looked at some paper on the table, "three hundred grams of methamphetamine in his possession?"

"He did not have anything in his possession. I think you need to look for Mr. Carter's associate."

Casey was dead right. Their investigation had been ass backwards. If they'd wanted to know where the drugs were coming from, they should have found a lab or something. I'd been straight up set up. Entrapment, a guy in the county lock up had said. That brother had called it right.

The other lawyer strained forward like he was a dog pulling on a leash. I could feel him wanting to lock me up tight for something. But they didn't have much of anything for a federal charge. This was straight buy-bust that all drug dealers had to write off.

"Why did he have ten thousand dollars in his possession?"

"My client declines to answer that question," my lawyer said.

She glared at the guy. He couldn't look her in the eye. Flipped through some papers instead. He was a straight up pussy. I looked back and forth between them. Ah, man, he'd dumped her and felt bad about it. Reading people was always easier than reading books. Interesting. I looked up at the bright ass light tubes and tried to figure a way to play the angles. I had to be able to wedge something in here to get me the hell out of trouble.

"You've been arrested before," he said, moving his hand down some small print.

My lawyer sucked in her breath far too quickly. "He's never been convicted of any crime," she said.

"Bang for the Buck? What's that business for?"

"My client runs a couple of sports bars," she said. Her mouth was a little bit tight around the edges. Little lines grooved in.

"Then why the promoting prostitution charge?"

"He has girls dancing in the back. Some overzealous cops thought they were selling more than lap dances. My client runs a clean operation. Fired the girls in question. Building violations were fixed. All clear. The places are back open."

I tuned out their legal mumbo jumbo. Wondered if my money had been delivered to Alisha. I could for sure use that cash now. I needed to bail my ass out of here. Get back to Cuyahoga County. Decide if I needed to disappear for a bit or what.

"Small time stuff," the government lawyer said. Sounded like a white boy. Definitely not Cleveland. He peered at Casey. "All right, you can go."

I stood quick, my wrist and ankle shackles jingling. I didn't want to give no one any damn excuse to shoot me dead in here. They'd take me out in a body bag and no one would think twice about another dead nigga.

Before the sheriff's deputy could close the door too quick, that lawyer was talking again.

"Funny," he said. "For a minute, I'd hoped this was the Container Case guy. He's got the perfect cover business. But he's just a small time drug dealer who decided to go big. Guess he didn't make it."

"Guess not," my lawyer said.

"We'll comb the car. Run the phone. But if that doesn't pull anything, we'll take the federal hold off him," the guy said.

The phone. Rida. The god damn phone.

42

"He didn't just cross the line, Casey. He jumped over it like the motherfucking Holy Grail was on the other side," Lulu said.

She was right. I knew that. But it didn't stop me missing him. Aching for that boyfriend to husband to family path that seemed so far out of my grasp. I squirmed under my friend's scrutiny. Turning my back on her, I peered out of the sliver of window over her overflowing bookcase.

For all the extra money in Lulu's paycheck at the end of the month, my office view was way better than hers. My best friend's bit of plate glass looked out on what I think was a war monument, or soldier memorial or something made of aged bronze. If I had to choose, though, I'd probably pick my Lake Erie view any day.

"Why you going back to Toledo?" Lulu asked while she picked at her stir-fried green beans. I looked at my battered, deep fat fried, sweet and sour chicken and envied my friend her good choices. Next time, I'd order vegetables as well. Slowly but surely, I would learn how to be thin again, not give into my desire to make food my faithful companion.

"Client got arrested there," I answered.

"And this has absolutely nothing to do with Miles?" Lulu didn't break her stare. I eventually looked away.

"The feds will probably pass on the case. My client's out on bail and out of Toledo. Maybe I can hand him over to a lawyer out there. Or I'll try the case. But Miles will be too busy climbing the career ladder to worry about me down in County. "

"We'll see about that," my best friend said like she hadn't believed the little tale I'd woven.

I pointed out the window toward the statue. "What is that, anyway?"

"Soldiers and sailors memorial," she said, for once her voice was totally straight. No faux urban speak.

"Oh, okay."

"My grandfather's on the 'M' panel under Mueller."

"Panel?"

"You can go inside," she said. "The names of those who served are there."

I tried to think how many times I'd passed that monument and never noticed it. Never knew there was something inside that marble or granite or whatever. Kind of like the girls Jarrod Carter ran. People had to have seen them every day, but nobody had ever said a thing.

I closed my eyes against the future of working on his case. I was proud of myself for extracting a promise that he'd stop working the girls while I was working his case. Though I didn't think he did it so much for me, but because he couldn't risk a federal charge. The feds still weren't sure he wasn't a player in the meth game and had been keeping an eagle eye on him after he bailed out. He'd even let a couple go home, he'd told me.

"Girl...don't think you're getting off that easy," Lulu said, back in casual girlfriend mode. "Tell me you aren't chasing that man."

I turned back to the talk about Miles. "We haven't really talked since he moved," I said. "I dropped off a couple of things he'd left at my place." When he hadn't been home, I'd left out. I hadn't had the guts to look him in the face after Toledo. I didn't want to be stared at by someone who'd looked at me and found me wanting.

"Did he say anything during the interview?" she asked.

"Nope. He was as cool as a cucumber. We were nothing more than prosecutor and defense attorney." Like it had been in the beginning. Like how maybe it should have stayed.

"You miss him?"

I pushed the gelatinous chicken aside, appetite gone. Not that I could swallow anything past the lump in my throat. I shook my head, then turned away and sucked in a breath. I wouldn't cry. I wouldn't cry, I repeated, trying to make it true.

"What client in Toledo?" Lulu said, trying to change the subject.

"Just a meth case," I said, keeping the rest as confidential as I should have the first time. I'd learned my lesson about sharing half-confidences.

"Fun," she said, spearing three or four beans. Her stare was as keen as a clinician's. "Are you unhappy because of the job or because of Miles?"

"Both. Neither," I said. I honestly had no idea anymore. By all accounts, most was right in my world. Bills paid. Weight lost. Cat aloof.

"Do you even like criminal law?" she asked, then chewed slowly, clearly thinking of ways to analyze all my life choices. "You don't seem any happier than when you were in Juvie."

"Criminal pays the bills," I said. "It's a regular schedule. The cases actually end. There's a lot to credit it." By all accounts, it was a huge step up from Juvenile.

"But you hate the clients?" Lulu surmised, getting right to the heart of it. But her saying it out loud made a ball of knots form in my stomach. Made a mockery of my belief in innocence and constitutional law. Made me feel like a total asshole.

"I don't hate them," I protested. Even I could hear it was a weak ass protest. "They just do some pretty terrible shit."

"Didn't you expect that?"

"Expect what?" I asked, playing dumb.

"Don't mess with me. You've seen the news. You saw what Judge Brody did. There are people who prey on the weak and vulnerable. They steal from them. They rape them. They kill them."

"I kinda thought it would be a lot of poverty crimes," I admitted. "Kind of the flip side of Juvie. I met a lot of the parents that stole to feed their families, or dealt drugs because that's the only job they could get. I thought I'd be defending those people who needed more from society than prison bars."

"And you're not?"

"Some are like that. Probably most. But it's the ones with no remorse that are hard to stomach."

"And you can't tell which is which coming in the door?" she asked.

I shook my head. If only it had been that easy. I'd never have let Jarrod Carter into my office. "The ones who are in it for the money can pay me my going rate," I said. "They don't advertise that they're sociopaths."

"And you like to eat," Lulu said, holding up a bean like a champagne flute.

"And I like to eat," we said in near unison as I toasted her bean with my reddish orange chicken.

It wasn't so bad, I'd told myself over the last few nights. Jarrod Carter would probably go to jail for a few years at least. Maybe Grand wouldn't be so smart and he'd get caught too. Maybe one or both of them would let the girls go and permanently close up shop. I prayed for those women when Carter made bail. After his brief incarceration in one of the county's worst jails, I hoped he'd learned mercy. My greatest fear was that he had not.

A well-timed knock came at the door, pressing pause on the hard questions. Maybe with this distraction, she'd forget about grilling me for a moment. An older-looking guy with light brown eyes and a suit to match let himself in. I was grateful for his intrusion. I didn't want to discuss how my reality wasn't living up to my ideals anymore. Not until I figured out how to wrap my head around it all.

"Oh, sorry, I didn't know you had someone in here," he said, eyeing me nervously.

I kind of wondered why big firm lawyers had guest chairs if they never had any clients come to see them in their cells. I couldn't be the first person to have sat in here.

"Hi, I'm Casey." I put down my fork and stuck out my hand in an attempt to put the anxious guy at ease.

"Ron," he said, fiddling with one of the buttons on his cuff. "I'll just leave these here," he said, dropping a stack of manila folders on Lulu's desk and backing out the door.

"What's that?" I pointed to the stack. Had to be less controversial than anything that could drop on my desk.

"Pro bono," she said, casually flipping through some papers. Then she got the inspired look on her face that may result in shopping for a gaudy bauble she thought worked for me or something equally outrageous. I and my wallet braced ourselves. "Hey, do you want to partner with me?" she asked.

"On what?" I asked. Didn't sound as crazy as the rhinestone dress she'd tried to get me to buy last week. We'd always had fantasies of working together until our paths diverged so widely. When the Brodys made it nearly impossible that I'd ever cross the hallowed ground she and her clients walked upon.

"The firm has a pro bono program that's helping finalize adoptions," she said.

"I thought that was a money business. What do they need volunteers for?"

"Bunch of reasons. But have you considered it? Still in the family realm, so you already have the experience. And like you said, there can be some big money in it."

For the first time in weeks, I sat up straight. "That totally sounds like something I should look into," I said. "Do you think the firm would mind?" I asked. It would be absolutely great to get in some supervised training in another area of the law I hadn't considered.

And maybe Mr. Jarrod Carter could be my last criminal case. Unless a miracle happened, he was going down for the drugs. After his case was done, I had been thinking it was high time I stopped dropping my card off in the arraignment room. Going purely domestic could be the break I needed. Adoption could get me halfway there.

"Nope," Lulu said. "I don't think they'd mind at all. Gimme a minute."

My best friend flipped through a well-thumbed spiral bound notebook on her desk. Finding what she was seeking, she dialed four numbers. After a short conversation, her secretary brought in a single sheet of paper.

"Sign this," she said, glancing at the white sheet, then handing it over to me.

"What is it?"

"Confidentiality and ICA stuff," she said.

I looked it over. The firm wanted me to keep my mouth shut, to make sure I knew they weren't paying me a dime, and I had to agree to arbitration should we ever disagree. I lifted one of the blue ball points from Lulu's desk organizer and penned my name.

"So what are we working on?" I asked after handing over the partially executed agreement binding me to big firm servitude—for the short run.

"Let's have a look," Lulu said, abandoning her meal. I closed the lid on mine as well. The cold chicken had lost my interest. "Foreign adoption. Family ran out of money, needs to finalize."

"I'm in," I said. "Helping an abandoned kid find a home seems like the right kind of work for me at the moment."

The buzz, buzz of my phone in my bag had me reaching for the little plastic gadget. The way I reacted reminded me of Miles and his crackberry habit. He'd always claimed the messages were important. I knew mine weren't.

I plunked the phone on the desk. It jumped around like a kid's motorized toy.

"Let me turn this off, and maybe we can strategize for an hour," I said, totally jazzed about thinking my future and not my recent past.

The name Velma Carter blinked up from the back of the phone while I thumb-wrestled the off button into position. "Feds h...," scrolled across the little screen before the display went blank.

"You going to answer that?" Lulu said, pulling out clean pads and new pens from her desk.

"Not now," I said. I was pretty sure it was Jarrod Carter calling. I'd had enough of his problems for a while. Whatever he had to tell me could wait.

"New beginnings?" my best friend asked, lifting her cola bottle in the air.

"New beginnings," I agreed, tapping her pop with mine.

ABOUT THE AUTHOR

Aime Austin is the author of the Casey Cort Legal Thriller Series. Casey is almost always in trouble. Aime's full time job? Rescuing her. Good thing Aime's got experience. She practiced family and criminal law in Cleveland, Ohio for several years—so she has the skills for the job.

When Aime isn't rescuing Casey from herself, she's raising her son or traveling between Budapest and Los Angeles.

www.ingramcontent.com/pod-product-compliance
Lightning Source LLC
Chambersburg PA
CBHW030937260626
47169CB00002B/519